OF NEPTUNE

OF NEPTUNE

ANNA BANKS

FEIWEL AND FRIENDS

NEW YORK

For my nephew Jason, and he knows why.

A FEIWEL AND FRIENDS BOOK
An Imprint of Macmillan

OF NEPTUNE. Copyright © 2014 by Anna Banks.
All rights reserved.
Printed in the United States of America by
R. R. Donnelley & Sons Company, Harrisonburg, Virginia.
For information, address Feiwel and Friends,
175 Fifth Avenue, New York, N.Y. 10010.

Feiwel and Friends books may be purchased for business or promotional use.
For information on bulk purchases, please contact Macmillan Corporate
and Premium Sales Department at (800) 221-7945 x5442 or by e-mail at
SPECIALMARKETS@MACMILLAN.COM.

Library of Congress Cataloging-in-Publication Data Available

ISBN 978-1-250-03960-6 (hardcover) / 978-1-250-06091-4 (e-book)

Feiwel and Friends logo designed by Filomena Tuosto

First Edition: 2014

10   9   8   7   6   5   4   3   2

MACTEENBOOKS.COM

1

I DIG my bare feet into the sand, getting just close enough to the water for the mid-morning waves to tickle my toes. Each lazy wave licks my feet, then retreats as if beckoning me into the Atlantic Ocean, whispering of adventure. Of mischief.

Of peace-and-freaking quiet.

Which is all I want after this past summer. What with Jagen's attempt to take over the kingdoms, our near discovery by humans, me leading a wall of fish to an underwater tribunal—we barely had room to breathe. And then our breath was all but stolen away from us when Rachel drowned.

We deserve a break from it all, Galen and I. But it doesn't look like we're getting one.

Behind me, the wind hauls with it the occasional shout erupting from my house. The bellows of Galen and his older brother Grom taint the air with a rancor that repels me farther from the house and deeper into the water. I roll up my pajama pants and, letting the saltwater have its way with my calves, try to ignore the words I can make out between the squawks of seagulls overhead.

Words like "loyalty" and "privacy" and "law." I cringe when I hear the word "grief." That word comes from Grom, and after it, no words come from Galen. It's a kind of silence I've come to recognize from him. One filled with anguish, torment, guilt, and the overwhelming need to say or do something to hide it.

But there is no hiding that Rachel's death mauled the deepest parts of him. She was more than just his assistant. She was his closest human friend. Maybe the others don't see the depths of it. If they did, they wouldn't throw it in his face or use it against him. But I do see it. I know what it's like to have so much heartache you come to despise the air that keeps you alive.

Galen doesn't cry. He doesn't talk about her. There seems to be a part of Galen that belonged to Rachel, and she took that part with her. What's left of him is trying hard to function without the missing piece, but it can't quite coordinate. Like a car running on empty.

I want to help him, to tell him I know how he feels. But comforting someone is different than being comforted. In a way, it's harder. I went through this after Dad died of cancer. After my best friend Chloe was attacked by a shark. But I still don't know what to do or say to make it better for Galen. Because only many, many sunrises can soften the pain. And it hasn't been long enough for that yet.

I feel bad that I left my mom in the kitchen to deal with this mess by herself. Poseidon princess that she is, this is a difficult problem to navigate alone. But I can't go back in yet. Not until I think of a fantastic excuse for why I thought it was okay to abandon a very serious and very-important-to-Galen conversation. I should be there with them in the kitchen, standing beside him, arms crossed, giving Grom the stank eye to reiterate that I am not his Royal subject and that I'm on Galen's side no matter what that might involve.

But it's hard to face Grom like that when I'm kinda sorta in agreement with him. Especially since the Triton king is one of the most intimidating people I've ever had the misfortune to meet. He would hone in on my reluctance. He would see through me if I put up pretenses about the trip.

This stupid trip.

Last year at prom—well, our own version of prom, which involved dancing underwater in Armani—we promised each other we would take a trip to the mountains. To get away from it all, or whatever. And at first, this whole summer jaunt inland with Galen seemed like a good idea to me. Actually, it seemed like unfiltered heaven. He's adamant that he wants to be alone with me. To make up for all the time we lost mutually denying our feelings for each other. Then the time we spent fending off Jagen's advance on both the kingdoms. And what could be better than that? Spending private time with Galen is about a ten on my Ecstasy-O-Meter. *Of course* I want to steal back all of the lost time—I'd steal the time *before* we actually met if I could somehow bribe the universe to grant wishes.

But the bigger reason—the real reason—I think Galen wants to get away is Rachel. I know he wants a change in scenery. He wants to get away from the house they shared together. Especially from the now maddeningly quiet kitchen where she used to click around in stilettos while preparing him delectable seafood dishes. The house used to smell of cooking food and swirling Italian perfume and possibly gunpowder if you came on the right day.

And don't I know how that feels? Waking up every day in my bedroom full of all things Chloe was like getting a daily, fast-acting injection of painful memories. Staring at my dad's empty place setting at the table felt like watching vultures of the past circling around his empty chair. But Galen hasn't allowed himself to start the grieving process. And this trip seems to be an attempt to keep it at bay even longer. Which can't be healthy. And since it's not healthy, I feel more like an enabler than a supporter.

Either way, I should go back now. I should go back and be there for Galen and tell Grom that no matter his reasons Galen needs this trip. Then express my own concerns with Galen privately. I should be there for him now and support him in front of the others, just as he would for me—just as he's already done for me.

I'll need to explain myself—why I left during the conversation in the first place—say something so that I don't look like the jerk that I am. Tact hasn't been my specialty lately. I'm thinking Galen's sister Rayna is contagious, and she's somehow infected me with her rudeness. But maybe tact isn't what I need. Maybe I should try her truth. *The truth would only embarrass Galen,* I decide. And make him feel even more alone.

Or maybe I'm just being a quivering chicken about the whole thing.

I guess I have to take an honest-to-God stab at tact. Lovely.

As soon as I turn to go back, I sense my grandfather in the water. The pulse of the Poseidon King Antonis coils around my legs like a tightening string. Fan-freaking-tastic. Just what we need. Another Royal opinion on the matter of our road trip.

I wait for him to surface, trying to think of a great excuse as to why he shouldn't go to the house. I've got nothing. Anything I say will come off as unwelcoming, when really, I'd like to see him more often. He's high up on the list of people—well, people who have a fin—I'd like to spend time with. But now is not a good time for spending.

It's not long before my excuse to shoo him away presents itself in the form of Naked Grandfather. I cover my eyes, irritation bubbling up against my will. "Really? You really forget every single time you change into human form to put shorts on? You cannot go in the house like that."

Grandfather sighs. "My apologies, young Emma. But you must admit, all these human traditions are a bit overwhelming. Where might I find a short?"

That clothes seem like a mountainous burden to him reminds me that our worlds are spectacularly different. And that I could learn a lot from him. Without unshielding my eyes, I point toward the water, in the exact opposite direction I know Galen has a pair hidden. When in doubt, stall. "Try over there. Under the slab of rock. And they're called *shorts*, not 'a short.'"

"I'm afraid you'll have to bore someone else with your

human expressions, young one. I couldn't possibly care less." I hear him disappear under the water, surfacing several seconds later. "The short is not here."

I shrug. "Guess you can't go in then." This is going better than I thought it would.

I can practically feel him crossing his arms at me. Here we go.

"You think I'm here to object to your going inland with Galen."

My mouth drops open. And I stutter excessively when I say, "Well. Um. Aren't you?" Because so far, he's done nothing but play hall monitor between me and Galen. A few months ago, he walked in on us while we were making out, and Galen nearly passed out because of it. Ever since then Galen has been terrified of disappointing the Poseidon king, so Grandfather's negative opinion on this trip might actually be a game changer.

Which is why he cannot go in the house.

I hear Grandfather melt into the water, and he confirms it with, "You can turn around now." Only his shoulders and chest are above the waves. He smiles. It's the kind of adoring smile I've always imagined a grandfather gives his grandchildren when they bring him their most hideous Crayola creation. "I'm certainly not happy about you going inland, of course. I had wanted to spend a bit more time together, too. But I know from past experience that Poseidon princesses are not inclined to care about my opinion."

It's kind of cool to be referred to as a princess, even though my mother is *the* princess of Poseidon territory. Still, I raise a get-to-the-point brow. Grandfather responds best to frank and direct.

"I'm here to speak to you, Emma. Only you."

Mortified, I wonder if there exists a Syrena expression for "the birds and the bees talk." Probably there is, and it's probably some god-awful analogy having to do with plankton or worse.

In the distance, we hear a shout of outrage. He cocks his head at me. "Why aren't you in there helping your prince?"

If I thought I felt guilty before . . . But then I remember that this business is not for Grandfather's nose. I'm actually doing Galen a favor by stalling now. "Because if I stay there any longer, I'll grow a beard from all the testosterone hovering in the air." Of course, my answer is over his head; he indicates this with a bored-silly eye roll. Syrena do not know—nor apparently care— what testosterone is.

"If you don't wish to tell me, that is fine," he says. "I have trust in your judgment." More shouting from behind me. Maybe my judgment sucks after all. I'm about to excuse myself, when he says, "It's better this way, that they're distracted. What I have to say is for your ears only, young Emma." A seagull overhead drops a bomb then, and it lands cleanly on Grandfather's shoulder. He mutters some fishy expletive and swishes saltwater over the offending white glob, setting it off to sea. "Why don't you come into the water, so we can close some of the distance between us? I'd rather someone didn't overhear. Here, I'll change back to Syrena form if that will make you more comfortable."

I wade into the Atlantic, not caring to roll up my pajamas this time. I pass a large crab who looks like he's tempted to nip at me. I squat in the water, submerging my entire head, and come face-to-face with the crab. "If you pinch me," I tell it, "I'll pick you up and throw you on the beach for the gulls." The Gift of Poseidon—the ability to talk to fish—does have its advantages. Bossing around marine life is just one of them.

I've come to realize crabs in particular throw mini temper tantrums. I wonder if that's where the term "crabby" came from in the first place. He scuttles away, as if I've ruined his whole day. When I resurface and reach Grandfather, I can no longer touch the ground. Gliding up to him, I say, "So? We're as private as we can be."

Then he smiles at me like I am the reason he is floating instead of the waves or his powerful fin. "Before you leave on your adventure, young Emma, I need to tell you about a town called Neptune."

2

GALEN GRABS an orange from the fruit basket in front of him. If only he could channel his rage into the orange. Somehow inject his fury into the confines of the peel instead of showing his indignation all over his face.

The same way his older brother Grom wears indifference as a second skin.

But I am not Grom, the impervious Triton king. Galen squeezes the fruit so hard it becomes a disemboweled mess of peel, seeds, and juice on the kitchen counter. It feels good to squeeze the innards out of something. Galen can think of a million feelings inside himself right now that he'd like to pour out onto the counter next to the juice of the orange. But it would have no effect on Grom. Grom is immune to feelings.

Grom rolls his eyes, while Nalia casually grabs some paper towels from the cabinet.

"Was that really necessary?" Grom says.

Nalia makes quick work of cleaning up the orange. Galen gives her an apologetic look. He would have cleaned it up eventually, after he and Grom came to an agreement on the matter of this road trip. But then Nalia returns a look of pity. Galen's so tired of everyone's pity. But Nalia's pity isn't about Rachel. Nalia feels sympathetic toward Galen because she thinks he won't win this argument. That he is no match for Grom.

Galen decides she can clean up the mess after all.

"Actually, I could think of something better to squeeze than an orange," Galen drolls. Like his brother Grom's hard head, for instance. Or maybe his throat. Rachel's expression "take a chill pill" comes to mind. Galen counts to ten, just as she taught him. Then he counts to twenty.

"You have much maturing to do, brother," says Grom.

"And you have an entire kingdom to run, Highness. Which is why I don't understand why we're still here. And those are my boxers."

Grom raises a brow, then shrugs. "I thought they seemed small."

"Grom—" Nalia starts, but he cuts her off with a huff.

"You just graduated from human school a few days ago, Galen. You don't want to relax for a little while?" Grom takes a sip of his bottled water, then screws the cap back on so tightly it makes a cracking sound.

"High school," Galen says. "We graduated from *high school*. If you keep calling everything 'human' this and 'human' that—"

"I know, I know." Grom waves his hand in dismissal. "Very

well. High school. What is so high about high school, anyway? No, no, don't bother to answer. I don't care enough to know. But, little brother, why are you in such a hurry to leave the beaches?"

"For the hundredth time," Galen grits out, "I'm not in a hurry to leave the beaches. I'm in a hurry to spend time with Emma before we go to college, or before the Archives change their mind about their agreement with us, or before something else catastrophic happens. Can you not handle the kingdom without my help, brother? You should have just said as much."

This cracks the shell that is Grom's face. "Careful, Galen. Will you never learn that diplomacy is an asset?"

"So is being direct," Galen grumbles. He runs a hand through his hair. "Look, I honestly don't know what the problem is here. We're taking a two-week road trip."

"Our treaty with the Archives is still delicate, Galen. It takes time to build trust. Your disappearing with Emma for so many turns of the sun will cause murmuring. You know this. And we've just witnessed how powerful murmuring can be."

Galen rolls his eyes. Grom's referring to Jagen's near take-over of the houses of Triton and Poseidon, a conspiracy that started with hushed whispers and speculation, and nearly cost the Royals their freedom and throne. But this is different. "Why would the kingdoms care about our spending private time to-gether?" He doesn't mean to yell. But he doesn't regret it, either.

"Well, for starters," Nalia injects so calmly it irritates Galen, "I'm sure there will be rumors flying about whether or not you're respecting the law and not mating before your ceremony."

Galen can't argue that. And he can't argue that the rumors would be somewhat founded. He can barely keep his hands off of Emma. And she's not exactly helping the situation, being such a willing recipient of his frequently wandering hands. He pinches the bridge of his nose. "They'll just have to trust us. They could give us the benefit of the doubt on this one thing."

Grom shrugs. "They could. But they're also eager to get to know the new Poseidon princess. She needs to spend more time in the kingdoms."

"So they can whisper about the Half-Breed behind her back?" The very thought makes Galen want to pick up another orange. Still, he knows Grom is right. Galen wants Emma to spend more time in the water, too. Dr. Milligan said she may eventually be able to hold her breath for much longer. Right now she's only able to hold it for hours at a time. Maybe that could be extended to days, with enough practice. And if it could, he and Emma wouldn't have to alternate between land and sea so often once they had mated.

"The more she's around them, the less her presence will affect them, Galen. They're giving her a chance. The least you can do is reciprocate. Someday, they won't even notice that she's a Half-Breed. Or at least, they'll learn to accept it and move on."

He must be joking. Everything about Emma screams Half-Breed, starting with her pale skin and white hair and ending with the fact that she doesn't have a fin. A stark contrast in every way to the Syrena.

Galen stands up from the bar stool. Maybe stretching his legs will keep him from satisfying the urge to jump across the counter. *Where has all this anger come from?* "It's just two weeks, Grom. Two weeks is all I'm asking for. Antonis is okay with it." At least, Antonis hasn't expressed any feelings *against* their trip. *And there I go again, raising my voice.* In front of a different audience, Grom would be forced to admonish him.

"Antonis is in agreement because he's so eager to please Emma, having never known his granddaughter. You're my brother. I've put up with your antics for too many seasons already."

"What does that have to do with anything? Why can't you just give me your approval so we can move on?"

"Because I get the feeling you're going whether or not you obtain my approval. Tell me I'm wrong, Galen."

Galen shakes his head. "I want your approval."

"That's not an answer."

"It's all I can give you." He does want Grom's approval. Truly he does. But Grom is right—Galen wants to get as far away from here as possible. Even if it means infuriating his older brother. The need to flee is almost overwhelming, and he's not sure why. The only thing he's sure of is that he wants Emma with him. Her touch, her voice, her laugh. It's like a seaweed salve to the gaping wounds inside of him.

Grom sighs, pulling open the refrigerator door. With deliberation he places the half-empty bottle of water next to a container full of green something. "I appreciate your honesty. You're no longer a fingerling. Emma is of the age of independence by human standards. You both know the difference between right and wrong. Your decisions are yours to make. But I have to wonder, little brother. I have to ask. Are you sure this is what you need? Because two weeks does not change everything. Some things . . . Some things cannot be undone, Galen. I hope you understand that."

"Stop making everything about Rachel." *Please.*

"Stop making nothing about Rachel. Grieve her, Galen."

"So I have your approval then?" Galen shoves the bar stool back in place. "Because Emma and I have to pack."

I wish Emma would come back in.

3

I DON'T deserve the way my grandfather smiles at me. It's as if I've never done one single bad thing in my whole life. It's as if he thinks I'm capable of anything—except wrongdoing.

Clearly he missed out on a good portion of my childhood. I hope he never finds out that Chloe and I baked chocolate chip cookies for my ninth-grade science teacher—only the chips weren't chocolate at all, they were laxatives, and we . . . Well, we got more time to study before a particularly hard exam.

I wonder if Syrena have or even need laxatives. What would they use? That's something I'll have to ask Mom. I don't think I could ask Galen without passing out.

I realize then that I've been contemplating laxatives instead of acknowledging Antonis. I don't know why it surprises me when my grandfather speaks or takes me into his confidence. Maybe it's because all the stories Galen and Toraf used to tell me painted the Poseidon king as an unsociable recluse. Or maybe it's because I'm not used to having a grandfather at all, let alone one who wants to talk to me. Or maybe, for the love of God, I should try to swallow the novelty and answer his freaking question.

Only, what was the question? Oh, yeah. If I'm up for an adventure.

"Sure," I tell him. "If Galen is up to it."

Grandfather scowls. "I was hoping you had one of those drawings on hand, Emma. The ones humans make of land."

Drawings humans make of land... "A map?"

The older Syrena scratches at his beard. By now I know him well enough to figure out he's stalling. Stalling must run in our family. "Yes, yes, that's it. A map. But before we talk about any map, I trust you'll keep this between us? Oh, no," he says quickly. "It's nothing bad. On the contrary, really. But it's something that I only want to share with you. The others wouldn't ... appreciate it as much as you will. And you may not appreciate it as much if they were to know."

I'm still trying to grasp not only the fact that my grandfather knows what a land map is but why he would need to know what it is in the first place. Apparently, "the others" are not aware of this knowledge. And it's clear he doesn't want "the others"— including Galen—to know. I'm not sure how I feel about this. But I'm too curious not to promise. Besides, Antonis said it wasn't bad. Maybe it's like when grandparents give you cookies and candy when your parents aren't looking. It's not bad per se, but your parents certainly wouldn't approve. That must be all it is. An innocent grandfather-granddaughter secret.

"I can pull up a map on my phone, but I left it on the beach. You'll have to come ashore with me, and if you come ashore, you'll need shorts. They're over there," I say, pointing in the opposite direction I originally sent him. "Under the driftwood stuck in the sand."

He nods. Grandfather gives me a quick piggyback ride to the shorts, then lets me loose so he can change to human legs.

When he's properly covered and sitting next to me in the sand, he gives me a knowing smirk, accentuating the small wrinkles tugging at his eyes. Syrena age well. For hundreds of years old, Grandfather's smirk is youthfully vibrant. The only telltale sign of his age is some saggy skin on his stomach—and that could just be the angle at which he's sitting right now. I pull up a map on my phone. "I can search the phone and find Neptune on the map."

He shakes his head. "It's been a while since I've been there, but last time I visited, Neptune was not on any human maps." He rubs his chin. "I know it from the waters offshore here. Show me the land map with the water next to it, and I'll know where it is."

"Sure." I pull up the East Coast of the United States, hoping I'm interpreting ancient Syrena speak correctly. "How about this?" I show him the face of the phone. The map is a bit detailed, with labeled highways and interstate signs. I doubt he'll understand what we're looking at.

Until he says, "Chattanooga. That's very close to it, if I remember correctly."

My half-fish grandfather knows how to read? What the what? "Um. Okay, I can zoom in a little more." With a swipe of my fingers, Chattanooga and its suburbs are the only thing on the screen now. I can't help but notice that Chattanooga is quite a distance from the Atlantic Ocean. In fact, I have to scroll over a few times. My curiosity is about to erupt into an onslaught of questions.

Grandfather studies me a few more moments, as if gauging whether or not he should tell me. Or maybe he's trying to decide where to begin. And maybe he should hurry up before I burst.

Finally, he sighs. "Emma. You haven't heard my story yet. The story of what I did when your mother disappeared."

This is the first time anyone from the Syrena world has said "disappeared" instead of "died," when referring to what happened to my mother all those years ago in the minefield. Or at the very least, now that she's been found, they all say, "when I thought she had died."

I have heard multiple versions of the story. First from Grom's point of view, as told to me by Galen: Mom was blown to bits in a minefield blast and assumed dead. Then my mother filled in the rest of the crevices with details from her perspective on what happened that fateful day in the minefield: She somehow survived, came ashore, met my father, and ... then there was me.

But sometimes stories aren't just crevices and holes waiting to be filled in. Stories, real-life stories, have layers, too. Layers built on foundations laid centuries and generations ago. It's those kinds of layers I see etched on my grandfather's face right now.

"I did what any father would do if their child disappeared," Antonis continues. "I searched for her." And just like that, another layer adds on to the story. A layer only Antonis could contribute.

He looks at me then, scrutinizing my reaction. I don't know what he's looking for. I glance away, digging my feet into the sand as if it's the most important task on the planet.

Satisfied, the old monarch clears his throat. He's hunkering down, I can tell.

I let out my breath. "Yes, I know. They said you kept your Trackers searching for a long time."

Grandfather nods. "That is true, young Emma. I did send out Tracker parties. During both the light and dark parts of the days. I kept Trackers out at all times. And each time they returned, they came back with nothing."

I already know all of this. We'd already dissected everything over and over again. Maybe my grandfather just needs someone to talk to, I decide. And I'm sort of honored that he chose me. Especially because of the way his voice transforms, tightening each word, choked by emotion. This is hard for him to talk about. But he's reopening old hurts that have barely scabbed over to tell me. Just me.

"They came back with nothing, and I began to lose hope," he continues. Antonis leans back on his hand, his focus set on the waves rolling in ahead of us. "Until one day. One of my most trusted and talented Trackers, Baruk, came to me. He swore on

Poseidon's legacy that he'd felt your mother's pulse. That it was faint and erratic. It would come and go so quickly that it was impossible to follow, even for him. Sometimes it would be toward the sunrise, others, toward the sunset. We figured out that she must have been adrift."

Okay, so maybe I didn't know all of this. In fact, I'm pretty sure my jaw is hanging open. "Grom said the same thing, that he felt her pulse sometimes. Did he tell you?"

"Of course not," Antonis says, his voice grave. "Just as I didn't tell him. You must understand, Emma, I did not know what had transpired between Grom and my daughter. All I knew was that she was gone and that he was there. No, I didn't tell him. I didn't tell anyone." Grandfather pauses, a wise kind of curiosity dancing in his eyes. "Of course, if your friend Toraf had been born at the time, I might have been diplomatic enough with the Triton house to take advantages of his tracking talents. There has never been another like him, you know."

I nod. It's all I can do. It's sad, how many opportunities had come up again and again for them to share information, to work together to find my mother. And if they had, I wouldn't be here right now. That said, there is only so much anguish I can devote to those long-ago circumstances. If my grandfather is waiting for a response from me, sympathetic or otherwise, he's not getting one. I know this story isn't over, and I don't want him to stop telling it.

He seems to sense this. "After a few days, her pulse disappeared. Baruk believed her dead. I refused to accept that. Baruk thought me mad, begged me to let her go and move on. But

I couldn't, you see. Nalia was all I had left. In the end, I ordered Baruk to point me in the direction where he last sensed her. I knew she might be dead. But I also knew something else about my daughter, young Emma. Something she doesn't realize to this day. Nalia always had a secret fondness for humans."

Yep, definitely didn't know that. I'm starting to realize I could fill a black hole with all the things I don't know. "What do you mean?"

"I mean that a good father knows what his fingerlings are up to. There was a time shortly before she disappeared when my Trackers reported her visiting the same spot each day close to the Arena. Each day, they followed her, but when they arrived, she'd already gone. They never found anything there, couldn't figure out the purpose for her daily visits. At first, I thought she was entertaining the thought of sifting with other males, since she was so opposed to Grom in the beginning. Yet, all the Trackers reported the absence of another's pulse. So I decided to investigate this myself. I almost passed by it, I tell you. But somehow, one of her shinier possessions captured one of the few rays of sunlight able to reach bottom. I figured I must have stirred up the murk in just the right place. That's when I found her cache of human things."

Ohmysweetgoodness. "My mother collected human things?" And my grandfather never busted her on it? "And you let her? What about the laws? You didn't care?"

He waves a disdainful hand in the air. "And which law was she breaking? Who could prove she'd had contact with humans? Who was to say that she didn't find these things on old shipwrecks?"

So he turned a blind eye. He chose not to question her. Somehow this just endears him to me more. "So because of her obsession with human things, you figured out she'd come ashore?"

Antonis shakes his head. "Yes and no. I thought she might have. I searched the coasts and then began to move deeper inland. I never found her, obviously. But I did find something else, Emma. Something I haven't told anyone."

And that's when I realize this is not just an innocent grandfather-granddaughter secret.

4

GALEN LOADS the last of Emma's luggage into the trunk of his SUV and lifts a brow at the two very different piles of personal effects. He didn't even fill one whole suitcase, yet Emma managed to fill two big ones and a small one. Not to mention that bulky purse thing she carries. He grins. Either she planned something big or she failed to plan.

Not that he cares. He's just happy to steal her away.

"What do you suppose that was all about?" Grom says, startling him.

Galen scowls. "Since when did you learn to sneak around on human legs?"

His brother gives him a lazy smile, then shrugs. "I'm a quick study."

"Obviously," Galen grumbles.

"Well?"

"Well, what?" Grom has already tried Galen's patience today. Forcing him to ask permission to take this trip in front of everyone—especially since they'd already discussed it countless times—was unnecessary and humiliating. Was he just showing off his Royal muscle for Nalia? *Or does he truly feel I'm taking liberties with my position as human ambassador?*

Because if he is, Galen is ready to turn the job back over to His Royal Majesty. Maybe the humans don't need to be watched. They have a blinking existence on the earth, much shorter than any Syrena, and then they're gone. Just like Rachel.

Grom crosses his arms, straining the fabric in the borrowed flannel shirt he's wearing. Emma's father must have been of slighter build than him. "What do you suppose Antonis had to tell Emma? They were too quiet when they came in from the beach. Antonis's shorts were dry. They'd obviously been out there a while."

"What do I care?"

"You'd be a fool not to care. Antonis has always been . . . secretive."

Galen leans against the back of the SUV and kicks at the gravel in the driveway. "Sounds like a Poseidon trait."

Grom nods. "Yes. Exactly. Which is why you need to find out what they're up to."

"They've missed out on each other's company for Emma's entire life. Maybe they're just catching up."

"You don't believe that. And neither do I."

Grom is right. Galen doesn't believe it. Sure, they have a lot to talk about. But Antonis rarely comes to shore. He'd have a purpose. A purpose he didn't want anyone else to know. Still, it's not worth starting off this trip with a potential argument. "Emma will tell me if she wants to."

He glances at Grom, daring him to protest. They both know the Triton king wouldn't try to force it out of his beloved Nalia. And they both know that even if he tried, he wouldn't succeed.

Grom sighs. "Maybe you could ask her leading questions or something."

But Galen can tell the subject is all but dropped. Grom hasn't reached that level of hypocrisy just yet. Which is good, because Emma has grown particularly sneaky on her human feet as well.

"What are you talking about?" she says behind Grom. Galen can tell she doesn't like the fact that his brother is wearing one of her father's old shirts. "And more importantly, are we ready to get this party started?"

Nalia brushes past Galen and throws her arms around Emma. "Have a safe trip, sweetie." Then she leans closer. Galen knows he's not meant to hear what she says next. But he does. "I'll have Grom in a new wardrobe by the time you get back. No more wearing Dad's clothes."

Galen walks away, giving them a moment. Even though he's irritated with his brother just now, Galen feels sorry for Grom because he doesn't even realize he's being talked about. Or how much he's imposing on Emma's patience. Galen lightly punches his brother in the shoulder. "So, about that permission, Highness?"

Grom rolls his eyes. "Enjoy, minnow. Just remember, you and Emma aren't mated yet so . . ."

Galen holds up his hand. "Grom." This is not a discussion he ever planned to have with his brother. Or anyone, in fact.

"I'm just reminding you," Grom says, looking every bit as uncomfortable as Galen feels. "Privacy presents many opportunities."

A fact Galen knows well. He's just not sure if he cares anymore. Keeping his hands off Emma is not something he's good at. And he's not sure how much he cares about the law anymore. The law was wrong about Half-Breeds, after all. Emma could never be an abomination. "I'm not talking about this with you."

Grom seems relieved. "But privacy does allow for more conversation, so it still wouldn't hurt if you could—"

He's cut off when Nalia links her arm in his. "Toraf and Rayna left already," she says. "Rayna requests that you bring her back something 'interesting.'" The couple had come to see Emma and Galen off, but when Toraf felt the tension between Galen and Grom, he'd made up a reason for them to be excused. Galen wishes he'd had some time with them before leaving.

Galen smiles. "Of course she does." He strolls around to the driver's side. "See you in two weeks." He doesn't wait for a reply, just in case Grom wants him to ask permission for the amount of time they're taking. Two weeks was just an estimate. Galen has the feeling that when he and Emma are actually alone together, two weeks won't be enough.

At least, not for him.

5

AHEAD OF us, the interstate looks like a river of cars running between the two mountains. My ears have been popping for at least an hour with the higher altitude. I keep glancing at Galen in the driver's seat to see if he's experiencing anything funky. Sometimes the water pressure affects my ears the deeper we go in the ocean. I wonder if Galen's Syrena ears can adapt to any kind of pressure, or just the pressure caused by the deep blue sea.

He hasn't complained about it, but that doesn't mean anything. Actually, he hasn't said much at all, which might mean something. Either he doesn't notice how often I look at him, or he's pretending not to notice. I get what that means: He doesn't want to talk.

But letting him keep his thoughts to himself seems counterproductive, given the underlying reason for this trip. When my best friend Chloe died, I wanted to hole up and stop living. The possibility that Galen could be going through the same type of pain drives me crazy. Rachel was his best friend, maybe even more so than Toraf. And a mother figure, too. To lose both of those in one fell swoop is a devastating thing.

I put my hand on his shoulder and squeeze. "Thinking of her again?"

Galen gives me a wistful, forged smile that lasts only a second before his face falls again. Rachel's death affected us all. We all could have done more. We all had a responsibility to look out for her. We all should have been more vigilant and kept track of her whereabouts the day we retrieved Jagen from the humans. Any of us could have prevented her drowning. But Galen is bent on stockpiling the blame on himself. And I'm bent on making him snap out of it.

I just haven't figured out how yet.

"Actually," he says, "I was thinking about what you and Antonis could have possibly talked about for so long yesterday."

Oh. That. I was wondering if/when he would ask. "Nothing much," I say. Maybe I don't want to talk after all. Not because I'm keeping a secret—I'm not. Not really. The truth is, I don't know why Grandfather insists we travel to the belly button of Tennessee. But I do know that this weird scavenger hunt is important to him, and for some crazy reason, I'm willing to go along with it. And until now, I thought Galen was, too. He didn't question it yesterday when I changed our course on the GPS from our original destination of the Cascade Mountains to the new target in the Smoky Mountains.

He turns the radio down. "What are we going to find in these mountains, Emma? Why is Antonis sending us here?"

My reflex is to be defensive, but I know Galen is on edge. Fighting with Galen is the last thing I want to do right now. I smile. "I'm just as curious as you are. Besides, he didn't send us here, remember? We already said we were going to explore the mountains. He just made a suggestion of which ones to visit." Meaning he pinpointed the entire middle of the state of Tennessee with his thumb on my cell phone. To scale, his thumb is about 150 miles on a map.

Galen shifts in his seat, leaning his elbow on the armrest of the door. "What exactly did he say?"

"He said to have a safe trip. And that he hopes I find what I'm looking for." Which is true, and at the time, it didn't sound nearly as questionable as it does now, even with the epic story he had to tell about searching for my mother. I'm not sure I'm adding anything new to what I've already told him about the conversation. It's not like I've kept anything from him—I already explained why we changed course. And I thought he already accepted that. But Galen appears to be mentally dissecting every word my grandfather has spoken since birth.

Which makes me just a little suspicious about Grandfather's motives myself. Did he anticipate Galen asking questions—and did he intentionally omit any solid answers? If so, why?

Galen glances at me sideways before looking back to the road. "He didn't say anything else? Something that could have had a double meaning?"

"Are these your questions? Or Grom's?"

Galen grimaces. "Grom did question me about it. But I have to admit, I'm curious. Maybe if you told me what he said, I could help figure out what he's really up to."

I wonder if the hatchet will ever be buried between Grom and my grandfather. And I'm not ecstatic that Grom is clearly influencing Galen's opinion. "He said, 'Freshwater fish are bland.'" I gasp. Obnoxiously. Dramatically. Flared nostrils and all. "Do you think that's code for 'I saw a spaceship'? Or maybe, 'I'm really a Soviet android'? We should totally turn around and go back. Beat the answers out of him."

At this, Galen flashes me the most heart-stopping grin. "Do you realize how gorgeous you are when you're . . ."

But his dimples have already reduced my vocabulary to "Um." And I'm in severe danger of relapsing to my old blushing habits.

He nods ahead of us. "I'm sorry to be grouchy. Let's take this exit. I'm tired of driving. Let's stretch our legs a bit." By stretching his legs, Galen means unleashing his humongous fin. I have to admit, it would be fun to explore the springs here. According to Google, there are lots of them in this area.

"My bathing suit is in my suitcase," I tell him. "I'll need to find somewhere to change. Maybe a rest area?"

"You could always just wear nothing."

Yep, totally blushing. And my mouth is dry. And my insides are goo. And I accidentally imagine Galen wearing nothing. Ohmysweetgoodness.

It seems Galen is a victim of his own teasing. His grin is long gone, replaced by what I would call hunger. He licks his lips then scowls, turning his attention back to the road. "Sorry. That slipped out."

Galen rarely lets these things slip. Sometimes I can see mischief in his eyes, and it's playful and harmless and flirty. But Galen has boundaries. Boundaries like the law and his conscience. Boundaries that have always stopped him from saying anything like that before.

"You've never apologized for teasing me before," I muse.

"Teasing you? Is that what you think I'm doing?"

"Don't tell me you don't say things to make me blush."

A smirk raises the corner of his mouth. "Of course I do. But I apologized because I wasn't teasing that time."

He's having a hard time keeping his eyes off my mouth and on the road. I'm having a hard time keeping my seat belt on and a respectable—not to mention safe by DMV standards—distance between us.

He swallows. "Emma. I'm driving." But he's not committed to his argument. Even now, he's scanning the side of the road and slowing his speed, probably in case I pounce on him.

"You could pull over," I offer helpfully.

To my complete surprise, he does. The cabin quiets as the sound of our hushed high speed turns to gravel crunching under the tires as he maneuvers the SUV onto the wide shoulder.

He puts it in park. Unbuckles. Faces me. "You were saying?"

I don't know if he pulled me to him or I did it all on my own, but in fast-point-five seconds I'm out of my seat, into his lap, and tasting every part of his mouth. I'm surprised and pleased when his hands slide up the back of my sundress. He's shy at first, just caressing my back lightly with his fingertips. But as I kiss him deeper, the lightness disappears, replaced by a want that matches my own.

I silently thank whoever invented tinted windows. We are a whirlwind of hands and groans and impatience. I'm near drunk from the way he smells, tastes, feels beneath me.

Galen is more ambitious than he's ever been, and I decide to analyze that later. I don't know why I think about it now; usually I take what I can get before he comes to his senses. And for now, I do take advantage of my good fortune. My thumbs slip under his T-shirt and glide up the rigid plane that is his stomach. He releases me for just long enough to hold his arms over his head, so I can relieve him of his shirt. Then I am back in his grasp, in his arms, against him, around him. Almost part of him.

He entangles his hands in my hair, trailing kisses from my ear down my throat, leaving what feels like a stream of lava in his wake.

I finally get brave enough to reach for his jeans button. I wait for him to end it, to put a stop to this craziness. The miracle is, he lets me undo it. I feel reckless and unstable and empowered, but the last thing I want to do is stop and think about this. What we're doing. Where we are. How far will he let this go? How far do I want him to let it go? And I'm suddenly overwhelmed by the answer. I pull away.

His hands drop.

I bite my lip. I'd gotten used to the idea of waiting for us to be mated. The idea of a mating ceremony and picking an island with him is crazy romantic to me. Sure, at first it felt like a burden, to wait until we were the Syrena version of married before I could fully enjoy Galen. And then I don't know when, but I started to view things differently. He was giving me so much—living on land and adopting a human way of life for me. And all he asked in return was that I observe this one tradition. What kind of lowlife would I be if I refused him that one thing? Sure, I enjoy tempting him and teasing him. But I always know he'll come around and do the noble thing—he always does. So why is he backpedaling now? Did I finally push him over the edge?

Words of remorse form in my mouth, but he presses a finger against my lips.

"I know," he says. "Not like this."

I nod. "Sorry. It's just that—"

He laughs. "Funny that you feel *you* should be apologizing to *me*."

"I tempted you and I shouldn't have. I'll keep up my end of the deal from now on, I promise."

This seems to startle him. "Deal?"

"That you'll wait for me if I wait for you."

He's quiet for a long time then nods. My legs are now falling asleep. This position wasn't so awkward five minutes ago, but now it's pretty close to torture. I brace myself on the driver's side door, ready to move back to my own seat, when Galen pulls me in for one last kiss.

And when he does, someone taps on the window. Fan-flipping-tastic.

Galen stiffens underneath me. "You've got to be kidding," he mutters into my neck.

That's when I have the good sense to be mortified. Not so much at how far we'd gone, how close we'd come. No, I'd already apologized for that, felt the appropriate shame. But this, this is a new kind of horror. Because it's a public one. We are still in a less-than-ideal position. On the side of the flipping interstate.

"Everything okay in there? Having car troubles?" a man says. Then that rotund stranger proceeds to make a mask of his hands and peer into the freaking window, pressing his porous nose onto the glass and blowing a circle of steam on it. Mother of pearl.

"Oh," he says. "Beg your pardon." He eases away from the window just as I'm positioning myself back into the refuge of my own seat. Galen has already somehow put his shirt back on. Which is, of course, both a relief and devastating to me at the same time.

He rolls the window down and somehow manages to sound polite when he says, "May I help you?" But his voice is thick, full of appetite. He's as affected as I am, just from the beginnings of a kiss.

The man's face is as red as the rash of kisses Galen left on my neck. "Sorry about that," the man says, tucking his thumbs into the straps of his overalls. "I was just making sure y'all were all right. I saw you had an out-of-state tag."

How he could have noticed that from the canal of speeding cars that is the interstate, I couldn't say. Unless, of course,

Tennessee is full of the type of do-gooders that would actually turn around and help someone. Any other day, any other second in the existence of the universe, I would appreciate that.

But as it stands right now, I want to choke this man. And curse Tennessee for churning out such helpful citizens.

Galen frowns at the man. "We aren't in need of assistance, thank you."

The man glances past Galen, making an obvious show of scrutinizing the situation. He looks like his name could be Herschel. Or Grady. "Everything okay here, young lady?" he says to me.

Galen must realize his purpose, because he leans back in the seat, allowing Herschel/Grady a good look at me. I'm going to kill Galen. And not just because a complete stranger is more worried about my virtue than he is at the moment.

"It was," I tell him pointedly.

The man clears his throat. "Well, I apologize for the, uh . . . interruption. Have yourself a good day." It looks as though he might grace us with his absence, but then he turns back to the window. He scratches the back of his neck in an almost superstitious way. "You know, a purdy rough storm is moving in. Might want to think about getting where you want to go." With this, he departs. We wait until we hear his truck door slam shut before we breathe again.

Or at least, I do.

Galen grips the steering wheel tightly with both hands. "I think we should stop for the day."

I know he's not great at driving in bad weather. But I don't think he's talking about driving. A tiny knot of rejection grows in my stomach. "Okay," I tell him. But what did I expect? He's just doing the right thing. Do I want him to, or not?

He whips his gaze to me. "No, I mean, if it's going to rain, then maybe we should . . . I mean . . ."

I laugh. "Tongue-tied?"

He catches my double meaning, too. "Emma."

It's then that I turn away from him. Looking at him for one second longer would guarantee another visit to his lap, which is clearly not what he wants right now. I'm starting to think I don't know what Galen wants. And I'm starting to doubt whether he knows what he wants, either.

Maybe by the end of this trip, we'll both have it figured out.

I pull out my phone and peruse the screen for the link I'd found earlier. I feel the heat receding from my cheeks. My lips still feel like they're on fire, though. "There are some touristy areas nearby. Springs. Caves. Sounds ideal for stretching."

Galen lets out a breath. "Sounds perfect, actually. The farther away from people, the better."

I can't help but search for double meaning in that, too.

6

GALEN STEPS into the shallow water, startling some nearby frogs whose songlike croaks stop immediately. Even as the wind chops up the surface of the spring, a school of frenzied minnows whip up some ripples of their own. Galen marvels that no birds are taking this opportunity to feed. He supposes all the winged creatures here are fat and happy though, what with all the potential food above water—frogs and insects and other crawly things—why bother getting wet at all? Birds are meant for the air.

Just as Syrena are meant for the water. He tries to stop it, but the thought pushes through anyway. *If Syrena are meant for the water, what am I doing here on land?*

Then the reason he is here shuts the door to the SUV. Emma must be done changing into her swimsuit—and hopefully it's a swimsuit that covers her well. After his slipup today, he can't risk letting her stroll around in just any state of undress at the moment. Even the law didn't hold him back this afternoon when he had her in his lap, intending on doing just exactly what he shouldn't. But Emma views his self-control— what's left of it, anyway—as a rejection. He's explained to her about the importance of the law, even though he's been questioning the importance of it himself.

It seems to him that Triton and Poseidon wielded superstition rather than reason when they concocted the law all those centuries ago. That they scared their subjects into subjection instead of reasoning with them. Grom is different, Galen knows. He's open-minded, taking what the humans call a progressive approach. And Galen has a suspicion that Antonis is, too, if the way the Poseidon king eagerly embraced the idea of a Half-Breed granddaughter is any indication.

But the Royals have already pushed the old law to its limits by accepting Emma into their fold. Adhering to all the other aspects of the law now is more important than ever if the Royals are to regain full trust from the kingdoms again. From the Archives. From the Commons. From the ex-Loyals, Jagen's brood of followers.

There is no room for distrust if they are to keep the kingdoms united.

Galen knows there will come a time when humans will discover them. Grom knows it, too. And when that happens, the Syrena have a better chance of surviving if they work together. No more silent wars. No more rebellions by those who can tickle the ear and not follow through with their promises. If there was ever a time they could not afford dissension, it would be now.

Galen is drawn from his thoughts by the sound of Emma's bare feet pressing into the leaves. With each step she takes, his blood seems to heat up, to flow more freely. The tension melts away from him, and all those kingdom problems are absorbed into the air to rain on him another time. Because right now he has Emma.

He thinks of what she said in the car. About their "deal." *She'll wait for me if I wait for her. But is there a real reason to wait anymore?* He shakes his head. *Of course there is, idiot. If not for the law, then to keep the trust of the kingdoms.*

He smiles as the sound of her footsteps becomes the sound of her stumbling, then gasping. She's not nearly as graceful on land as she is in the water. Maybe he could show her that, how much more she belongs in the water than on land. How much easier it is to live in the oceans than to come ashore and build relationships with humans who will eventually die and—

"Wow, look at those clouds," she says from behind him, sloshing the water as she wades in. Then slender fingers lace through his, and the rest of his anxiety hitches a ride on the strengthening wind. "Will we be safe in the water?"

He presses a quick kiss to the tip of her nose, which is the only safe place for his lips to be at the moment. Before she can pout, he pulls her deeper into the water. To his relief—and his disappointment—she's wearing a one-piece swimsuit and has also opted for a pair of matching shorts. "We'll be fine."

"Outswim lightning, can you?" Half of her sentence is

above the surface, half is below. She giggles when her voice distorts for a brief moment.

"I'm not saying I can outswim lightning," he says, pulling her in deeper and deeper. "But I'm not saying I can't, either." *After all, the Gift of Triton makes me faster than any other Syrena alive.* He knows if Emma were in danger, he'd give lightning a fair race.

For a split second, the tendrils of Emma's hair interlace with the tendrils of the last of the sunlight tickling the surface of the spring, and suddenly she's enveloped in a halo of gold warmth. It's all Galen can do to remember how to breathe. If he'd known spring water could be this glorious, he would have sought it out sooner.

"What?" she says. "Is there something behind me?"

"Now I know why humans bring cameras everywhere they go. You never know when perfection will sneak up and show itself to you."

She eases closer to him, but he keeps an arm's length between her body and his. He turns away from her, hoping to redirect her attention from what he knows she will see as a rejection, and to focus it on what's below them. "There's a cave entrance down there. Do you see it?"

She nods. "Do you think it's safe to go in?"

He laughs. "Since when were you concerned about your own safety?"

"Oh, shut it," she grumbles as they near the opening.

Still, he motions for her to stay behind him. "If anything is down here, then I want it to be busy eating me while you're getting away, angelfish."

"That's not your decision."

Galen pauses. He knows it takes a moment for Emma's eyes to adjust to the darkness of the deep water, and when they enter the cave completely, even the occasional glow of lightning from the surface won't be able to find them. "Better?" he says after a few moments.

She answers him by trying to swim ahead. He reins her in to his side, closer than is wise, and yet not as close as he'd like. The heat from her body seems to jump at him, even through the cold current and his thick skin. *And since when did heat send shivers through me?* "Fine," he says, more exasperated with himself than with her. "We'll go together. But I swear by Triton's trident, if you try to get in front—"

"Side by side is always okay with me, Galen." Before she can come up with another smart remark, she stops them both. "Look. That is amazing."

He follows her line of sight to a row of pointed rocks ahead of them. It reminds him of the entrance to the Cave of Memories. All the rocks spearing up from the ground look like teeth, ready and able to chew anyone brave enough to swim through them.

And if Emma is impressed with this, he can't wait until she sees all the caves have to offer. Not only this spring-fed cave, but all of them. The ones in the deepest part of the ocean where the only inhabitants are the marine life that create their own lights to attract their prey. Maybe one day, after things have settled a bit, he'll take her to the Cave of Memories. She would truly love that.

"This is the part in a horror movie where you're supposed

to turn back," she says as they pass the first row of "teeth." Her voice is light, but when he stops, she clings to his arm. "What? What's wrong?"

Gently, he pushes her away from him and drifts a few feet backward. "Do you feel . . . heavier in this water?"

"No. Why? Do I look heavier?"

He rolls his eyes.

"Well, then what do you mean by heavier?"

He flicks his tail back and forth, watching as the wake stirs up some muck. "It feels different here. It takes more effort to get through the water. You haven't noticed?"

She shrugs. "A little, I guess. Maybe it's the freshwater. In saltwater, everything is more buoyant."

"But you don't feel a difference?"

"I don't think I would have noticed if you hadn't mentioned it."

He retrieves her hand and laces his fingers back through hers. "I'm that distracting, huh?"

She smiles. "You have no idea."

He leans in, intending for the smallest of kisses on her lips. Just something to tide him over, really. Just an innocent, controlled kiss, nothing like the raw passion he almost couldn't contain this afternoon. At least, that's what he intends. . . .

And then it hits him. A faint thrum of electricity that comes and goes. Prickly and intrusive one second, then fluid and soft the next. There's no way that's lightning.

It can't be. He's felt lightning in the water before. It's almost like a rogue wave that sweeps through, and before you can blink, it's gone—passing through your body without permission or apology. Yes, it's tingly. But not like this.

This feels like . . . But can it really be?

He shakes his head to himself. No. *There's no way that I'm sensing a pulse.*

Because Syrena do not have pulses like that. A Syrena pulse is strong, not like the watered-down thrumming he barely feels against his skin now.

Then what could it be?

7

IT'S A rare thing to see panic on Galen's face. So when alarm takes over his expression and his entire body tightens like a drawn rubber band, I'm pretty much on the verge of freaking out. Especially since we're in the stomach of a foreign cave with sharp teeth, and every time the thunder rumbles behind us, it sounds like said cave is hungry. And by Galen's face, he's also thinking we might be the appetizer. "Galen, I know you're busy being all heavy and everything, but you have to tell me what's going on, rightfreakingnow."

Why is it that when someone clamps their hand on your mouth, it makes you want to scream? "Be very still, angelfish," he whispers against the back of his own hand as he tightens it over my lips. A scream builds up inside me, rapping on my vocal chords to set it free. Swallowing doesn't help. "I...I think I sense something."

"Something?" I say, but through his hand it sounds like "Umfin?" I thought Syrena could only sense each other, not objects or animals or whatever other "things" Galen could be talking about. Already, this hand-over-mouth thing has grown old. Slowly, I peel his fingers from my face to show him I'm not going to do anything rash. No sudden movements, no loud noises, no swimming ahead.

Definitely no swimming ahead.

"What do you mean, 'something'?" I hiss.

Galen won't tear his eyes away from the tunnel ahead of us. Just a few more feet and the cave takes a sharp turn to the right. To think we were actually about to go down there, into the bowels of this place. "I sense . . . something," he says quietly. "It's not Syrena, of that I'm certain. I've never sensed this before." He tucks me behind him, and for once, I let him. "Whatever it is, it's right around that corner. It's getting closer."

I press my forehead into his broad back. "Are you trying to freak me out? Because it's working."

He chuckles and I relax a little. "I'm not trying to freak you out, I promise. It's just . . . interesting. You're not curious to see what it is?"

That's when I notice that we're moving. Ahead. Since when did Galen become curious? He's usually the one pulling *me* back. "But you don't know what it is. What if it's dangerous? What if it's like, Jaws's prehistoric cousin or something?"

"What?"

"Nothing." I admit to myself that I do sound a bit panicky. My voice slams against the cave walls, and when it returns to me, I can hear the distinct rattle of hysteria in it. I peer over his shoulder. "Do you see it yet?"

"Not yet."

"Should I call for backup?"

Galen pauses. "Actually, have you even seen any fish in here? I haven't. That's weird."

It's not weird; it's terrifying. There should be fish here. But so far, there's not a single living thing in this hull of rock. Which probably means a natural predator has set up shop in here.

"Hello?" a voice calls from around the bend.

So the natural predator here is male and speaks English. My first thought is a scuba diver or at the very least a snorkeler. But the words are clear, without the muffling of a mask or mouth-piece. And wouldn't he need a light down here? Yet there is no light striking through the water. Or maybe my eyes have adjusted enough to where I wouldn't notice.

A large swarm of fish burst around the turn of the cave and blow past us. Before they get too far, I call after them. "Where are you going? Who's chasing you? Come back." I also want to say, *Take me with you*, but that wouldn't be very brave.

The entire group comes back and encircles Galen and me. The fish here are not as colorful as they can be in the saltwater, but they're still interesting to look at—and apparently they think I am, too. Some have stripes and razorlike fins. Others are long and speckled with pink bellies. Then there are short, paunchy-looking fish with spots like a leopard. But despite their differences, they all have one thing in common: They understand the Gift of Poseidon.

It takes me a moment to realize that Galen isn't looking at the halo of fish around us anymore. He's looking straight ahead, his jaw clenched. "Who are you?" he says.

The boy swimming toward us cautiously is muscular and, apparently, bold. His blond hair is a bit longer than Galen's, maybe shoulder length, but I can't tell because it floats above his head like a fan. He eases closer, wearing only blue swimming trunks and an easy smile, despite the fact that Galen feels taut under my fingertips, ready to spring. Behind him is a rope snaking through the water, and at the end of it, a bunch of dead fish pulled together by the rope through each of their gills.

Either this boy has a death wish or his brain doesn't have the ability to process fear because he drifts steadily toward us, as if on a current. He could be our age, or very close to it. He wears no snorkel, no breathing equipment, and carries no light. Not in a particular hurry to get to the surface for air, either.

My own breath stalls.

"You have the Gift," he says, cocking his head toward me. He's not asking. He's not even surprised. If anything, he's pleased.

My legs jerk beneath me as if I've forgotten how to swim.

"And you are?" Galen says. Which I'm grateful for, because right at the moment, my mouth won't form words.

I realize then that I can sense him, too. Not like I sense Galen or Rayna or Toraf. It's different. It's more a faint sweeping caress, a phantom touch. Maybe that's what I thought was lightning. But the truth is, I felt it as soon as we stepped in the water. Before a vein of lightning ever splayed across the sky.

The boy shows us his hands, that they're empty. "I'm Reed."

A fish swims in front of us, blocking our view. "Oh, come on!" Reed says. "I've told you to stay out of people's faces. Go find someone else to bother, or *you'll* be on the end of this rope." He looks back at me. "You don't have to be so polite with them, you know. They're an unruly bunch."

My heart drops to my feet when the fish scatter. But it's probably because he startled them. Not because they under-stand what he's saying. *Right?*

All the fish are gone, except for a long pink-bellied one who swims to Reed with familiarity, like a dog would approach its beloved owner. "I call him Vac, short for Vacuum, which is ex-actly what he does when he gets around minnows. He's a serial killer, this one."

Galen is not amused. "What are you?"

I feel it's a valid question, but Reed thinks otherwise. "Well that's not good manners, now is it?"

"You're a Half-Breed," Galen says. He tucks his arm behind him, a visible show of protection. A shudder runs through me, but I stamp it down before it bubbles to the surface. A Half-Breed? *This is not happening.*

But . . . It's so obvious, isn't it?

Blond hair.

Pale skin.

Violet eyes.

No fin.

In an underwater cave with no breathing equipment, bonding with fish.

Reed's smirk reveals a tiny dimple in the corner of his mouth. "And you're especially observant."

Nofreakingway. Another Half-Breed. Like me. *How? When? What? Holy . . .*

"How did you find us?" Galen barks.

I still can't figure out the danger here. Reed is not armed. And so far, he hasn't shown us any aggression. In fact, he seems pretty much amused by us.

"Find you? That implies I was looking, now doesn't it?" He eases toward us some more, and I feel Galen tense up. "Ironic, but I was trying to get away from strangers."

I know Galen doesn't want me to talk to this boy. It's one of those unspoken things where body language—the fact that he's still pushing me behind him—is the greatest communicator.

But Galen doesn't always get what he wants. "Where did you come from?" I say, maneuvering around Galen. I figure that's a good place to start. He grabs my wrist, so I stop, waiting for Galen to be comfortable that I've come out from hiding.

Reed offers me the kind of smile that says, *At your service.* "I'm from Neptune. I didn't catch your name?"

"She didn't give it to you," Galen says, tightening his grip.

"Emma," I say, not daring to look back at Galen. "My name is Emma. Are there others like you?"

"That's an odd question to ask," he says. Curiosity drips from his handsome features.

I guess it is odd. I mean, if there are two of us Half-Breeds, there are bound to be more, right? But why? How? I shake my head. In his statement is a question, and answering one way or the other would be a half lie. I knew there was something here in Tennessee. Grandfather was adamant that Galen and I travel here, that there was something of interest I'd want to see. Now I understand why he didn't tell me what it was, why he let me find out on my own.

Grandfather knew I would tell Galen. And somehow he knew Galen would not like it.

"How far away is Neptune? Can you take us there?" I blurt.

Reed is already nodding even as Galen grabs my wrist. "Emma," he growls. "We don't know him."

I turn on him. "Antonis sent us here to find it. I think it's pretty clear why." Immediately I feel guilty for chastising him in front of a perfect stranger.

"Why wouldn't he just tell us about it and let us decide for ourselves?"

And suddenly the guilt is gone. At first I don't answer. Anger percolates in my gut. Because Galen doesn't mean, "let us decide for ourselves." He means "let me decide for both of us." And I'm not okay with that.

I turn back to Reed. "I've decided for myself that I want to see Neptune. Will you take me?"

8

GALEN'S FOCUS darts between the two-lane road ahead and the stranger in the rearview mirror. Reed takes up a good portion of the backseat, leaning his elbow on the middle console that separates the driver from the passenger. The passenger being an all-too-attentive Emma.

"It's about twenty more miles ahead. There won't be any signs for Neptune. We were only recently added to GPS. Like, this year," Reed tells Emma. He seems almost proud of this unimpressive feat. And so does Emma.

"And there are more Half-Breeds in Neptune?" she says, not even trying to hide her excitement.

Reed answers with a smirk.

Galen feels as though he's entered a bad dream, one that he can't wake up from. He silently curses Antonis for his involvement in this. *What was he thinking, sending us to a town full of Half-Breeds, whose very existence breaks the law? Right when we're trying to earn back the trust of our kingdoms, no less! And he places Emma right in the middle of it all.*

What's worse, Emma seems to be completely comfortable with it.

"It's a small town," Reed concedes. "But there are full-blooded Syrena there, too. And humans. Humans who keep our secret."

Galen whips a glance at him. "How is that possible?" And how have Trackers not discovered this cache of deserters? Especially Toraf, who can sense Syrena anywhere in the world. Or does the freshwater affect his Tracking, the way it affects Galen's ability to sense?

The only other community mix of Half-Breeds and Syrena Galen has ever heard of is Tartessos—which was destroyed by General Triton thousands of years ago. The story goes that all of General Poseidon's Half-Breed children were destroyed, and all the full-blooded Syrena returned to the oceans never again to return to land.

How could another community have started without the knowledge of the kingdoms? Who are these stray full-blooded Syrena who've initiated another generation—or more—of Half-Breeds?

Reed pauses, scrutinizing Galen in the rearview. "Look, I appreciate the ride back to town and all. But I've answered all your questions, and so far, you haven't offered any information about yourselves. Doesn't seem very fair."

Emma nods. "What would you like to know?"

Galen casts her a warning glare, but Emma pretends not to notice. In fact, she's trying at all costs not to look at him at all.

"Well," Reed says, leaning forward just enough to make Galen want to readjust his jaw with an uppercut, "I know you're from the ocean. At least, he is. You're obviously a descendant of an ocean-dwelling Syrena."

Emma's mouth drops open.

Reed shrugs. "Oh, don't worry, I'm not psychic or anything. Ocean dwellers send different pulses than freshwater Syrena. The best we can figure is that over time the lack of salt in the water changed the way we sense each other. That somehow our bodies adapted to being in freshwater." He studies Emma more closely, if that were possible. "But my question is, Why have you come? And how can I get you to stay?"

Galen nearly fails to brake for the car slowing in front of them. "We're not staying." He doesn't miss Emma's frown.

"It's a long story," Emma says, melting into a smile for Reed. "My mother is Syrena; my father was human. I grew up on land. My grandfather visited your town once, I think. He's the one who sent us here."

Antonis must have visited Neptune. That's how Reed already knew that we sense each other differently in freshwater. What else did Antonis share with these strangers?

"Sent you here?"

"Well, it was actually more of a scavenger hunt, I guess," Emma says quickly. "He pointed us in your general direction but didn't tell us what we would find in Neptune."

"Why would he do that?" Reed looks Galen square in the eyes.

Galen decides Reed has a gift for discernment. "We were wondering the same thing," he mutters.

Emma laughs. "It's obvious he wanted us to find you. Oh, um, no, Neptune," she stutters. "I meant he wanted us to find Neptune."

Reed shifts his attention back to Emma. "I'm glad he did."

Galen is quite certain Reed is not under any false impressions about his relationship with Emma. And he's just as sure Reed doesn't care. Reed is thoroughly enchanted by Emma, and Galen can't blame him.

But I can knock his teeth out. . . .

Reed continues to ask questions, and Emma continues to offer vague but truthful answers: Her mother has lived on land all of her life. Her father was a human doctor, who knew her mother was Syrena. She met Galen off the coast of Florida. The kingdoms are aware of her existence, and for the time being are okay with it.

To Galen's relief, Emma doesn't offer any information about their Royal heritage or the recent events that led to her discovery. He knows she feels a connection with this new stranger, and while he doesn't like it, he at least understands it. Reed is a Half-Breed like her. With that carries novelty and curiosity, and for Emma, a certain sense of belonging. Especially if they're approaching a town full of Half-Breeds.

But Galen's not about to trust this blond boy who oozes charm. Galen has been fooled by a good-natured smile before. It won't happen again.

9

IT'S LIKE Galen's not even in the car with us. Reed and I converse while Galen broods over the steering wheel. At Reed's direction, he pulls us onto a winding gravel road, leading us farther and farther into the woods, closer and closer to the cleavage of two nearby mountains.

To the town of Neptune.

There is a wooden sign at the edge of town with the words WELCOME TO NEPTUNE carved in big letters at the top and TOWN OF MEMORIES at the bottom in smaller, more elegant letters. The sign stands in a flower bed lined with white-painted rocks. Galen's gaze seems to linger on the bottom words as we pass. I want to ask him about it, but I know better than to do so in front of Reed.

Galen's quiet saturates the air between us, a silent disapproval of my immediate acceptance of Reed. It occurs to me that Galen could be jealous, too, which is moderately insane. Especially given our afternoon make-out session just hours before. So I decide to give him the benefit of the doubt and treat his withdrawal from the conversation as caution. Actually, I'm kind of hoping this is about Reed in some way and not about the existence of Neptune, or my excitement about it. Because *of course* I'm excited. What's not intriguing about a town of Half-Breeds? Surely Galen can understand why I'm so interested. And if not, he should make more of an effort here.

The SUV pulls onto what looks like the main street of Neptune. A row of small, endearing stores and offices line both sides of the street. To me, it's the cliché depiction of a town in the old West, only there are cars parked in front of the businesses instead of horses tied to wooden posts. A medley of people promenade the concrete sidewalks. Some are obviously Syrena— olive skin, black hair, violet eyes, classic muscular build. Others are obvious Half-Breeds. And then there are those who could be human—or a cocktail of all three species combined. There are blond pale Asians. There are blond lighter-colored African-Americans. Old and young. Male and female. A walking jumble of species and races and ages and genders.

I take it all in, ignoring my growing excitement and Galen's deepening scowl. "So all these people live around here? Where?"

"They live in houses, just like regular people. We live like humans here. Because most of us are partly human." Reed gives me a meaningful look, which I pretend not to notice.

"So what do you *do* here?"

"What do you mean?"

"What is the purpose of the town? Is this—" I sweep my hand toward the buildings and people around us. "Is all this just for show? Or are those shops really open?"

Reed laughs. "Of course, they're open. We need hardware stores and post offices and grocery stores just like any other town. We have electric bills, too, you know."

Mind-blowing. "So how does it all work? How do you pay the electric bills?"

"This is turning into a social studies lesson."

I roll my eyes. "You know what I mean."

"We are pretty self-sufficient. I work part-time at the grocery store after school, but I take off summers for fishing. Some of the humans commute to neighboring towns to work at banks and insurance companies or whatever. I guess I don't know how else to explain it. We're just a normal town."

Reed doesn't know how to explain it, and I don't know what else to ask. I guess I thought maybe it was all for show and they were all independently wealthy like Galen. But Reed is right, they really are a normally functioning small town. As normal as a town full of Half-Breeds could be.

We halt at the only stoplight in sight, in front of what appears to be a three-story cottage-like bed-and-breakfast—a big sign in the front indicates there are no vacancies. A man sits on the front porch in a white rocking chair. So far, he is the only one who seems out of place, and maybe that's just because he's wearing a white lab coat covered with the soil he's packing into the potted plant in front of him. He looks up and pauses, watching the SUV as if it were an approaching predator. Once again, I'm grateful for the tinted windows.

I look at Reed. "Who's that man?" Not that I think Reed could possibly know everyone in town, but this guy lends himself to speculation.

He glances at the man on the porch. There is an underlying tension when he says, "Mr. Kennedy. He's been staying at Sylvia's place for about a month."

I nod. "Why is he here?" Which might seem like an odd question, but really, all the other humans I've seen seem to belong here. All of them seem privy to the secrets of the little town of Neptune. All of them except this guy.

Reed shrugs. "We try to make the town as uninteresting to tourists as possible—for obvious reasons. But Mr. Kennedy is not a tourist, exactly. He's a botanist, and he's here to look for new plant species. He's kind of a nut, actually. Always talking to himself and running into things. And he always has black fingernails from digging around in the dirt." Reed's face scrunches up as if playing in the dirt were the same thing as playing in a pile of crap.

The light turns green, and we pass the bed-and-breakfast, but I don't have to look back to know Mr. Kennedy is still staring after us. "And what makes him think he'll find new plant species here?"

I can practically hear Reed shrug. "Not sure. He's not really a talker. And he's mostly in the woods all day, searching for his eco-treasure."

"You can't get rid of him?" Galen says, startling me.

"Get rid of him? You mean kill him?" Reed laughs softly. "I don't know how you do things in the ocean, but here, we don't go around killing people. That sort of thing is kind of frowned upon in these parts."

"That's not what I meant," Galen clips. "Why don't you drive him away? There are more of you than him."

"It's not as easy as it sounds. Back in the 1950s, all the residents here decided to incorporate as a real town. Which meant Neptune fell under the jurisdiction of the county and the state and all that garbage. Sure, we had to follow human laws before that, but it wasn't until then that we had to keep a close eye on who we ran off and who we let stay. Nowadays, someone can cry discrimination based on the size of their shoe, and then we're in one huge mudslinging competition." He turns to me and winks. "We had to change our bullying ways."

Galen snorts. I give Reed a reproving look. "Well, *were* you discriminating?"

Reed grins. "Of course," he says, and my tongue is gearing up to unleash all the things my temper is about to say. Galen almost looks amused. That is, until Reed covers my mouth with his hand. "Before you haul off and say something you don't mean, I was just kidding. We filter the people we tell our secrets to, of course, but it doesn't have anything to do with race or religion or whatever."

"Get your hand off her," Galen says. "If you want to keep it."

I second the motion, returning his entire arm to him in the backseat.

"He's a bit touchy, huh?" Reed says without looking at Galen. "Not that I blame him."

Really? He's going to go there? Galen's jaw locks. His patience is almost obliterated. "I think we should establish—"

But Reed interrupts him, unaffected. "Here it is. Here's my house."

As soon as Galen pulls into the dirt driveway, Reed is out of the vehicle and hopping up the three steps to his front porch with his rope of fish slung over his shoulder. The house is old and dilapidated, but not without appeal. Bright baskets of pink and white pansies line the porch railings, drawing attention away from the peeling paint and chipped wood.

Galen and I get out but wait in front of the SUV. It's not like we've received an invitation to come in. Reed has disappeared inside the house, but we can hear him stomping around and calling, "Mooooom! We have company. And I caught fish for dinner."

Galen throws me a look that clearly says, "Let's make a run for it."

But I shake my head. I'm sure this is what Grandfather wanted, for me to come here and meet others like me. Galen crosses his arms. I walk over to him and plant a soft kiss on his lips.

"What was that for?" he says, noticeably pleased.

"For cooperating when I know you don't want to."

He's about to say something else, but Reed materializes in the doorway and beckons us inside. "I guess Mom's not here," he says over the slamming screen door behind us. He's got a chocolate chip cookie in each hand. He offers me one. "They're still warm."

I decline, a little perturbed that he didn't ask Galen if he wanted one, too. Not that Galen would eat it, but it's the principle. Reed seems to read my mind.

"We've always got some sushi handy," he says to Galen. "I know most Syrena hate the sweet stuff. My dad included."

"No, thank you," Galen says, though I think robots sound more courteous.

Reed gives us the shorthand tour of the house. The three bedrooms upstairs belong to him, his parents, and his little brother Toby. There are homemade crafts decorating every wall, beautifully constructed quilts gracing each bed, and the smell of a fire going somewhere, even though it's midsummer. The floor squeaks in a kind of charming serenade.

He circles us back down to the kitchen, where he swipes another cookie from a well-endowed plate. This time, I accept his offer for one. I know Galen thinks I'm throwing caution to the wind, but it's more like I'm throwing it up as a kite and seeing if it will fly.

We take a seat at the retro orange-and-yellow kitchen table.

"So," I say around a mouthful of chocolate goodness, "How old are you?"

Reed grins. "Twenty. You?"

I'm about to tell him eighteen, but I've managed to get another year older during all the chaos. My birthday pretty much went unacknowledged by me—and apparently, by everyone else. It's been a busy year. "Nineteen."

He glances at Galen. "And you?"

"Twenty-one."

Reed nods, more to himself than to us. Then the stringy sound of a banjo fills the air, giving us a reprieve from yet another awkward moment. Reed jumps up and grabs the cell phone erupting with country music on the counter. Apparently it's his mom. He walks it into the living room, and all we hear are a few hushed words and then, "See you soon."

This makes Galen uneasy. Not that everything doesn't make Galen uneasy nowadays. When Reed returns, he brings with him his laid-back smile. "Mom wants you to stay the night and visit with us. Galen and I can take the couches in the living room, and you can sleep in my room."

"We don't want to impose," Galen says quickly. "If we're going to visit," he glances at me as if he's asking me if we are, instead of agreeing to it, "then we can stay at the bed-and-breakfast. What did you call it? Sylvia's?"

"The sign said there's no vacancy," I say.

"The sign always says that," Reed says. "Mr. Kennedy creeped out poor Sylvia, so she's not accepting new out-of-towners. I'm sure you'll be the exception though, since you're one of us."

A frown tugs at Galen's mouth. He doesn't like being referred to as "one of us." It makes me feel guilty that I do like it. In fact, I'm kind of delighted by it. But for now, I'm relieved to check in to our room and have a private discussion about the day's events. Staying here at Reed's house would feel too . . . public. Which is silly, given that the inn is about dead center in town. Anyone who's curious could come up there to see us—including the spooktastic Mr. Kennedy.

I admit Mr. Kennedy wouldn't have registered on my weirdness radar under normal circumstances. It's just that Reed seems to view him as "different," and it's nice to view someone else that way instead of feeling like the outcast, as selfish as that sounds.

Reed offers to accompany us to Sylvia's, but Galen holds up his hand. It's a finalizing gesture. "No, thank you. I remember the way back."

Our new friend doesn't miss a beat. "Just be back here at six o'clock. I told Mom you were coming to dinner, at the very least. Don't make a liar out of me."

When it looks like Galen might protest again, Reed supplements, "Toby caught some trout over at the creek. I'd love to know what you think of freshwater fish, Galen."

Galen runs a hand through his hair. "Fine. We'll see you at six o'clock then."

I pretend not to notice that Reed is smiling at me like a canary-gobbling cat.

10

GALEN HAULS the suitcases to the second floor of Sylvia's Starfish Bed & Breakfast. He waits while Emma opens the door to her room before he drags her belongings in behind her. Since he and Emma aren't mated yet, Sylvia insisted on them staying in separate rooms, as all of them were "romantically designed" with only one bed.

Apparently the town of Neptune picks and chooses which of the old laws is most convenient to follow.

Emma falls onto the bed, a beautifully appointed wrought iron creation with light blue satin bedding and lacy ruffles around the bottom. The bed squeaks with her every movement, and she giggles. "It's not that romantic, if you know what I mean."

Galen grins and sets the suitcases underneath the window. Then he takes a spot on the bed next to Emma. The air in here smells stale to him, as if this room hasn't been used in ages. "What do you make of this place?"

What he really wants to say is, "What do you think about Reed and his infatuation with you?" but that would just start a fight, not to mention bring all the jealous feelings he'd had bubbling up back to the surface. Reed's fascination with Emma has gotten Galen's imagination stirring on so many levels.

First, he imagined bringing the SUV to a sudden stop that pitched Reed straight through the windshield and landed his bloodied, broken body on the gravel road ahead.

Then there was the fantasy of using his fist to relieve Reed of every one of his teeth, thereby creating his own version of an easy smile.

Not to mention the daydream of punching Reed in the stomach hard enough for him to choke on whatever remnants he forgot to chew of his chocolate chip cookie.

"I think it's too early to tell yet," Emma says, startling him from his reverie.

"Really? That's not what it looked like."

She rolls her eyes as he rests his elbow on the mattress, propping his head up so it rests just over hers. Their noses almost touch. *Triton's trident, her skin is flawless.* "I don't think you give me enough credit. And I don't think you give Reed enough credit, either."

"That's what I was afraid of." He leans back and stares at the ceiling. "Emma, we don't know these people. And what we do know about them is that they shouldn't exist. That they're here living on land, risking our discovery."

"I think it's safe to say they're risking their discovery, not ours. Can't we agree on the fact that they've stayed hidden—even from us—for long enough to prove they mean us no harm?"

"You're a Half-Breed, angelfish. If they're discovered, you're discovered."

"How so? No one's going to point me out of a crowd and start shouting."

"You don't know that. And I don't want to find out."

Emma sighs. He can tell he's aggravating her, but what does she expect? For him to embrace all of the strangers like long-lost cousins? It just doesn't work that way. Especially not under the circumstances.

"You don't want to be here." She says it as if he's betrayed her somehow.

"I want to be wherever you are."

"That's a generic answer."

He pinches the bridge of his nose. "No. I don't want to be here." He rolls over again, looking down on the glory that is her face. Tracing the back of his hand along her cheek, he says, "Truth be told, my first instinct is to run. To get as far away from here as possible."

She doesn't like the honesty in that answer. He can't help it. "Why?"

"Because they're breaking the law."

"But you said yourself the law is a bunch of superstition. Have you forgotten? I'm an exception to the law. Couldn't they be?" It's true, he's back and forth about the law. But right now, the law seems to have reinvented itself into good common sense.

"Well they're not exactly asking to be pardoned, are they? Besides, what *I* think about the law doesn't matter. It's what the *kingdoms* think about the law—and they still have a law against the existence of Half-Breeds." He winces when a glint of pain flashes across her face. "Of more than one Half-Breed," he corrects. "Right now, I think we should concentrate on keeping the peace between the kingdoms and not throwing another Royal scandal in their faces." Every time he opens his mouth, Grom comes out.

"It doesn't feel like a scandal to me, Galen. Besides, my grandfather knew about this place. He's been here. And obviously he doesn't think it's such a scandal."

"Actually, I'm quite certain he does," Galen says dryly. "Otherwise he wouldn't have kept it a secret." And Galen's first instinct is to be furious about it. *What was Antonis thinking?* "Why was he here, anyway?"

"He said he was looking for Mom."

"On *land?*"

She shrugs. "Turns out, Mom had a fascination with all things human. Kind of like Rayna."

Galen doesn't appreciate the comparison. Rayna only collects human things. She would never abandon the Syrena way of life to actually live on land. Still, he doesn't feel confident enough to say that out loud. Rayna is unpredictable, after all. Just like Nalia, Emma's mother.

And just like Emma.

Galen is tired of everything being unpredictable; he's ready for things to settle down. But the human world seems too tainted with complications for that to happen. Look where it got Nalia. She lived among the humans, all the while missing out on Grom's devotion and love. Look at Emma. She's willing to shorten her life span, to deprive him of what could add up to years of her company, just to spend time on land. To go to human school. To do human things.

And look at Rachel. She *belonged* on land. But even one of the world's most resilient people proved too perishable—too human—in the end.

I was right all along to be wary of humans. And now I'm in too deep.

He's startled to find that Emma is watching him. He wonders what she sees. Can she tell how bitter he is? How desperate he is to tell her how he feels? And how terrified he is of her rejecting him?

But Emma seems to have some concerns of her own. Her whole face gives way to pleading—and Galen already knows he has very little power to resist whatever she's about to request of him. He wonders—and doubts—if he'll ever develop an immunity to that face of hers.

"I know you don't feel comfortable here," she says softly. "But the thing is, I do, Galen. In fact . . . In fact, it feels like I *belong* here. I'm not some weirdo outcast in Neptune. The only weirdo outcast here is Mr. Kennedy—and he's human."

You belong *with me,* is what he wants to say, which is a little more possessive than he cares to admit. But he can't help it. She's acting as if this place is the answer to her dreams. And deep down, he knows it's no use arguing. Emma has it in her mind to explore this place.

"You're not an outcast," is all he can say. He hates himself for hiding his true feelings, but he senses that now is not the time to argue. Emma wants to stay for a while, so they will.

But what will I do if she decides she permanently *belongs here?*

He puts his arm around her waist and pulls her closer against him, and she snuggles into the crook of his arm, relaxing. But no matter how close his body is to hers, there seems to be a new space between them. And Galen tightens his hold.

11

REED'S FAMILY is just as easygoing as he is. In fact, the dinner table is like a sort of center stage, and each of them takes turns occupying the spotlight.

His father, Reder Conway, is full-blooded Syrena, with a muscular build showing through his flannel shirt and olive skin glowing attractively in the relaxed lighting in the dining room. He has the same icy blue eyes as my mother—just more proof of how Syrena eye color changes after so much time spent on land. I wonder how long it will take for Galen's eyes to fade to blue. And if I'll be able to bear it when they do.

Reed's mother, Lauren, is unapologetically human. Blonde hair that I can tell would be curly, but that is French braided into submission with the occasional rebellious tendril sticking out. Large brown eyes that seem to miss nothing and a pear-shaped figure that could only be gotten by enjoying the sweeter things in life.

Toby, Reed's nine-year-old brother, is a classic Half-Breed—blond hair, pale skin—and a classic pain-in-the-butt, loud-mouthed younger sibling. I've always wanted one of those.

"Reed says you have the mark of a trident on your stomach," Toby says to Galen, so enthralled he almost passes the bowl of rolls to the floor instead of to me.

The clink and clatter of silverware stops. Mr. Conway takes a swig of his buttermilk, then leans back in his chair. He's trying to look casual. He's failing. "Is that right?" he says.

Galen cuts into a new potato that we both know he's not going to eat. "It's a tattoo," Galen says, shrugging.

Suddenly, dinner feels like a game. Mr. Conway is interested in Galen's Royal birthmark, and Galen is not interested in telling him about it. Lovely.

"Aww, crap," Toby says, crestfallen. "We were hoping you were a real-live Triton Royal. No one's seen one before."

Galen offers him a good-natured smile from across the table. Only I notice the slight flex in his jaw. "Sorry to disappoint, minnow."

"A tattoo, huh?" Reed says. "We haven't had much success with tattoos here. Some nonsense about our skin being too wa-terlogged for the ink to stick."

Galen shrugs. "Must be a freshwater thing."

What the heck? I can understand why Galen would be guarded—these people are still strangers, after all—but to flat-out lie? Especially when they already know what the trident means. Who cares if they know he's a Royal? If anything, his status could be used to open up communication with them. To start bridging the gap between freshwater and saltwater Syrena.

Unless Galen's not interested in bridging the gap.

I push that thought aside and pop a whole red potato in my mouth. It will keep me from blurting, and I'll have to concentrate on not choking instead of sifting through reasons why Galen wouldn't want to bridge random gaps.

"Not to question your judgment, Galen," Mr. Conway says. "But wouldn't the kingdoms see a human tattoo as . . . Well, as not only breaking the law, obviously, but also as a kind of sacrilege against the Royals? Especially a trident, like yours. Or have things in the ocean changed that much?" He glances with meaning at me, the Half-Breed girl Galen brought to dinner. Touché, right?

But for once in my life, I don't feel out of place as the Half-Breed girl. In fact, Mr. Conway winks at me, and I can't help but return a smile. At least, I hope it resembles a smile, but I may have literally bitten off more than I can chew. Maybe he's smiling because a *Half-Breed* brought a *Triton Royal* to dinner. That seems more of a noteworthy scandal here in Neptune.

Galen sets his fork down. I try not to notice the deliberation in the action. "No offense, Mr. Conway, but you don't give the impression of being overly concerned with the laws of the ocean."

Milk. I need milk. I take a bigger swig of it than I intended. It's the only way I can keep from gasping/choking/speaking out of turn. At this point, I expect Mr. Conway to throw us out. And I wouldn't blame him if he did.

"Please. Call me Reder," Mr. Conway says, oozing hospitality. "And you're right, of course. The laws of the ocean dwellers don't concern me. I'm just curious. What brings you to our neck of the woods? We haven't been visited by your kind for quite some time."

I wonder how old Reder is—and if my grandfather is the last "visitor" he's speaking of. Surely there aren't many dirty little law breakers among the ocean Syrena?

"Our way of life is very different from yours," Galen says. "We still have a healthy fear of humans. Which is why I've been appointed as an ambassador to them. I've been assigned to watch them and to report back to the kingdoms."

Since when did Galen fear humans? And is he trying to offend our host? "Galen has made some valuable human contacts," I blurt. "People who help him watch the human world. But he knows that not all humans are bad."

Under the table Galen grabs my knee. If he's trying to shut me up, it won't work. He does know that all humans aren't bad. *Doesn't he?*

Mr. Conway crosses his massive arms. It's a good intimidation move. Galen appears unimpressed. "And what will you be reporting about us, Galen?"

Galen smiles. "So far? That Mrs. Conway has a talent for making freshwater trout actually taste good."

Mr. Conway is about to parry, but Toby, oblivious to the tension, slurps the rest of his buttermilk and near slams it on the table. "Galen, Reed says you have the biggest fin he's ever seen."

Galen smirks at Reed, then nods his head toward him ever so slightly. "Thanks. I appreciate that."

Reed responds with a scowl.

I can tell that Toby was really asking a question instead of making a statement, and Galen probably realizes this, too, but he's not budging on any insights into why he'd have a ginormous fin. Of course.

Toby gives up on Galen and turns to me. "Emma, Reed says you have the Gift of Poseidon, too."

"Too?" I ask, glancing at Reed. So he really was bonding with the fish in the cave. Poseidon-style.

The older brother offers me his carefree grin, only one corner of his mouth bothering to rise. "Toby and I both have the Gift," Reed says.

Okay, didn't see that coming. "Really?" I squeak. "So that means . . . Are you both descendants of Poseidon?" Because that's the only way they could have the Gift.

"There are many descendants of Poseidon living here, Emma," Mr. Conway says, all the strain gone from his voice. Neptune has now become my personal jackpot. "You see, long ago—"

"Ugh! Not that story again," Toby grunts.

Mrs. Conway laughs. "Toby, don't interrupt your father."

Toby rests his elbow on the table and plops his chin in his hand. "But, Mom, it's such a boring story, and Dad draws it out forever." Toby has a slight problem pronouncing his r's, which makes "forever" sound like *fowevew*. Might be the most angelic thing I've ever heard.

"Our heritage is not boring," Reed corrects.

"I'd have to agree," Galen says. "I would love to hear the story." He locks eyes with Mr. Conway.

Mr. Conway gives a small smile, then stands abruptly. "Maybe another time. Obviously, I need to brush up on my storytelling skills." He takes his empty plate, stacking his silverware on top. Before he exits to the kitchen, he calls over his shoulder. "But if you want to be entertained, you could ask Reed why he refuses to use his Gift."

"Oh, nice Dad," Reed says, sinking in his seat.

Toby snorts beside him. "He thinks it's cheating. Unbelievable, right?"

What's unbelievable is that I'm really having this conversation. With Half-Breeds like me. Half-Breeds who have the Gift of Poseidon. *Like me.* "Cheating?" I ask, trying my hand at low-key.

Reed rolls his eyes in surrender. "It *is* cheating. It gives me an advantage over other fishermen. An advantage I don't need. Besides, it's not like it's my *job* to fish."

I raise a brow. "But it's not cheating to lure fish to your rope of death?"

"That's a matter of eating, which is what the Gift is for, right? I'm talking about competitions. I can handle a pole just as well as any of them."

Toby shakes his head at me. "He wishes."

Reed pulls his little brother into a headlock. "Take it back!"

"Oh, here we go," Mrs. Conway says, leaning an elbow onto the table in mock boredom.

A small scuffle ensues, which results in both brothers sprawled on the floor, and Toby still in a headlock, though in possession of some of Reed's elbow skin between his teeth. Even Galen appears amused. I wonder if—and don't doubt that—he's been in this same position with Rayna.

"I won't take it back!" Toby growls, but his tenacity is markedly reduced by his uncontrollable giggles.

"You don't even know who the better fisherman is," Reed says, releasing his brother. He looks at me, brushing imaginary dust off his shirt. "He won't fish without using the Gift."

"Why would I?" Toby takes his chair again. "I've won every fishing tournament I've ever entered. Got the trophies to prove it."

Mrs. Conway nearly spits out her wine. "You told me—you *promised* me—you wouldn't use the Gift for those tournaments, Toby Travis Conway. You're in serious trouble, young man."

"Aw crap," Toby says. "I just got un-grounded yesterday."

"Welcome back. Go to your room. And we don't say 'crap.'" Mrs. Conway's brow furrows in that kind of betrayed-mother disapproval. It's a look I know well.

"Do we say 'crud?'" Toby asks.

Mrs. Conway considers. "I suppose 'crud' is okay."

"Hey! You didn't let me say 'crud' when I was his age," Reed protests.

"No saying 'crud' then, Toby Travis." Mrs. Conway is an experienced rebounder.

"Thanks a lot, Reed," Toby grumbles as he passes his brother.

"Hey, you brought it up," Reed says. "I'll bring you up some dessert later."

"You most certainly will not," Mrs. Conway snips, standing. She collects as many plates around her as she can. "You boys are going to be the death of me. Wrestling on the floor like cavemen in front of our guests." She's muttering to herself about fishing trophies when she vanishes into the kitchen.

"It seems we've run everyone off," Galen says. And he seems more jubilant about it than strictly polite. "We should probably be going."

"So soon?" Reed says, but he's not looking at Galen. Reed has a way of making me feel like the only person in the room.

I glance sideways at Galen. His face shows no expression at all. He's turning into Grom in front of my eyes. And I don't like it.

Galen stands. "We've traveled a lot today," he says, turning to me. "I think we should call it a night."

I wonder what he would say if I said I wasn't tired. If I said he could go back to the inn, and Reed would bring me home later. I mentally cross that thought out of my head. I would never do that. It would be childish, and it would hurt him if he knew I'd even considered it for a shaved second.

What has gotten into me?

I take a stab at faking a yawn. It turns out just as I expected: dramatic. "I am pretty tired," I say as an understatement. Then a real yawn takes over, a really obnoxious one, and Galen and Reed share the same expression as they stare at me.

Maybe calling it a night isn't such a bad idea. After all, I have a lot of information to take in, process, and then dump in order to fit in more info tomorrow. I wonder how many mind-boggling facts a person can handle at one time. I have to have set some sort of record already.

Reed walks us to the car and watches us leave with his hands shoved in his pockets. His expression is full of all sorts of doubt.

The car ride back to Sylvia's is thick with silence. The way the air gets thick and humid right before a storm rolls in. It gets sticky and heavy and suffocating. Galen walks me to my room, and I motion for him to come inside. He hesitates. It's then that I realize he's holding something back. Something bigger than what happened at dinner.

"What's wrong?" I say.

He still doesn't come in. By this time, I'm already throwing my purse on the bed. He's acting like a complete stranger, and it's setting me on edge. "You're not coming in?"

Leaning against the frame, he sighs. "I want to come in. You know I do. But . . . I just feel that before we go further, we should talk."

"Further? Into what?" I peel off my ballet flats. The carpet is high and feels luxurious between my toes. Or maybe the carpet is average, and I'm trying to distract myself from looking at Galen's troubled expression.

He shuts the door behind him but doesn't come any closer. "Further into our plans, I guess."

"Plans?" *Plans?* When a guy says plans, he's usually talking about the next meal or movie or game on TV. When Galen says plans, he's talking about Plans.

He runs a hand through his hair. Not a good sign. "The truth is, I've been thinking about our deal. How we said we would wait until our mating ceremony until we . . . And that our mating ceremony would wait until after college. Is that . . . Is that still what you want?"

I pull my hair around front for fidgeting convenience. Twisting it, I say, "I'm not sure what you're asking me right now." Is he saying he doesn't want to wait to be mated? Just the thought of it, and the intimacy of the "romantically designed" room in general, makes my cheeks smolder. Or is this about Reed? Is he asking me if Reed has changed our plans to be together? Surely, that can't be it. Surely, he's not that insecure about his ability to make me swoon.

Galen laces his fingers behind his head, probably to keep from fidgeting himself. I've never seen him this nervous before. "Triton's trident, Emma, I don't know how much longer I can keep away from you—I really don't. No, no, it's not even about that. This is coming out all wrong." He lets out a slow breath. "What I'm asking is this: After all that's happened, do you truly want to stay on land?"

Whoa. What? "Everything that's happened?" And staying on land as opposed to . . . ?

"You know. Finding out that your mother is the Poseidon

princess. That at the first chance she got, she mated with Grom, and now they spend most of their time in the water. I mean, if it weren't for—" Galen shifts to one foot and leans against the antique dresser.

"If it weren't for what?" My insides suddenly blister with anger. *"First chance she got?" I guess that could be the short, rude version of what happened.*

"Nevermind. I told you, it's coming out all wrong."

"You were going to say, If it weren't for me, Mom would live in the water permanently, weren't you?" He doesn't try to deny it. He can't. It's all over his face. Along with some appropriate guilt. But the worst part is, he doesn't just mean that she would live there permanently. He means that she would be happier if she did. That she *should* live there permanently.

Is he saying that I'm somehow standing in the way of my mother's happiness? Is he saying that I'm standing in the way of his happiness? Or am I reading this all wrong? I try to rein in my feelings and filter them into useful conversation. "You don't want to wait until after we graduate college to be mated? Is that what this is about?" And if it is, how do I feel about that?

But my brain won't answer the questions my heart is asking.

He sighs. "I didn't mean to upset you. We can talk about it later. We've both had a long day."

"You know you don't have to attend college, Galen. We already talked about this. I can take classes, and you can . . . We can get an apartment off campus, remember?"

He grimaces. "No. Yes. Sort of." He crosses his arms over

the dresser and rests his chin on them. "Look, I'm not asking for a decision right now, and I'm not trying to pressure you."

"Pressure me into what? Galen, so far I haven't heard you ask me to do anything. I don't know what we're talking about here." And I'm getting pretty frustrated with it. He must be, too, because he buries his face in his arms.

Finally he looks at me again, meets my eyes. "I don't want to go to college," he says. "All I want to do is have our mating ceremony and go back to the ocean. With you. Now. Ten minutes ago, actually. The sooner the better."

My jaw may never close again at this point. Shock pirouettes through my veins in precise, intense waves. Is that why he didn't have a problem stopping before things got too serious on the side of the interstate earlier today? Was he trying to get me to break my promise to wait until after our mating ceremony so he could break his promise to stay on land with me? "You're backing out of our plans?" I almost choke on the words.

He jerks his head up. "No. I'm just . . . offering an alternative to the whole college thing."

"You were the one who wanted to come on this trip, Galen. To get away from the ocean. And now you want to get away from land?"

"I needed to think."

"And so this is what you came up with? That college is a bad idea and that you'd rather live in the water—where I can't breathe, if you recall?"

"Dr. Milligan said that over time you could—"

"No."

"You would live longer. You wouldn't be as fragile as humans."

"Absolutely not."

"You're angry."

Understatement of the millennium. "You think?"

"I shouldn't have brought it up yet. I was waiting for the right time, but I can see this wasn't it."

"There is no right time to ask me to live in the ocean with you, Galen. I can't do that."

"Can't? Or won't?" Now he sounds mad.

I feel so waylaid by this conversation. I just told him I can't breathe in the water. But even if I could, would I? I wish my brain and my heart could call a truce. I really need them to be on the same side right now. "That's not fair."

"Really?" he says, incredulous. "But it's fair that I give up everything I've ever known?"

I feel the tears spill out of my eyes, roll down my hot cheeks, and land on my chest. When he puts it like that, it doesn't seem fair. But it's what we agreed on. He said he would go anywhere, as long as I was with him. "You made that decision, Galen. You said you didn't mind."

"That was before."

"Before what? Reed?" I regret it as soon as I say it. I can tell I've practically pounded on a very sensitive button.

He snorts. "If I never hear that name again, it will be too soon." He paces toward the curtain and makes a show of peering out the window.

"If this isn't about Reed, then what is it about?"

He faces me. When he does, some of the anger is gone from his face, replaced by the sadness that's been haunting him the last few months. "Neptune is just an added complication to this whole mess. What I mean is, I've been thinking about this for a long time." He shakes his head. "Just forget I mentioned it. I'll deal with it."

I stand. "Really? Like you're dealing with it now?" I'm still not even sure what "it" is. This is probably the most unnerving exchange with Galen I've ever had. "Are you sure this isn't about Ree—Neptune? I mean, everything is going great, we're on a road trip that *you* wanted to go on, by the way, and now we've come across a town of Half-Breeds who are defining themselves instead of letting some arcane law do it for them—but none of this has anything to do with your sudden decision to keep me prisoner in an underwater castle?"

He flinches. "I didn't realize you felt you were my prisoner," he says softly. He closes the distance between us and brushes his fingers over my cheek. "I want so much more for you than that, angelfish."

I put my hand on his. "Galen, I—" I'm going to say I'm sorry but I can't force it out. I am sorry. But I'm just not sure what I'm sorry about. That we had a fight? No, because we're going to fight sometimes, and apparently these things needed to be said. Sorry that I don't want to live in the ocean with him? No. Because I never misled him into thinking I did. He knew from the beginning where I stood about college and staying on land.

I guess what I'm sorry about the most is that we're at odds—and there doesn't seem to be a solution. And that I said something I don't mean. I absolutely do not feel like his prisoner. I feel more like his warden, like I'm holding him back. Apparently what he wants is no longer what I want.

The problem is, I still want *him.*

"I have to go back," he says quietly. "I hope you understand."

"Back?"

"To Triton territory. I have to tell Grom about this place. It's my duty."

"Are you sure Grom doesn't already know about this?"

"Grom wouldn't keep this from the kingdoms. Even if Anto—under any circumstances. I know my brother. I have to tell him." He visibly braces himself for what I'll say next.

I step away from him. "You can't do that, Galen. You just can't. You know what the law says about Half-Breeds. You would let them do that to these people? You would let them kill Toby?"

His features are weighed down with anguish. "I don't know how we've come to this point, Emma. I don't know what I've done to make you think of me this way."

"I'm not going with you."

He nods, and brushes past me. "I gathered as much." Opening the door, he turns back to me. "Stay here then, Emma. If you feel you belong here, if this is what you want, then stay. Who am I to stop you? We both know you're going to do what you want."

And then he is gone.

12

WHEN HE can't keep it in any longer, Galen pulls over on the side of the road. Turns off the lights. Slams the door behind him. He makes his way into the woods just far enough to be unseen by any cars passing by. And he takes his frustration out on the nearest tree.

Over and over and over, he punches it. The bark gives way to wood, and still he punches. Only small ribbons of moonlight shine through the trees, barely exposing his misery, for which he's grateful. "I'm such an idiot," he yells at the massive, newly assaulted trunk.

He turns around and sinks down the length of it, drawing his knees to his chin. *She feels like my prisoner. And why wouldn't she? I follow her around like a seal pup. I barely give her room to breathe. But I don't want to miss a single waking moment with her.*

And what hurts worse is that all this time he thought she

felt the same about him. The way she kisses him, pressing her body to him as if she can't get close enough. The way she always absently finds some way to touch him, by resting her hand on his arm or crossing her leg over his under the dinner table. How could he have misjudged her feelings like this?

He'd wanted to explain to her how he felt. *What an excellent job I did!* He starts off by announcing that he doesn't want to go to college and that he can barely keep his hands off her. He groans into his fists. *Way to act like a stalker, idiot.*

Right when he was about to get around to explaining why he wants her to live in the ocean—that it will give them more time together—she tells him that she already feels like his prisoner. Which means that she feels they spend enough time together as it is.

Centuries wouldn't be enough time for him. He knows that with his whole being.

But she doesn't feel that way. *Open your eyes, fool! She just told you that Neptune is where she belongs.* And why wouldn't she want to stay here? The residents are like her. She doesn't have to worry about people asking about her pale skin or her white hair or her violet eyes. They know what she is, and they'll accept her.

No, they'll embrace her, once they really get to know her. She is one of them.

And it's more than Galen could ever promise her. Even if she agreed to live in the ocean with him, they would always have to endure curious glances and whispered gossip. And if he stayed on land with her, she would always have to be cautious with other people, always have to hide what she is. And so would he.

All this time he'd been thinking Antonis was cruel to send his Half-Breed granddaughter here and get her hopes up that her kind wouldn't always be an abomination to the Syrena. The Poseidon king had to know she would want to somehow make peace between Half-Breeds and the two ocean kingdoms.

But that's not what Antonis intended at all. He didn't care about peace between them, or he would have done something about it long ago, when he first discovered this sleepy little town. Instead he told no one. Ever. Until he met Emma, his Half-Breed granddaughter. Then he gladly sent her here because he cares about her happiness. No matter who she is or what she is or where she is. He was giving her another option, another choice. And he trusts her with this secret. *Or did the Half-Breed exception made by the Archives spring Antonis into action? Are his plans truly to pursue peace with Neptune after all?*

He also knew I would try to keep her from this place. That's why he didn't tell her what exactly she was looking for. She would have told me, and I would have refused to bring her.

Oh, and he *would* have refused. Vehemently. He knows deep down he would have. Back at the inn, he basically accused Emma of being selfish, of letting him make all the sacrifices. He's certain he would have tried to stop her from coming here. From breaking the law. From angering the Archives. From finding companionship with others like her.

All so he could steal her away to the ocean with him. Which is what she never wanted.

It doesn't change the fact that he can't keep this place a secret from Grom. Too much damage has already been done by keeping secrets. The kingdoms were almost torn apart by secrets. He and Emma were almost torn apart by them.

It kills him that Emma thinks he's capable of hurting an innocent minnow like Toby. That he means to bring Grom here to destroy them. That she thinks he would help bring harm to this town. She should know that he—more than anyone—is particularly sympathetic toward Half-Breeds. And, really, so is Grom, what with a Half-Breed stepdaughter.

But he doesn't have to go all the way back to Triton territory to tell Grom. It's something that can be accomplished with a simple phone call. He doesn't have to—and doesn't want to—leave Emma here by herself.

He was testing to see if she'd come with him. And he got his answer.

Still, he'll make the phone call. Galen knows Nalia will be coming ashore every few days to check in with Emma. It may take a few days to make contact with Nalia and Grom, and that's fine. And maybe that's what Emma needs—a few days to explore what could be. *Whatever she decides, I'll be there for her. I have to go back and ask for another chance to explain.*

Just as he starts back toward the SUV, headlights from the road send an intrusive beam of light into the woods, forcing him to close his eyes against the brightness. When he opens them, he realizes the beam is not going away. It's heading straight toward him. He stands, his instincts telling him to run. The truck stops within a few inches of him. It takes all he has not to step away. Two large men—or Syrena in human form, that is—hop out and stride to the front of the truck.

"Woods ain't no place for a boy like you," the bigger one says. He spits on the ground in front of Galen. The bottom of his mouth protrudes as if he's got a chunk of food tucked there.

"There are actual laws against my being in the woods?" Galen says, hands in pockets.

The short one laughs. "Tyrden was right. He is obsessed with laws."

"Which is why you're coming with us. Galen, is it? Now there's no sense in backing away, boy. You're surrounded. If you make a run for it, it'll just hurt more."

Nonetheless, Galen runs.

13

SLICES OF sunlight leak through the blinds of the room. I'm sure it would be breathtaking to behold if my eyes weren't almost swollen shut from crying all night. The fight Galen and I had is serious. And it's not just because it's the first real argument we've had as a couple and now we've officially erased the new feeling, the euphoria from the relationship, blah blah blah.

It's not just a surface scratch that can be buffed out by an apology and some roses or whatever. It's a huge dent in what each of us envisioned our relationship to be. It *could* be proof that we may not be right for each other. It seems like the death of our dreams together somehow. And I mourned all night over it.

I want to go to him. Knock on his door and tell him that I'm sorry, that I don't feel like his prisoner, that I love him and I want to fix this. But I can't.

Because Galen never came back last night. Sylvia confirmed

it for me. She'd knocked on his door early this morning, and when he didn't answer, she went in, finding that his bed had not been slept in. The room appeared untouched altogether.

Which is something I wish I could say about my heart.

He actually left me here. He stole away to Grom and now he won't answer my calls. Maybe he's already reached the water and doesn't have access to his cell. Maybe he hasn't, and he's ignoring me.

When the room phone rings on the nightstand, I jump, pulling the blankets tightly to my chin. Galen. He's not ignoring me after all. I snatch the phone from the receiver. "Where are you?" I blurt. I hope he can't tell that I've been crying. My voice sounds pretty rough, all things considered.

"Um. I'm at my house," Reed answers. I slump back under the covers, bringing the phone with me.

"Oh. Hey. I thought you were Galen."

Silence. Then, "You've misplaced Galen?"

I can't help but smile. "You could say that."

"Do you know when he'll be back?"

"I don't know that he *will* be back."

"For real? Did you have a fight or something?"

I sigh into the phone. "I really don't want to talk about it, honestly." For one, I might start crying again. Also, rehashing the fight would involve divulging that Galen left to tattle on the entire town. But shouldn't I say something? Shouldn't I warn them that they may be in danger?

"Sure, sure. No worries," Reed says quickly. "Listen, I was going to take the both of you around town and introduce you to some folks. The offer still stands. You know, even if Galen isn't back yet."

And there is the dilemma. Galen leaves town less than twenty-four hours ago, and I decide to haul off and go gallivanting with another guy? Not just any guy, a guy that Galen may or may not be jealous of.

But the thing is . . . *Galen* abandoned *me*. I can stay here and bathe in my own misery all day like a pathetic weakling. Or I could get up, get showered, and explore the town, just as I had intended to do before Galen left. Not only would the latter be good for me, but it would also be good for Galen. It wouldn't hurt anything if he changes his mind and comes back, only to find that *I've* abandoned *him*, that I've gone on an adventure without him. Well, not abandoned, just . . . found independence in a tight spot. Or something.

The point is, it wouldn't hurt anything at all to stand my ground. Except maybe his pride. Or his feelings. But he's not the one who cried all night.

"Absolutely," I tell Reed. "Give me time to shower and dress, and I'll meet you in the lobby in an hour."

It's true. You can hear someone smile on the phone. "Awesome. See you in an hour."

So Reed pulls up in this dumpy blue antique truck. A rash of rust covers the whole thing, which reminds me of someone with a bad case of acne and the pain of a tetanus shot all at once. One headlight is foggy. The front fender has a dent, the kind of dent a bowling ball would make if chucked from a canon. The dash sports a web of cracked, light blue vinyl, either maimed from the sun or from consistent abuse over decades.

That said, I've never been more thrilled to hop into the front seat of a truck in my whole life. This truck means distraction, adventure, curiosity satisfied. Independence.

This truck is my new BFF.

"I know it's not svelt like you're used to," Reed says apologetically. "But either Galen is the richest Syrena I know, or he's an extremely effective car thief."

I laugh. I'm feeling generous today. "He sells things he finds in the oceans. Lost treasures from old shipwrecks and things like that."

Reed's eyes widen. "Son of a biscuit eater. That's brilliant."

I almost tell him that Rachel thought of it first, but then I'd have to explain who she is—and what happened to her. And that feels more like a betrayal of Galen than anything else.

And that's when I remember something that Galen said last night. *You won't be as fragile as humans.*

"Oh, no," I groan, burying my face in my hands. I've been so selfish. I should have seen this coming. I should have known that his change in attitude is all because of Rachel. He wants me to live in the ocean so that I'm safe, so that I'll live longer. So that he doesn't lose me, like he lost Rachel. I'm such a moron.

"Reed, before we go, I need to make a quick phone call," I say as I unbuckle.

"Is everything okay? You're not having second thoughts, are you?" He places his hand over mine on the seat between us.

I relinquish my hand, open the door, and slide out.

"Everything will be okay. And I'm not having second thoughts. I want you to take me around town. I want to see it all. In about ten minutes, okay?" Actually, I am having second thoughts because of my sudden revelation. But how rude would it be to tell him to get lost? After all, he was going to take *both* of us around town today. It's not like he singled me out.

I find a quiet corner in the lobby of the B and B. Feeling too unsophisticated to sit in one of the fancy French-silk parlor chairs, I pull out a metal seat from the breakfast nook. Then I dial Galen's number. Of course, he doesn't answer. I don't expect him to.

When the digital lady advises me to leave a message, I do. "Galen. I'm so sorry. I just realized how selfish I acted. I didn't listen, didn't hear what you were trying to tell me. I'll listen now, I promise. Please . . . Please just call me back." I squeeze my eyes shut, not allowing any tears to escape. My throat feels raw, as if the words I just spoke were miniature blades leaving behind tiny incisions. But it's not that I don't mean every word. I do.

It's that I'm terrified that he won't call me back. That it's too late. That I blew it.

My feet feel like anvils as I make my way back to the truck. It doesn't go unnoticed by Reed.

"Are you sure you want to venture out today? You probably didn't sleep last night, huh? Maybe you should—"

"That's nice of you, Reed," I say, buckling back in. "But I need to get my mind off things for a while. I was hoping you could help me with that." Which isn't untrue.

"Ten four," Reed says, and the worry all but melts from his

face. "I was going to take us to the market first. That's where everyone who's anyone gets their open-faced roast beef sandwich for lunch."

I nod. "Lunch. Roast beef. I'm in."

Reed is right! Everyone in town comes to the market for lunch. Mismatched tables skirt the street, people line the serving buffet set up on the sidewalk, and steam clouds rise in smoky ribbons over the buffet itself. My stomach gives off a vulturine growl.

Reed laughs. "So you skipped breakfast, huh?"

I nod.

He does, too. "Well, I've got a trick up my sleeve. Come on."

We make our way to the line, and all I can think is that I'm going to start eating my own arm if people don't start moving. Then Reed rolls up his proverbial sleeve.

"Excuse me, Trudy?" he says, tapping on the woman's shoulder in front of us. Trudy turns around, then eyes me with surprise. I remember that Reed says they don't get many visitors here. "This is Emma," he continues, wrapping his arm around me. I can't decide if it's harmless or not. "She's a descendant of Poseidon, and she's visiting us from New Jersey. Do you mind if we cut in line so I can introduce her to everyone?"

Trudy grabs my hand and shakes it. "Emma, is it? So lovely to meet you! I had no idea we had relatives in New Jersey. Oh, you'll want to meet everyone, for sure. Go ahead and cut, Reed. It's okay by me." That's it. No questions asked. I'm immediately and wholly accepted.

I wonder where else they *do* have relatives. Because meeting a Half-Breed from Jersey doesn't seem like the marvel I would have pegged it for.

And that's how we make it to the head of the line—Reed introducing me to other Half-Breeds, and the other Half-Breeds greeting me and being all unsurprised.

A server plops roast beef and peas and a piece of white cake onto my Styrofoam tray. When we sit at one of the wrought iron tables, a few people pull up extra chairs, and it becomes quickly overcrowded. But I don't care. I have food and good—if not a tad overwhelming—company.

These people know what I am, and they accept me because of it. It's like I've been a part of their secret society since the day I was born.

And deep down inside me, I think I have.

14

THE ROOM has two metal chairs including the one he's tied to, a blanketless cot, and a card table boasting a small lamp that has seen better days. No carpet. No pictures. No windows—which Galen is grateful for at the moment. Any kind of substantial light would make his head pound twice as hard.

He can only remember fragments of how he came to be here. He remembers running. Tripping. Something hard and heavy connecting with his head. Nausea, angry bile rising as he was transported in the back of his own vehicle to ... to ... here.

He becomes aware of the cloth in his mouth. It tastes of vomit. It's wrapped too tightly around his face and head, making his eyes bulge with pain. His hands and feet have grown numb from sitting in the same position too long. His neck feels permanently disfigured from the angle at which he passed out.

He stretches and turns and works his hands and feet as best

he can to relieve some of the tension, but the rope is tight. Just as his muscles relax, just as his neck adjusts to the task of holding up his head, the single white door to the room opens.

The fattest Syrena Galen has ever seen closes the door behind him. Sure, by human standards, he's not fat. Paunchy maybe. But by Syrena standards, the guy is obese. This anomaly swaggers to the other metal chair, scrapes it across the floor to face Galen, then plunks into it. He studies Galen for a long time, holding the vague grin of a shark who's just supped on a school of fish.

"So. I'm in the company of a real Triton Royal," he says. Then he spits on the floor between them. He has the same bulge in his mouth the other Syrena did. "My name's Tyrden. You'll want to remember that."

Galen doesn't grace him with a reaction, much less a muffled reply through the cloth in his mouth.

"You don't have to play dumb, boy," Tyrden says. "Everyone knows all about you. But just so we're clear..." He stands and moves to lift Galen's shirt. Again, Galen doesn't resist. What is the point in denying it now? They believe him to be a Royal. So much so that they went to the trouble of abducting him. If anything, Tyrden is probably just curious. With a town full of Poseidon descendants, he most likely has never seen a Triton Royal.

Tyrden rests his eyes on Galen's trident. "I've never seen a real one," Tyrden says, as if reading Galen's mind. He drops the shirt and walks back to the chair. Taking his time getting comfortable, he shifts and adjusts himself until the metal legs squeak and threaten to buckle.

Galen wonders if Tyrden is making this kind of show to build anticipation. Grom does this when he's trying to intimidate someone. Acts like the other person doesn't even exist. Usually it works.

But not on Galen.

When Tyrden finally looks at him, he has a smile on his face that can only be described as disturbing. "I'm here to ask you some questions, boy. And if you don't cooperate . . . Well, I'm here to see to it that you do cooperate. I hope we understand each other." He leans forward, and the chair groans with the movement. "So. How is it that you found us so far inland? What are you doing here?"

Galen huffs into the cloth invading his mouth.

Tyrden jumps to his feet and unties it. Galen flexes his jaw several times, working some relief into the joints. Tyrden sits back down, this time with much less zeal.

"Thank you for removing that," Galen says calmly, looking Tyrden in the eye. He is perfectly capable of being unsettling, too. And of being unpredictable. Grom was a great tutor.

But Tyrden is not easily unsettled. "You're welcome. If you scream for help, I'll harvest each of your teeth and keep them in a jar in my kitchen." When Galen says nothing, his captor crosses his arms. "Did you think I removed your gag for the fun of it? Answer my questions."

Galen cocks his head. "In fact, I did think that. Surely you don't actually expect me to tell you anything."

"Is that right?"

When Galen nods, Tyrden rises from his chair and walks

across the room to the table. Then he reaches under it, re-trieving the biggest knife Galen ever recalls seeing. With ease, Tyrden removes the duct tape that secured it in its hiding place.

The blade is rusted in some places—or is that dried blood?—and the grip is well worn. Tyrden handles it expertly, spinning it in his hands as if it were some sort of toy baton. He sits back down.

"You'll have to do better than that," Galen says, trying not to visibly swallow. "I'm not sure about you land dwellers, but we ocean dwellers tend to have very thick skin."

Tyrden chuckles. "Not impressed yet, boy? Well, give me a chance to change your mind." He leans back in the chair and clearly relaxes. "Have you ever seen a rhinoceros, Highness?" He rubs his shirt over the blade as if to clean it. The question-able stains do not budge. "You see, here on land, rhinos live in a place called Africa. Humans have a silly formal name for them, pachyderms, which means thick skin. Their skin is actually as thick as any full-blooded Syrena. In fact, some parts of their skin are double the thickness of ours. That's the part we used to test our weapons. We had to make sure that if you Tritons stirred up trouble for us again, then we'd be ready for the fight. We based all our designs on the ability to penetrate rhino skin. This knife here can slice the thickest part of a rhino with one swipe, boy. Impressed yet?"

In a word, yes. Not just by the knife, but by what Galen suddenly realizes is all the time and trouble these land dwellers took in preparing for some sort of war. The defenses they'd already thought of. Making weapons just for Syrena skin.

Choosing a location too far inland for Triton's gift to do any damage. Forging bonds with humans, multiplying their numbers and respective skills.

Yes, Galen is very impressed. But giving Tyrden the answers he craves is still out of the question. Mainly because, if all the citizens are armed this way, that means Neptune seems to be expecting a conflict with the ocean dwellers, instead of just preparing for a potential attack.

When Galen's rebuttal is still silence, Tyrden presses his lips together into what isn't quite a grin. "Hard to excite are we, Highness? Let's see what else I can do to convince you."

In an instant, Tyrden is on his feet and hovering over Galen. He brings the blade close to Galen's cheek, so close he can almost feel the knife quiver in his assailant's hand. Out of nowhere, Tyrden raises his hand to show Galen his palm. Then he raises the knife to it. Raking it across slowly, delicately, Tyrden breaks through his own skin. The laceration is so thin, so precise it's as if his hand has forgotten to bleed for a few seconds. But bleed, it does.

With a blank expression, Tyrden lets Galen watch the blood drip down his hand, snake across his wrist, and drop like silken beads to the floor. Strange as it may be, it appears as though he enjoys watching the blood pool at his feet. He then uses the knife to slice off a piece of Galen's T-shirt, barely missing the flesh of his stomach. In fact, if Galen hadn't reflexively sucked in, it could have gutted him. His reaction doesn't go unnoticed by Tyrden.

"You see, boy, rhino skin can get up to two inches thick."

He displays an estimate of two inches between his fingers. "And this blade here? This blade can cut right through it."

Satisfied with himself, and with Galen's newfound attentiveness, the rotund Syrena wraps the T-shirt material tightly around his wound and sits back down. "Now, Highness," he says, turning the blade over and over in his good hand. "Let's talk, shall we?"

15

GALEN NEVER called me back yesterday. I left two more messages after I got back from my afternoon with Reed. If I'm being honest, I did expect him to call by now. I expected us to be talking about how dumb we both were—me especially— and telling each other ridiculous things like how we'll never fight again.

I can feel myself growing desperate. I don't want to be one of those girls who can't get over a relationship when the relationship is clearly over. Still, the relationship, how hard we worked to have it . . . It can't be over. In fact, I always thought nothing could ever truly come between Galen and me. I never thought we'd have a last kiss.

It's been two days. I'm not about to give up. I sit on the edge of the bed and dial his cell. This time it doesn't ring but instead sends me straight to voice mail. Have I left that many messages? Or is someone else trying to get hold of him?

"Galen, please. Please hear what I have to say." I bite my lip, because if I don't, my voice will crack. Finally, I say, "I love you. We can fix this." And I hang up. What else can I tell him? I'm practically begging now.

My fear is that he really is becoming just like Grom. A hard outer shell that won't let anyone in. Except—Grom let my mother in. Surely, Galen won't barricade himself from me. Right?

When the cell rings in my hand, I nearly fall off the bed. I scramble to answer it, but let it ring one more time when I see that Reed is calling. Reed. Not Galen. Again.

"Hello?" I say, trying to sound cheerful.

"Hey, Ms. Popular, ready to go fishing?"

Now I *am* genuinely enthusiastic. Reed introduced me to practically the entire town yesterday. I'd left the hotel room last night to walk down the street and grab some snacks and got nothing but kindness: "Hello, Emma! Good to see you again" and "Can I help you carry anything?" These people, these Half-Breeds, these humans, these Syrena. They've made me one of their own in the space of two days. It's just the opposite of what I'm used to. Back home, I had to fight for any freaking tidbit of recognition or acknowledgment. Here I'm some sort of celebrity.

And it's fantabulous.

Still, Reed gets most of the credit. He's the one who isn't shy, who goes after what he wants. The problem is, it's becoming more and more obvious that he wants me. Small touches here, lingering glances there. Yesterday at lunch, someone even called me his girlfriend and he didn't correct them. It was me who had to set things straight. Because until Galen says otherwise, I'm taken.

"But we're not going to keep the fish we catch, right?" I say. "You promised."

Reed sighs into the phone. "I was hoping you'd forget that."

"Not a chance. I don't kill fish."

"How else am I supposed to prove that I caught a bigger fish than Toby?"

"Get ready to have your mind blown. There are these new things called cell phones, and they actually have a camera built in—"

"Smart-mouth."

"Just saying."

"I'm pulling up to the hotel now. Get your butt down here before I decide to leave you behind."

I laugh. "I dare you."

Reed snorts. "Just get down here, Miss Congeniality." Then he hangs up on me. He's going to pay for that.

The rickety dock is just skinny enough that two people can't stand side by side. Reed hops in the small fishing boat, and it rocks like it's being tossed around in a typhoon. Then he holds his hand out for me to jump in. I haven't yet explained to him how clumsy I am. That I don't jump into anything, let alone an unstable object floating precariously close to a dock full of potential splinters.

"I'm not a little sprite like you," I tell him, sitting on the edge of the dock.

He snickers. "You think I'm little?" He holds out both his hands, so I can scoot off the dock without causing too much pandemonium in this tiny vessel.

Do I think Reed is little? No freaking way. He's actually very athletic-looking, a fact accentuated exponentially when he takes his shirt off. He's not quite as big as Galen, but he is well-defined in all the right places. Which is why I look away.

He doesn't miss it. "Didn't think so," he says.

God, he's irritatingly confident.

"Now, remember," he says as I sit on one of the wooden planks posing as seats, "once we get to where we're going, absolutely no talking. When we get close, I'll give you a signal that it's time to be stealthy."

"What's the signal?" I hold my hand up to shield my eyes from the sun.

He holds up a fist, a gesture a soldier might make if he wants to halt the troops behind him.

"Okay. Got it."

Reed zigzags us along the bends of the creek, avoiding fallen logs and overgrown brush from shore. The wind breathes through the trees as if it's telling secrets. Birds chime in with treble, and a nearby woodpecker adds percussion to the mix. Then there's the steady, quiet hum of the boat dividing the water ahead of us. It's possibly one of the most relaxing moments of my life.

Until I notice Reed smirking at me.

"What?" I say.

He shrugs innocently. "I was just trying to imagine you using the Gift in the ocean. And I was getting a little jealous of it." He gently steers us clear of some drooping tree limbs that hold a masterpiece of a spiderweb. "What's the biggest fish you've ever talked to?"

The answer immediately pops into mind. "A blue whale. I named him Goliath. You've never been in the ocean?"

"Of course not."

"Why?"

"Well for starters, it's against our law. And secondly, didn't you hear what Triton did to Tartessos? Not pretty."

No, it wasn't pretty. I can't imagine the same thing happening to Neptune. "Understandable."

"Besides, I'm not trying to get speared by the almighty ocean dwellers." The way he says it carries a sudden hardness. Like when you get to the pit of a cherry. "You're friends with a blue whale?" Apparently, Reed can go from smug to incredulous in snap-point-two seconds. "Weren't you afraid?"

Terrified is a closer description. But I can tell Reed is in awe of me right now, so I decide to sit back and enjoy the moment. "I was at first. It was before I knew I had the Gift. I thought he was going to eat me."

"Blue whales eat krill. If he ate you, it would have been an accident."

"Comforting. Truly."

"So he didn't eat you. You're a horrible storyteller, you know that?"

So much for awe. "I realized that he was gentle—and that he responded to my voice when I told him what to do. I knew then that he wouldn't hurt me."

"How often do you see him?"

I'm aware that my shoulders sag a little as the regret broils from my stomach to my throat. "Actually, a few months ago he was harpooned by some idiot fishermen. I didn't see him for a long time after that. Then one day a few weeks ago, he came to me out of nowhere. I could still see the scar, and I gave him some extra love. But I don't care what scientists say about how fish have no feelings. Goliath acted differently. He wasn't as playful as he was before that happened. It's like he was trauma-tized or something."

Reed gives a solemn nod. "Um. Whales are mammals. They definitely have feelings. But touchy-feely feelings? Not sure about all that."

"Well, I'm telling you they do."

"Right. So. We don't have to fish if you don't want to. We can turn around and go back."

I tilt my head at him. "But you said we weren't going to keep the fish. Did you mean it?"

"Of course I did. I would never lie to you, Emma. I'm way too scared of you." He chuckles. "But sometimes when you're fishing, they swallow the hook. I've never thought of it, but to me, swallowing a hook and having it ripped out of you could be kinda traumatizing, don't you think?"

Of course it would. Which is why I never intended to let him catch a single fish. But I still want to see his face when I thwart his plans. "Are you trying to back out now? Afraid you can't beat Toby after all?"

Reed sits a little straighter. "I changed my mind. We're not turning back now. Not even if you ask."

I'm becoming very good at baiting males. The rest of our ride is spent in silence. I can tell we're getting close to our destination because every time I try to chit-chat, he mumbles his answer and glances over his shoulder. Guys really take this sport-fishing thing to a whole new level of weirdness.

At last, Reed holds up his fist and shuts off the engine. The lulling song of frogs and the fast-moving current over a sandbar contrast against any silence we might have had. We come to a halt in the widest part of the creek so far. Reed makes quick work of hooking two crickets on his line. I can't help but wonder if the scientists are wrong about insects, too. What if they actually do feel pain, and here I've let him impale two live crickets?

"Life's too short to use dead bait," he says almost superstitiously. I wonder what kind of fishermen's lore he just satisfied by telling himself that. Ridiculous.

So Reed is not in an eco-friendly mood right now. He's all determination and focus and testosterone. He turns his back to me and casts off the back of the boat in one smooth motion.

Finally, my time has come.

With glee, I pull back my hair and shove my face in the water. I open my mouth to shout and large air bubbles escape first, tickling my face as they rise to the surface. But I will not be deterred. "Swim away!" I scream. "You're all in danger! Swim away!" I see the backends of fishtails scatter, just as they're told.

Minnows, a water moccasin, a turtle. Other bigger, striped fish that I can't identify make a whooshing sound with their speedy departure. When I come back up, Reed is reeling his line in with a scowl.

"I just knew you were going to do that," he grumbles.

"I should have done it before you murdered those two crickets. See something, say something, you know?" His pouty face is borderline adorable. It makes him look like an older version of Toby. And Toby corners the market on pouty face.

"Are you going to do that every time then? Is there any use in trying to find another hot spot?"

"Pretty much, yes. And if wasting time is your hobby, by all means, look for another fishing hole." Or whatever they're called.

A mischievous smile stretches across his face. *Oh no.*

My startled cry never hits the air, only the water as he bulldozes me off the boat. The water is clear, more clear than any part of the ocean I've been in. Even through my thick skin, I register the drop in temperature from Tennessee summer day to Tennessee summer creek.

Reed grins so big his dimples look almost like holes punctured in his face. "You realize you had that coming."

"I didn't figure you'd take it lying down." I laugh. In fact, I sound delighted under the circumstances.

"With you, I'll take it any way I can get it."

Awk-ward. Also, ew. "Reed—"

"Too much too soon?"

"Too much anytime. I'm with Galen. We're going to be mated." But I recognize the trace of doubt in my declaration.

He makes a show of looking around. "Really? I'm not seeing Galen anywhere. As far as I can tell, it's me and you here."

"That was a low blow." I turn away from him, intent on swimming back to the boat. Within seconds, I feel his pulse grow stronger, and I know the exact moment he's about to grab my wrist. I swirl around. "Don't touch me, Reed."

His face is all remorse. Genuine anguish. "I'm so sorry, Emma. I know he'll come back. Heck, he's probably on his way right now. If you want, I'll take you to the hotel so you can wait for him."

I don't like how pitiful that sounds. *So you can wait for him.* My emotions engage in a tiny skirmish. On the one hand, I left my phone in my room, telling myself that taking it fishing would be asking the universe to throw it in the water. On the other hand, I didn't take it because I already doubted Galen would call, and I'm sick of checking my phone every thirty seconds to see if he has at least texted me.

My phone and Galen's empty hotel room are anchors weighing me down. Things will work out with him, I just know it. But for now, I have to let it go. Yes, Reed is morphing into a scandalous flirt. But once he realizes I won't budge, he'll give up.

All I really know is that I can't stay locked away in my room waiting for a phone call that may not come for days. I have to live life. I have to have my own identity outside of Galen. It's only fair.

"Why don't you take me cave diving?" I say finally. "If Galen does come back and finds me gone, he'll know that I'm exploring Neptune. He knows that's why I wanted to stay a few more days."

Reeds nods. "Are you sure? I'm so sorry, Emma. That was mean, what I said."

"I'm positive. Stop groveling. It doesn't suit you."

He grins. "Well, then. The nearest cave is quite a swim away and against the current. You up for it?"

I eye the boat behind him. "I want to cave dive. Not exhaust myself getting there."

"Come on, princess," he laughs. He tries to put an arm around me, but I slither away from him. He takes it in stride. "We'll take the boat until we have to make a swim for it."

And that's when I discover that getting into a boat from the water is like trying to catch a fish with my mouth. Not gonna happen.

16

GALEN WON'T look up at his captor, which forces him to look down at his now-shredded shirt hanging like a loose net from his body. There are still small cuts on his side and on his back where Tyrden missed the fabric and connected with skin. Every time Galen adjusts in his chair, the shallow slices burn in protest, reminding him that they're still there.

Tyrden had used the blade quickly, in quick chopping motions, stripping Galen's shirt from his body piece by piece, sometimes forcing him to suck in or lean away to avoid getting deep gashes in his skin. Every time Galen gave an evasive answer—which was most of the time—Tyrden took to swiping the blade erratically, not caring if he hit or missed. Galen maneuvered away as best he could. Sometimes it worked. Sometimes it didn't. The scratches were mostly grazes, but some nicks here and there were just large enough to cause Galen some discomfort.

He wonders what Tyrden will use the blade for once the clothing is gone. He has come to learn that the older Syrena is very good at the art of anticipation. *It would help if I could figure out his motives.* At least then he could give him passable—though untrue—answers while also avoiding the lacerations he'd earned by being impassive.

But so far, Tyrden has asked such random questions that Galen can get no sense of what his purpose is, which is probably the point. Questions like, How many Syrena are loyal to the kingdoms? Have they started any new traditions? How far can your Trackers sense? What do the ocean dwellers do for fun? Do they still use lionfish venom for their spears? How many come ashore nowadays? What is the ratio of males to females?

All Galen knows is that Tyrden has an insatiable curiosity about the makeup of the kingdoms—and that he's designed at least one weapon that easily cuts through Syrena skin. Not a good sign.

The sound of the heavy boots walking back toward him makes his stomach simmer. This could be much worse, Galen tells himself. He thinks of Rachel and what she'd told him about methods the Mafia used for torture. This isn't torture, not compared with that. This is . . . intimidation.

Suddenly, the air is saturated with the smell of cooked fish and Galen can't help but look up this time. Tyrden takes a seat in front of Galen and crosses his legs, careful not to spill the steaming plate of food in his hand. Galen hates his stomach for growling so loudly.

Tyrden chuckles. "Nothing like a big pile of fish to keep you going, huh, boy?" He scoots the chair closer to where Galen sits, so that their feet almost touch. Then he waves the food inches from his face, making sure the white steam undulates right into Galen's nose. Galen's stomach groans ferociously. *Traitor.*

His last meal was at the Conway's house—and even then, he'd barely touched his dinner. He's guessing that was two days ago—two days that have passed with Emma thinking he'd returned to the ocean to tell Grom about Neptune. Two days since he all but disappeared from existence, with no one realizing he's missing.

Did Emma stay? Did she go home? Did she come to look for me? He hopes she didn't go in search of him and stumble across Tyrden herself. *Or what if she did?* He quickly dismisses the thought. If Tyrden had Emma, he would have already used it against him.

The older Syrena leans back in his seat. He forks a big chunk of fish into his mouth and moans in appreciation. The plate could easily feed two. "I have some more questions for you, Highness. I'm hoping you answer them this time, because to miss out on a meal like this would be a shame."

Watching Tyrden eat makes Galen slightly delirious. Even more so than the hovering and cutting technique his captor used the day before. But it's not so much about enduring the agonizing hunger as it is about regaining some strength. Each day he stays here without food or water, he loses energy and strength— both things necessary to escape. And by how comfortable Tyrden has made himself here, he looks like he might be in it for the long haul.

My best chance is to escape—but how? For all he knows, there could be someone standing guard at the door, though only Tyrden comes and goes. Galen remembers the men who captured him in the woods. Where are they now? Not to mention the thick ropes holding each of his limbs to the metal chair, cinched so tightly they threaten to cut off circulation.

"What do you want to know?" Galen grinds his teeth. *Think of the energy food will give you.*

"Emma already divulged to Reed how you came to be in the good town of Neptune. So Antonis sent you here. Why do you think he would do that?"

"Reed?"

"Oh, yes. They've been spending all their time together. Does it hurt not to be missed?"

The idea of Emma spending enough time with Reed to tell him anything worries Galen, but at least he knows she's not being held prisoner somewhere like he is. Still, Reed has the presence of a trumpet fish slithering around, stalking its colorful—and unsuspecting—prey on the reef. So slow and casual that it looks harmless. Until it strikes.

Galen clears his throat of bitterness and concentrates on the question. *Why would Antonis send us here?* "I don't know. Why don't you ask Reed? He seems helpful enough."

Tyrden helps himself to another heaping bite, taking his time to savor it. "Reed is an entitled fool who uses his daddy's position for his own gain. I have no use for Reed."

Galen can't decide if Tyrden is purposely all over the place or if he's genuinely skittish.

If he's not on speaking terms with Reed, where is Tyrden

getting his information? Then Galen realizes the full picture. He must be getting the information from Reder himself. Reder must be the one who ordered his capture. It makes perfect sense, given the way Reder was withdrawn at dinner, the way he scrutinized Galen under the pretense of hospitality. Reed must tell his father about his ventures with Emma. Then Reder tells Tyrden.

Which means Tyrden could just be a pawn—pawns are much more pliable than leaders.

Tyrden seems to read his mind. "I'll tell you a secret, Highness, about Reed's father. Reder isn't all he's cracked up to be. He's not the savior of this town, as he would have you believe. Too soft, if you ask me."

This is too soft? "When will Reder be visiting us?"

Tyrden tilts his head. "Why would you think Reder would bother himself to come visit you? Maybe he wants to give Emma and Reed a chance to bond. Get you out of the way for a while." At this he seems amused. "Seems to be working all right."

"Reed is not Emma's type."

Tyrden swallows another bite and leans forward, eyeing Galen. "No? But what if it's not about types? What if it's about what Reed can offer her? That's one thing I've learned about women. They like security."

"What do you mean?"

"Let's say you get out of here by some miracle and somehow you two run off into the sunset. All you can offer her is a life of hiding what she is. Or... you're *not* considering living in the ocean, are you? Let her surface for air every few hours like a whale?" Tyrden chuckles. "Reed—Neptune—can offer her so much more. She told him all about how your Archives begrudgingly voted to let her live. How generous of them."

Galen closes his eyes against the truth. "Neptune is still in hiding. You're not all completely safe from humans."

Tyrden makes a show of looking around. "What humans? Oh, you mean the rest of the world? Let me tell you something, Highness. The rest of the world couldn't care less about this little speck of a town. Do you know what I do for a living?" Tyrden sneers. "There's a cannery on the edge of the city limits. Real shack of a place. We've got three full-blooded Syrena, descendants of Poseidon himself, using their Gift to keep the cannery busy stocking fish. We've got shipments going out daily to big cities. We can hardly keep up with the demand. To them, we're just a quiet little fishing village etching out an existence in the mountains. We're beneath them. What do they care about us?"

"Someday they will."

Tyrden waves in dismissal. "Just like a Triton to be skeptical. We've survived this long without discovery, haven't we? Heck, we've survived this long without even the kingdoms knowing!"

Galen can't argue that.

Tyrden places the fork on the plate and slowly lowers it to the floor next to his chair. He clears his throat and dabs the corner of his mouth with his shirt collar. When he looks at Galen again, he's all focus. "Tell me about Jagen."

This is unexpected. Galen's mind races. How does he know

about Jagen? How does Neptune connect with Jagen's attempt at taking over the kingdoms? Galen decides to use a favorite strategy of his—answering a question with a question. "What about him?"

"Are Jagen and his daughter Paca in power yet?"

"No." *Yet.* So Tyrden and Reder don't know that Jagen's attempt to rule the Triton kingdom failed. Galen figures it's a good exchange, trading simple answers for telling questions.

And this answer seems to infuriate Tyrden. He sits straighter in his chair. "What happened?"

Galen glances at the food on the floor. "Don't I get a bite first?" The sound of longing in his voice is genuine.

At this Tyrden's lips pull up in a menacing smile. "Excellent idea, boy. We'll swap, you and I. A bite for an answer." He picks up the plate and forks up a piece of fish—smaller than Galen would have liked—then gestures for him to open his mouth.

Galen complies, and Tyrden makes a point to jab his tongue with the fork before retracting it. But Galen doesn't care because the fish is delicious and warm and his stomach seems to bubble up in anticipation of the next bite.

Tyrden waits impatiently while Galen appreciates the small sample. "Now, tell me what happened."

"Do you think I could have some water?"

Tyrden's eyes narrow. "Oh, I'll give you plenty of water. After you tell me what I want to know."

Galen thinks about negotiating, but he can tell Tyrden has reached his threshold for patience by the way he taps the fork on the edge of the plate. "Jagen was removed from power when we discovered that Paca was a fraud. That she didn't really have the Gift of Poseidon."

"And how was that discovered?" Tyrden holds up another forkful of fish. Instead of tapping the fork, the energy moves down to his leg, which bounces with a fast rhythm.

"Emma. She showed the council her own true Gift, which proved that Paca's was inferior." Galen remembers the pride he felt when Emma put Paca on the spot, telling her to save her father from two sharks that Emma would have ordered to kill him—or so Paca thought. Paca crumbled right then and there. If Emma wouldn't have come to the tribunal, Galen is sure that things would have turned out differently. The Royals would no longer be in power, and Jagen would be ruling the Triton kingdom under false pretenses.

But how does this relate to Tyrden? To Reder? What interest do they have in Jagen's rule? Were they the ones who trained Paca to use hand signals to control the dolphins? He accepts the next bite of food from Tyrden, watching his captor closely. Something about his expression has changed.

"That's very inconvenient," Tyrden says.

"Inconvenient for who?"

"Shut up." Tyrden pauses. "Where are Jagen and Paca now?"

No wonder they're so hungry for information about the kingdoms. Now that Jagen and Paca are imprisoned back home for what they did, Neptune has probably had no communications about the kingdoms—until Galen and Emma showed up.

"Where are Jagen and Paca now?" Tyrden barks.

"They're in the Ice Caverns. Where they belong."

Tyrden stands with the plate and scoops more fish onto the fork. He extends it to Galen. But just before he can wrap his mouth around it, Tyrden snatches it away, pitching the fish to the floor. Then Tyrden puts all his strength and frustration into throwing the entire plate of food at the wall, shattering the glass and scattering what was left of Galen's meal.

"Enjoy dinner, Highness," Tyrden snarls. "Now for dessert." He rears back and Galen closes his eyes, preparing for the blow. There is more anger behind it than he originally expected.

Tyrden's fist connects with Galen's cheek, whipping his neck back. The impacts don't stop there. They keep coming from each side, different angles, landing blows on his nose, his jawbone, his mouth. Over and over and over.

Galen tastes blood, feels it running down the back of his throat. Feels it pooling in his ear.

Then everything goes black.

17

IT TAKES a minute to adjust to the darkness, even though we made a gradual descent into the cave. Reed swims ahead, as if he can see perfectly or as if he's been here a million times before. Probably both.

Maybe my eyes don't adjust as well in freshwater. Maybe the saltwaters of the oceans help them in some way, which strikes me as funny. Usually saltwater in the eyes sucks. Unless you're part fish, or fish mammal, or whatever. Either scenario, Reed is impatient to get started. "Are all ocean dwellers this slow?"

He grabs my wrist and pulls me behind him. His pulse wraps lightly around me, like the whisper of a fishing line not pulled tight. A tangle of sensations. "Can you sense me?" I say, almost to myself.

"Of course. Don't you sense me?"

"I do, but it feels different than the way I sense Galen."

"Oh, geez." Reed rolls his eyes. "You don't believe in the pull, do you?"

This is the legend that Galen is on the fence about. Normal Syrena tradition says that when a Syrena male turns eighteen years old—or "seasons"—he suddenly becomes attracted to several match-worthy females—females who would complement him well. Then he gets to "sift" through them, which is the Syrena version of dating. But in cases of "the pull," the male is only attracted to one female, and that one is supposedly the perfect match in every way. The explanation is that the pull produces the strongest offspring possible, that it's some natural phenomenon among Syrena that ensures the survival of their kind.

Galen didn't believe in the pull—until he met me. Now he's torn, because I'm the only one he was ever drawn to. Our mating would actually back up all the hype behind the pull, and since I have the Gift of Poseidon and Galen has the Gift of Triton, our offspring could potentially have both.

Still, the law and Syrena customs appear to be crunked-up superstition. If our child was to possess both gifts I'd rather chalk it up to genetics than to some magical, whimsical myth that always makes the Syrena generals right.

"No," I pronounce. "I don't believe in the pull exactly. I believe in love. And genetics." I didn't mean for it to sound like, "so screw you," or anything, but by his expression, I think Reed takes it that way.

"I told you I get it, Emma. You're in no danger from me stealing you from Galen. *Great guy that he is*," he mutters. He swims close to me, so close I think he's going back on his word. His mouth is just inches from mine when he says, "Not that I don't want to steal you away. Oh, I do. And would if I thought you'd let me."

I try to back away, but he holds my wrist. I could snatch it out of his hand if I wanted to, but his eyes tell me he's being sincere instead of creepy or possessive. "I would steal you in a heartbeat, Emma McIntosh," he continues, his voice devoid of any kind of games or sarcasm or Reed in general. "But I'd have to kiss you first, and I don't want to do that."

For some reason, I'm offended by that. He notices and smiles.

"Don't get yourself all worked up. You're very kissable. But I won't kiss you. Not until you want me to. Because I know if I do, I won't be able to turn back. I won't ever be the same." He leans impossibly closer, tightening his hold on my wrist, and I swear I'm being bombarded by both his heartbeat and his Syrena pulse. "So know for sure, Emma. When you kiss me—and I think you will—know for sure who you're going to choose."

I ease my wrist from his grasp and give a lighthearted laugh. Even though lighthearted is the opposite of what I'm feeling. Reed seems so easygoing and laid-back, but now he's practically handing me his beating heart for me to do with as I please, which kind of waylays me. I mean, what kind of crazy speech is this? We've only known each other for days and he's putting this on the table for me to consider. Does he think we've been going on dates or something instead of him just acting as my (devoted) tour guide?

I feel guilty now. Because spending more time with Reed feels like leading him on. It's clear his intentions are not strictly platonic, but I've been transparent from the beginning that I love Galen. Our relationship is obviously not perfect, but isn't that the "work" part of it? I've always felt that the dynamics between us are like a musical snow globe. Wound tight some-times, shaken and shaken, but never broken. Always intact and really something to behold on the inside.

It would help if Galen showed me a sign that he still loves me. That our snow globe isn't leaking. Or worse, shattered.

And there is still my need to explore Neptune. Reed is my guide—and that's all. I've already chosen who I want. A kiss from Reed will never change that. I'll simply continue to rebuff him, and eventually (freaking hopefully) he'll lay off the whole "let me love you" spiel.

I realize I haven't answered him. I wonder what he sees on my face that has him so fascinated. "Got it," I say casually, which makes him wince. But this conversation has to come to an end for so many reasons, and the only way that's happening is if I start a new one. "Tell me about how Neptune came to be."

He blinks, once, twice. Then his lazy smile appears once more, free of anguish or jealousy. "I would, but Father is best at telling it, really. He has Archive abilities, you know. So don't ever try to argue with him based on memory. You'll lose."

"You have Archives here?"

He nods. "And Trackers. We have everything you have. Ex-cept the ocean."

I'm starting to understand Reed's obsession with the ocean.

It's not the ocean itself, although the oceans are endlessly fascinating. Reed's problem is the freedom of choice. He wants something he can't have, which makes him want it even more. And can't I relate to that?

I decide to give Reed a break. "But your father seemed reluctant to tell us at dinner the other night. I wouldn't feel comfortable asking him. You don't have to do that if you don't want to."

"I think your precious Galen was weaving awkward into the air or something at dinner. I'll talk to my dad. He'll call a Huddle."

"A . . . 'Huddle'?"

Reed nods. "You know how humans have city hall meetings and everyone gets to attend and talk about how the town is run? Well, a Huddle is just like that, only we meet secretly because what we have to talk about has nothing to do with streetlights or sidewalks."

"We?"

"Sometimes the whole town. Sometimes a few of us. Just depends on the occasion, really. But this Huddle will be big, I can guarantee that."

"Oh, well. I don't really want to put your dad through all that mess. Couldn't you just summarize for me?"

Reed grins. "Oh, yeah. I definitely could. But if I did that, you might decide that you learned everything you need to know from me. Then I won't see you anymore."

"Reed, I—"

He holds up a quiet-child hand, startling some minnows

around us. "Besides, he really does love to tell the story. And everyone loves to hear him tell it. It will be great—you'll see. Worth not getting rid of me. And then you can meet even more Neptune citizens. You're going to have a long list of people to e-mail when you leave."

When I don't appear convinced, he crosses his arms. "If you promise to come, I'll show you a secret about yourself. One that I'm pretty sure you haven't figured out."

Crap, crap, crap. "What is it?" I blurt, sealing the deal. Well, what did I expect? I'm sure Grandfather sent me here to learn about Half-Breeds. If I didn't agree, then I'd be wasting this informative—and very weird—trip.

"That's what I like to hear." He pulls me to one side of the cave, where the light fades into shadows.

Reed holds up his hand, ceremoniously turning it side to side like a magician does when he's about to produce something from thin air. "You see these are my real hands right? Would you like to touch them?"

"I trust you didn't pack any extra hands with you, thanks."

I'm not sure if he's conscious of it or not, but Reed slightly sticks his chest out. The only reason I notice is because I'm a bit compelled to float away. Confidence like that is dangerous, especially after the talk we just had. "I'm going to start from the beginning," he says, "because I'm not sure how much you already know."

I nod. Even if I already know it, getting a mini refresher course couldn't hurt. Of course, I don't know what we're talking about yet, so that helps the surprise factor.

"Okay," he says, almost preening. "So. Syrena can Blend when they feel the need to, and it works from the inside out. Say they need to Blend because they're afraid or whatever. Their skin reacts to what their brain tells them, so the stimulation to change comes from within. In our bodies, we still have the same pigmentation points as a full-blood Syrena, but ours responds to *outside* stimulants. Watch."

He holds out his arm against the cave wall beside us, then starts rubbing it furiously with his other hand for what seems like for-freaking-ever. If we were on land, he'd be giving himself one heck of a friction burn. Minute after minute drags by. I realize this is why I never figured this out on my own. I would have quit after the first forty-five seconds.

Finally, something happens. The middle of his forearm seems to be disappearing. There is a hand and then cave wall and then an elbow. After a few more seconds, the middle of his arm becomes altogether invisible. Reed has just Blended in front of me. With my eyes, I trace where his forearm should be between his hand and elbow. Only a vague outline shows, kind of like looking at a hidden 3-D puzzle. "Cool, huh?" he says, still rubbing madly. "You have to get through a few layers of human skin before you hit the Blending skin cells. That's why it takes so long."

"Holy crap," is what I think I say. Half-Breeds can Blend. If we don't mind being refurbished one patch of skin at a time.

When Reed stops scouring, his Blended state quickly materializes into a now-red forearm.

He shrugs. "So obviously it's too much trouble to try to

use as protection, but it's still pretty impressive. Ready to try yours?" He takes my hand and puts it against the wall, which puts us in a more intimate position.

I pull away. "I'm more than capable of rubbing myself." Then I blush at how that sounds. I want to squeeze Reed's lips together, to discontinue the knowing smile sweeping across his face. Without giving myself further opportunity for embarrassment, I start rubbing my own arm. Ferociously. It's exhausting. The water resistance hinders my efforts a little, so I have to work harder and faster to get the job done. Suddenly, I wish for Reed's muscular biceps. *No, Galen's. I wish for Galen's arms, and not just rubbing me mindlessly, but I wish for them to be wrapped around me.*

It takes me much longer to produce the same result. But I do. When it starts to fade, I can still feel that it's there, but my eyes refuse to see "arm" instead of "cave wall." It's kind of like the sensation when your foot falls asleep and you can touch it with your hand, but it doesn't feel like it's attached to your body. Your hand doesn't register what it's touching and your foot doesn't register that it's being touched.

A big part of my arm has disappeared now, and for once it's not my pale skin camouflaged by white beach sand. "Whoa," I say, more to myself than to him. "That's crazy." It doesn't feel any different, except maybe for a warm sensation creeping up my arm. Other than that, I'd never know I was Blending.

And if I can't feel it, I definitely can't initiate it with feelings, like an octopus does when it's afraid or nervous. Which might be a good thing. If my whole body turned invisible instead of blushing, I'd never need a mirror.

"So I did teach you something new." Reed beams. And at that moment, he's all child-like wonder and adorable and harmless. Until he comes to his senses. "If you want to make your whole body disappear, you'll clearly need my help. And for the record, I'm in."

This time I shove him. Hard. "Sounds like you need *my* help with a concussion."

And I'm not even joking.

18

GALEN AWAKENS with a groan. No part of his face was left untouched by Tyrden. His lips are crusted with dried blood and dehydration. His nose carries the steady thrum of his heart in it, beat for beat. His left ear rings, and he can hear the muffled sound of his own breath from the inside out.

But now his scalp crawls with what feels like tiny fingers exploring through his hair. His legs throb with the need to stretch. His feet tingle to the point of hurting.

He feels a drop of something hit his forehead. Slowly he peers up, willing his neck to stop trembling with the weight of his head. Small tributaries of what feels like water roll down his face, his neck. Above him hangs a blue tarp stretched across the ceiling, heavy at the center, where a small hole allows a drop to fall on him every few seconds.

It's then that he notices that what's left of his shirt is soaked through. The rim of his jeans is dark and wet. But he doesn't care about that. He has water. One precious drop at a time.

Opening his mouth, he leans farther back, aiming for the next drop. It hits his cheek and stings an open cut there. *Again.*

He repeats the process, three, four, five times. Finally a drop hits his tongue and spreads like a single tear on tissue paper. Salt.

It's saltwater. Soaking through his shirt, his hair, down the length of him.

A frustrated growl escapes Galen's lips, echoing off the walls.

I have to get out of here.

Tyrden opens the door then, walking in with a bucket in tow and an evil grin. Without a word or warning, he pitches the contents on Galen, dousing everything the tarp failed to saturate. The force of the splash is so great that some of the new saltwater finds its way into Galen's mouth, his nose, all the cuts and scratches. He spits vehemently.

Tyrden snickers. "I thought you were thirsty?"

Galen doesn't trust himself to speak. His throat is too dry to close around the words inside him. Anything he says will sound like a wheeze. *I won't let him think he's broken me.*

Tyrden drags the other chair across the room to face Galen, his usual interrogation move. Galen settles in for what could possibly be next, though he can't imagine anything quite as bad as this.

Tyrden smiles at him through tight lips that maneuver a toothpick back and forth. "You look rough, Highness." He removes the pick and rolls it between his fingers. Galen eyes it, wary. Tyrden glances up at the tarp above Galen and scoffs. "It's almost half empty already."

Galen groans in reply. It's all he has left. Beneath him his legs begin trembling with the need to unfold, to elongate.

"What's that?" Tyrden says, delighted. "Oh, you got a frog in your throat? Let me help you." He pulls a silver flask from his shirt pocket and shakes it. The liquid in it makes a swishing sound. "Can I interest you in some fresh water?"

Galen nods, which makes his head throb harder. He's in no mood to play games.

Tyrden stands and unscrews the flask. Galen doesn't trust that there's really freshwater in it, but what choice does he have? He's been three days without a drop to drink. It's a chance he has to take. Besides, if Tyrden wanted him dead, he wouldn't be sitting here now. *Right?*

The older Syrena eases the flask to his lips and Galen takes a swallow. It's fresh. He leans in for more but Tyrden pulls back. "Oh, sorry. I've got to save this for more questions." He settles back down in his chair and tucks the flask away. Galen feels his shoulders sag.

"So I've been thinking," Tyrden says. "Jagen and Paca failed, obviously. But how many followers did they round up? A lot? A few? Remember, a drink for an answer."

Galen complies quickly; this is an easy question. "I don't know," he rasps. The words feel parched and he coughs.

"Guess for me."

Shaking his head, Galen coughs again. He tastes blood in his mouth this time instead of the precious water. "I don't know. Maybe a third. Maybe more." It was more, he knows. Jagen's number of Loyals multiplied each day Paca displayed the Gift of Poseidon. There were enough of them to persuade the Archives to put the Royals on trial at the tribunal.

Tyrden gives Galen a heaping drink from the flask. "See how that works? Honesty goes a long way."

Another maddening drop of water falls on Galen's head and his legs ache with the need to wrap around each other, to become one. It's been three days since he used his fin to maneuver through the freshwater caves where they found Reed. It's been more than that since he used it to glide through his own saltwater territory.

"Jagen obviously convinced a good amount of followers in a short time," Tyrden says. "Someone more competent could pull twice those numbers. Sounds like the ocean dwellers are ready for change. Maybe the Royals are out of style, eh?" He scratches his chin thoughtfully. "Did you know that we don't have Royals here? Sure, those who possess the Gift of Poseidon are obviously descendants of the general himself. But we don't put much stock in that. Here, we elect our leaders." He makes a face as if the words taste tart in his mouth. "Sometimes democracy works. Not lately though." With a blank expression he scrutinizes the flask in his hand.

Galen feels liquid draining down the back of his throat again. In case it's remnants of freshwater, he swallows. The metallic taste suggests more blood. He wonders if his nose is broken. "More questions," he says. He has to take in more water. Though he doesn't like that Tyrden is sharing information with him. *Would he be divulging so much if he was going to let me go?*

Tyrden laughs. "You disappoint me, Highness. For a while there, I thought you'd hold out until the bitter end." He leans forward. Galen's eyes never leave the vessel of water in his hands. "Grom is the Triton king and your brother, right?"

Galen nods. Tyrden readily gives him another two swallows of water. Galen's not sure why he's being rewarded for obvious answers. If Tyrden knows about Jagen, he knows about Grom.

"So he wouldn't like it if he knew you were in so much trouble. Surely, he would come fetch his Royal brother if he knew he was being held prisoner somewhere. He would be angry with whoever did this to you."

There is no question here—and no need for one—but nonetheless Tyrden peers at Galen expectantly. It's not difficult to follow Tyrden's line of thought. "No," Galen says flatly. "He would be thrilled." They both know if Grom were aware that Galen were in such danger, he would come immediately. He would play right into Tyrden's hands.

Tyrden seems to appreciate sarcasm; he gives Galen another drink, tilting the flask up so that he gets several swallows. "This is a mercy drink, Highness. From now on, dishonest answers get punishment instead of reward. You're lucky that I need you alive for now."

Galen feels the water seeping down into his stomach. He imagines his bloodstream absorbing it, hydrating him. He sits up straighter. "Grom . . ." Galen says, then clears his throat. "Grom won't risk the kingdoms. Not even for me."

Tyrden puts the toothpick back in his mouth, rolling his eyes. "Of course he wouldn't. And I asked for honest answers, not your opinion." He reaches around to his back pocket and produces Galen's cell phone. "Grom have one of these?"

Until now, the idea of Grom coming here was just theoretical. A phone changes everything. "I won't call him." Galen hates himself for flinching when Tyrden jumps to his feet. He reminds himself that Tyrden is unpredictable.

"No?" Tyrden barks. He holds the flask in front of Galen's face and starts pouring the contents out slowly onto Galen's lap, giving him a chance to recant.

But he won't. Can't. He closes his eyes, unable to watch the rest of his lifeline soak into his jeans.

Tyrden grabs a handful of Galen's wet hair and puts his face directly over Galen's. "You will call him, I swear it." He tightens his grip. "It means your life. Think about that, boy." He shoves Galen away then, so forcefully that the chair almost tips backward.

Tyrden throws the flask to the floor, onto the pieces of broken plate by the wall, and stalks toward the door. He pauses when he reaches it, giving Galen a knowing smirk. He glances up at the tarp overhead. "You feel like stretching yet, Highness?"

Galen can't help but scowl.

Tyrden's grin widens. "I've always wanted to see the fin of a Triton Royal." Then he slams the door behind him.

Galen feels a new rage surge through him like a tsunami.

Shaping a fin would shred his jeans, leaving him completely naked—no doubt Tyrden's idea of ultimate humiliation. It would be one thing if Tyrden had removed all his clothes in the beginning to shame him or deter him from escaping. It would be quite another if Galen couldn't control his need to shape a fin amid the saltwater saturating him and accidentally destroyed his own clothing—and maybe even injured his fin in the process. The ropes are new and thick and strong; either they'll break or they won't, and then where will he be?

Another drop plummets to the tip of his nose and Galen lets it slither down over his lips, licking it defiantly.

Tyrden wants to see the fin of a Triton Royal? I'll show him one.

19

MOM CALLS me right as I'm about to walk out of my room and meet Reed in the lobby.

"Hey, sweetie, you called? Everything okay?"

My lip almost quivers at the concern in her voice. I sit on the bed and get comfortable. You'll-never-believe-what-has-happened kind of comfortable. Reed will just have to wait. "Did Galen tell you we were fighting?"

"Galen? What do you mean? Galen is with you. Right?"

"He left, actually." I don't skip a beat. This isn't the hard part of the conversation. Not yet. "A few days ago. He said he was going back to talk to Grom." Okay, so maybe it is a little hard. "Wait, you haven't seen him?"

So he hasn't made it to Grom yet? Why is he taking his time? Hope cartwheels through me. Maybe he's coming back. He has to be. He got all my messages, and we're going to work things out. I don't know why I feel so relieved, but I do. Maybe he'll even make it back in time to go to the Huddle. I'll have to get Sylvia to give him directions. I take out the hotel stationery and start scrawling my request for her.

Suddenly, I regret calling Mom, getting her involved in my relationship issues. I'm an adult now, right? Shouldn't I be dealing with this on my own?

"He *left* you? You're alone?" The outrage in her voice is unmistakable. I hear Grom mumbling something in the background, and then the phone goes all white noise dissention among the married ranks. Mom must be covering it with her hand. Then she says, "Grom says he hasn't seen Galen. Why on earth would Galen leave you all alone? What are you fighting about?"

I bite my lip. If Galen hasn't told Grom about Neptune, then maybe I shouldn't either. After all, the Triton king couldn't in good conscience keep this from the kingdoms. It's his Royal obligation to confront the leaders of this Neptune. I get that now.

Also, Galen is the fastest of his kind. If he was swimming with any sort of purpose, he would have reached Grom long ago. Maybe he's just taking some time to clear his head. If anyone can understand that, it's me.

But in the meantime, I wouldn't want anything to happen to this lovely little town just because of some centuries-old prejudice that has very little to do with its descendants now. And it's more Galen's place to tell Grom than mine. So if he didn't go home and tell, I've got no reason to.

"It's not a big deal. Just stupid stuff. He's probably on his way back now anyway." I try to sound casual. But Mom is the bloodhound of secrets.

"Galen doesn't fight over stupid stuff, sweetie. He'd hand you the world if he could. Now tell me what's going on with you."

Okay, now I really regret calling Mom. I want to tell her—as tactfully as possible—that it's none of her business. The thing is, *I* called *her*. I opened the conversation, and now I can't find a way to close it. Even if I wanted to tell Mom about Neptune, just to have someone to talk about it with, I couldn't dump it on her—she'd feel obligated to tell Grom. I feel guilty about what I say next. "Galen's just been different lately, you know? Ever since Rachel. He has these mood swings." I squeeze my eyes shut. *Oh God, I just betrayed Galen in the worst possible way.* It's one thing to be hanging out with Reed while I'm waiting to hear back from Galen; it's another to cover my own butt by taking advantage of his grief.

I want to drop the phone and cry.

Mom's silence is impossible to read. Then, "I'll give you that. Rachel's death was hard on us all. But Galen fought so hard for this road trip, Emma. Are you sure you're telling me everything?"

Nope. "Yep."

Another thread of silence, and I almost fool myself into thinking it's just a natural phone delay, the pause between her words leaving her mouth and her words hitting my ears. But I know better. When Mom is quiet, she has all sorts of things percolating in her head.

Crappity crap crap crap.

"Well, someone is waiting on me," I say quickly. "I've gotta go."

"Who is waiting, Emma? Where are you?"

"We stopped in this little town in Tennessee—I don't remember the name—but anyway, since Galen left I've made a few friends here. Just trying to get the most out of a vacation turned sour, you know?"

"What town? Have you lost your mind?" Mom half shouts. "You don't know these people, and Galen isn't there to protect you. I'm coming to get you. Call down to the front desk and get the address. Me and my GPS will be there shortly. Galen can sort out what he needs to sort out on his own time."

"Wow, overreaction much?"

Another pause. "Emma, I'm worried about you. Even if you're grown, you're still my baby."

Ew. We've had this talk before. "Look, I get it. You're worried. But I'm just doing what we came here to do. Strike out on our own and all that. I'm fine. You can hear me, right? You can hear that I'm fine?"

Mom sighs. She's fighting her instincts and I know it. What kills me is, her instincts are usually right. "Just tell me where you are at least."

"Promise you're not saying that as you start the car."

"I promise."

"I'm in a little town called Neptune." I hold my breath, waiting for a motherly explosion. It doesn't come. Apparently, Grandfather really didn't tell anyone but me about this place.

A little more confident, I say, "And I'm loving it. So don't worry."

Another long, obligatory pause from the mother, but still no freak-out. "Okay, Emma. Just be careful while you're having fun. Stay alert." I expect her to tell me not to accept candy from strangers and to always say please and thank you and to avoid big white vans in parking lots.

"Will do. Gotta go, okay?"

"Okay. Love you."

"Love you, too."

She lets me hang up first. She always lets me hang up first.

I throw the phone on the bed and head toward the door.

Reed is probably having a conniption; I've noticed that when he's ready to do something, he's ready to do it right freaking now. Everyone has secrets. I wonder if Reed's is that he's secretly OCD.

I take the stairs to save time, and I hit the lobby as Reed is pushing the elevator button to go up. "You meeting someone here?" I call to him.

He smiles before he even sees me. "Yeah, but don't tell my friend Emma. She's starting to have feelings for me, and I don't want to ruin it with her."

Alrighty then. "Are you some sort of man-whore?"

"Do you want me to be?"

"Nope. It would be nice if you were a little less creepy though."

He winces dramatically as I punch his arm. "Ouch. On both accounts."

I'm about to tell him something ridiculously clever when a third party joins our reverie. "Oh, hello there, Reed."

We both turn to see Mr. Kennedy walking toward us, arms full of different kinds of plants, white lab coat smudged with ten kinds of dirt and double that amount embedded in his worn-out tennis shoes, which don't match each other, much less the rest of the outfit. Not that I think a pair of wedges would save him or anything.

I'd actually forgotten all about him. Even though he's staying here at Sylvia's, I haven't seen him since that first day we arrived in Neptune. That day, he looked somewhat normal.

Today, he looks . . . frazzled. A close-up reveals that his hair is so grimy you can hardly tell the actual color. Probably brown, but light brown? Dark brown? Mousy brown? Who knows. Thick glasses magnify the fact that he also has brown eyes, and that the left one wanders.

Reed gives him an easy smile. One that I've come to know is actually fake, the manners kind of smile, since it doesn't climb all the way to his eyes. Reed is especially good at BSing for manners' sake. "Hey, Mr. Kennedy. You need some help there?"

Mr. Kennedy's eyes light up. "Oh, no, thank you, Reed. I've got to keep these little gems on lockdown." He lowers his voice and leans in, giving us a powerful waft of BO, probably earned from spending the day in the field. "I've found what I believe to be a crossbreed between *Asclepias viridis* and *Asclepias syriaca*."

"Gosh," Reed says, "that sounds exciting, Mr. Kennedy." My mother is very good at sniffing out lies, even the little white ones. I wonder if she could sniff out Reed right now.

Mr. Kennedy nods, shifting his weight from foot to foot. "Oh, it is exciting. If I'm right, it's a new species. One that could help sustain much more wildlife here in the mountains than we originally thought. Oh, yes, Reed, it's all very exciting."

"Congratulations, Mr. Kennedy. I knew you'd find what you were looking for here. Oh, and have you met my friend Emma? She's visiting from New Jersey." I decide that Reed learned his hospitality from his father.

Because his arms are too full to safely pull off a polite handshake, Mr. Kennedy nods to me, smiling big. "It's a pleasure to meet you, Emma." Then he eyes my dress and Reed's fancier-than-normal khakis and becomes visibly distressed. "Oh, are you going on a date? I didn't mean to interrupt. You both look very nice. I remember going on a date once."

I open my mouth to object, but Reed takes my hand. "Yes, sir, we're heading a few towns over to the movies. You didn't interrupt anything." He starts dragging me toward the front door. "But if we don't get going, we'll be missing more than just the previews. Evening, Mr. Kennedy."

"Have a good time, you two lovebirds," Mr. Kennedy calls over his shoulder. Sylvia rushes past us as we reach the glass lobby doors. Behind us, we hear her press the elevator button for Mr. Kennedy, accompanied by his frenzied thanks.

When we get in the truck, Reed pats the seat in the middle. "You can sit here, since we're picking up Toby."

I raise a you-wish brow. "Then Toby can sit in the middle."

Reed winks. "Worth a shot."

"What don't you get about—"

"So anyway," he continues as if I'm not talking, "I have another secret to tell you. If you don't know how to Blend, then you definitely haven't figured this out yet."

Why does he have to be so mysterious? If there were ever a time I would have appreciated a straight-up info dump, it would be now. But noooo. Reed is determined to string me along until . . . ?

I decide not to play his game anymore. I peer out the window, pretending to drink in the nectar that is the winsome town of Neptune passing us by.

He gives me a few seconds, then he starts squirming. "I know what you're doing."

"Huh?" I say, without looking at him.

"You're dying to know. I can tell."

But when I don't answer, he starts to show signs of weakness. First, he taps his fingers on the steering wheel to the tune of the song humming fuzzily through the speakers. Problem is, he doesn't appear to actually know the song. Or he has the rhythm of a worm.

Then he takes to checking the rearview. A lot. He adjusts it as if looking for something in his teeth. Then he adjusts it to view something terribly important-looking behind us. After that, he makes a show of waving to every. Single. Person. We pass.

Now I'm starting to think he's playing me. Because I'm about to blow a freaking gasket.

Thankfully, we pull into the driveway of a house I've not been to yet. Reed unceremoniously beeps the horn, and a few seconds later, Toby is sitting in between us.

"I thought you were grounded?" I tell Toby.

He scowls. "I am. I have to go to Mrs. Buford's for tutoring, 'cause I almost failed math this year. Which is stupid, because I *almost* failed it. I didn't *actually* fail it."

"Better get that out of your system before we meet up with Mom and Dad," Reed says, not unkindly. "You've had a smart mouth lately."

Toby rolls his eyes. "Says the King of Comebacks."

It's then that I realize that Toby reminds me of Rayna. And that I miss her. Me. Missing Rayna. Even her Tabasco-sauce temper. In. Sane.

I poke Toby in the ribs. "Your brother says he knows a secret about me. Yesterday, he showed me how to Blend. Today, he says he knows how to do something else."

Toby glances at his brother, but I can tell his mind is already made up to divulge it to me. After all, he does blame Reed for getting him grounded. "He's talking about the time he shaped a fin."

Okay. So now I'm the one fidgeting. In front of me, my knee begins to bounce. "A fin? What do you mean?" But I know what he means. And it's not possible. But then, twenty-four hours ago, I didn't think Blending was, either. Not for Half-Breeds.

"Aw, Toby, you little jerk face. You just cost me a kiss," Reed whines.

I'm starting to get really good at my you-wish brow.

"Yeah, right. Like Emma would kiss you. You've met Galen, right?" Toby shakes his head in mock sympathy toward his brother. Then he beams up at me. Apparently, the Triton prince made an impression. "Where is Galen, anyway?"

My stomach turns into a kaleidoscope of emotions. According to Reed, I'm meeting the rest of the town tonight at the Huddle. People will ask where Galen is. They know we arrived together. And I'd love to think of something to say that doesn't make me look like The Girl Who Got Dumped.

But then again, why should I make Galen out to be a hero? He did leave, after all. Maybe he's on his way back, or maybe he decided to take his road trip alone. All I know is that he hasn't called to tell me anything. Not that he's sorry, not that he loves me, not that he's coming back.

After all that jealousy over Reed, he suddenly leaves me alone with him? Nice.

Or . . . Or . . . Something could be wrong. I hadn't really thought of it like that. I've always considered Galen supercapable and independent. But . . . he didn't make it to Triton territory after all, according to Mom and Grom. Did he intentionally go off course, or did something happen? The realization that Galen could have been in an accident and lying injured or worse on some scarcely used road makes the churning kaleidoscope in my stomach feel more like a pot of melted crayons.

"Do you think he's okay?" I blurt.

Reed glances at me in surprise. "Who? Galen?"

I nod. "Because he's never left me like this. Ever. I know he was mad when he left but . . . This isn't like him not to check in with anyone." So now Toby knows he left me. And now I'm not so sure that he did.

Reed sits straighter in his seat and mindlessly adjusts his seat belt. "Anyone? Who would he check in with?"

"Well, I talked to my mom this morning, and she said he hasn't checked in with his brother."

"Your mom is Antonis's daughter? And his brother is . . . the Triton king, right?" I can tell what's going through his mind, the domino effect of what would occur if I told my mom about the good citizens of Neptune.

"Yes," I say impatiently. "But I didn't tell her about Neptune. Not the important part, anyway." Reed and I already talked about Mom and Grom before. I decided in the beginning not to keep secrets. I didn't think Grandfather would view my being cagey as productive in my short stay here. Still, while I sympathize with Reed's valid concerns, Galen could be *missing*.

"What does your mom think about him leaving you here to fend for yourself?"

Toby looks up at me, eyes wide. "Galen actually *did* leave you here? You weren't joking? Did you guys have a fight?"

Ah, hello, renewed humiliation. I nod. "We had a fight and he left, Toby." I wish I could say it happens all the time, because that would at least be a sign of normalcy or consistency. But it doesn't happen all the time. Galen has never done this before.

And I'm an utter simpleton for not thinking he could be hurt. For not worrying about it.

"We should look for him," I tell Reed decidedly. "He could

be broken down on the side of the road. Or . . . Or . . ." I can't say it. Not out loud, not when just thinking it makes me want to curl into a ball.

This time Reed raises his brow at *me*. "First of all, cars like his just don't break down, Emma. Even if it did, cars like his come with roadside assistance or some fancy thing like that. Plus, a Syrena is never stranded. Not if there's water close by."

This is all true. Still, apprehension undulates through my veins in waves. This hasn't felt right from the start, has it? Haven't I had that underlying feeling of . . . weirdnesss? And haven't I just pushed through it like the stubborn monster that I am? "We should look for him," I say again.

"You mean right now?" Reed says, incredulous.

"I heard 'now' is always the best time to look for a missing person."

"Missing person? Emma—"

I sigh. "I know it could be that he's missing on purpose and that he doesn't want to be found. I get that, Reed. But just in case. We have to find him. Or at least get him on the phone somehow."

Reed lets out a slow breath. "Okay. This is what we can do. Neptune's sheriff is going to be at the Huddle tonight. As soon as we get there, I'll introduce you to him, and we'll tell him about Galen. Neptune takes it seriously when one of their own goes missing, trust me. He'll probably form a search party right then and there."

"I want to go with them," I say. If Galen is really missing, then he's been gone longer than forty-eight hours now. Even as

I think it, I imagine a window shutting, the opportunity for us to find him now diminishing.

"I know you do," Reed says. "But despite how Podunk we all look, the sheriff and his boys have had real law-enforcement training. They're real cops, believe it or not. They know where to start looking. And they'd never let a civilian come with them. You need to trust them to find Galen—if he really wants to be found. It's dark out. If the boys don't find him tonight, we'll form a town-wide search party in the morning. We'll cover where the sheriff didn't, I promise. But coming tonight to the Huddle will help your cause. If they know you, they'll be more motivated to help."

My brain rebels against all this common sense. I know it's the right thing to do or whatever, but I know Galen would look for me if he thought something was wrong. He wouldn't be attending any Huddle, and he wouldn't be waiting for morning to start looking. No matter how many people were expecting him to be there.

But I feel like I don't have a choice.

Toby shakes his head. "You have to go to the Huddle, Emma. Sheriff Grigsby will find Galen. Please don't leave. I don't want you to go missing, too." The boy's eyes are filled with raw emotion.

Reed scowls. "Toby, buddy. Emma's not going to go missing. Right, Emma?"

I nod but Toby's not looking at me. "Alexa went missing and didn't come back." His voice is tight. He's trying to stop whatever's inside him from erupting.

Reed takes a turn down a red-clay road, and we're temporarily blinded by the setting sun at the end of it. "Alexa was a TV character, minnow. It's not real."

"They looked for her forever, Emma," Toby nearly wails. "They never found her car or anything. She just disappeared."

Reed peers at me over Toby's head, a look that clearly says, "Can we talk about this later?"

I nod. The last thing I want to do is upset Toby. I slip my arm around him. "I'm sure she's okay." Because what else am I going to say?

"That's what everyone says, but they don't really know for sure." Toby leans into me, lets me comfort him. I suppress a grin at his utter adorableness and try to remember what it's like to be so innocent.

Reed gives his brother's arm a light punch. "Listen, you let it out of the bag about my fin, little monster. Do you want to tell Emma the story, or shall I?"

20

GALEN WORKS at the ropes holding him to the chair. He wriggles and squirms but can hardly budge the expertly tied knots.

I just have to keep loosening them, wear them down somehow.

Still, the knots refuse to give even a breath of slack.

The tarp hanging above has long since run out of the salt-water, but the effect on Galen's body stayed. His need to shape a fin burns through him like fire on an oil slick.

But timing is everything; second only to loosening the ropes, injuring himself during transformation might cost him his only chance for escape. The looser they are, the easier to break free.

Footsteps fall heavy on the dirt outside, and Galen lets his arms and legs fall instantly. Seconds later, the door swoops open and Tyrden strolls in. He's carrying a bottle of water and a lantern. Setting the latter on the floor in front of Galen, Tyrden paces around Galen's chair. His shadow takes turns dancing on each wall.

"Evenin', Highness."

Galen glares at him, which is not a little painful with swollen eyes.

"I've brought you more water." Tyrden chuckles to himself, shaking the bottle. He makes several more laps around the room, circling Galen with the smell of sweat and fish. Finally, he takes his usual seat across from him. "I think we might have gotten off on the wrong foot. I've decided I don't want to make an enemy out of you, Galen." He unscrews the bottle and hands it to Galen's helpless torso. "Oh," he smiles. "You're all tied up." He leans close enough for Galen to take a sip.

But Galen hesitates. Tyrden's newfound hospitality has all the makings of another trick. He regrets not having the ropes loosened by now.

This amuses the old Syrena. "What? Don't trust me? Well, I guess I can't blame you. Here, take a tiny sip. It's fresh, I swear."

Galen decides that a sip doesn't make or break his plans. Worst-case scenario, this is saltwater—another mind game, plus another step toward dehydration. Best-case scenario, it's actually fresh water, in which case Galen needs it very badly. He angles forward and tastes it. *Fresh.*

Tyrden stands abruptly then, and to Galen's amazement, unties one of Galen's wrists and hands him the bottle to hold. A small twinge of hope whirpools in his stomach.

Tyrden backs away from him slowly and takes his seat

again, pulling the big knife from the inside of his boot. "Try anything and I'll fillet you. Keep your hand in front of you."

Galen nods, downing the bottle of water in all of three gulps. Now is not the time, he realizes. He won't be effective with one hand free. But he can possibly use this as an opportunity to earn Tyrden's trust. Something he should have thought of much earlier. He says he doesn't want to make an enemy out of me, right? *So let's take him at his word.*

Galen turns the empty bottle over and over in his hands. "Thank you," he says quietly, without lifting his gaze to his captor. If he did, Tyrden would know how insincere his gratitude is.

"You're welcome." He spits on the floor between them. "Are we friends yet?"

"No." Galen yawns for causal effect. Then a real one takes over, one so big it tugs at the corners of his cracked lips.

"How have you been sleeping?"

"In a chair."

Tyrden smiles. "Well, you're in luck. I've come to tell you a bedtime story."

Suddenly, Galen feels exhausted. He supposes that's normal, with no food and hardly any water for days, plus the effort he's been putting into escape. Plus, Tyrden is a taxing person in general.

"Do you know what a Huddle is?" Tyrden continues.

"No." Another yawn escapes him. The room seems to get smaller. *Or am I closing my eyes?*

Tyrden seems pleased. "Go on and make yourself

comfortable. Tonight, my friend, I'm going to tell you about the story of Tartessos."

"I already know about Tartessos."

"What you know is what you've been told."

A sudden warmth steals through Galen's body, reaching every part of him. His muscles begin to relax against his will. The need to shape a fin is no longer as urgent. His free arm falls to his side, and he feels himself slumping in the chair. *Oh, no.* "That wasn't water."

Tyrden scoffs. "Of course it was. With a little bit of something else."

"Why?"

"I just wanted you to get some real rest, Highness. I can't present you to your brother looking like that, now can I?" Tyrden's face grows hard. "And not to mention, your wrists are looking awfully raw. You should have told me you were bored. I can give you plenty of activities to keep you occupied." The chair creaks with Tyrden's weight as he eases back. "But for now, a story."

Everything becomes blurry. Galen squints to clear his eyes. Are the walls growing fur? Is the lantern going out?

"That's right, get comfortable, boy. You'll want to hear this." Tyrden leans forward slowly, the light from the lantern casting an eerie glow on his face. "Because everything you thought you knew about the destruction of Tartessos is wrong."

21

"TAKE OFF your clothes," Reed says with glee.

I roll my eyes and peel my dress off. "I didn't peg you for a perv."

He greedily eyes my bathing suit. "Gross. I hate that word."

"What? Peg?"

He snorts and strips off his khakis, then takes the rest of our clothing and tucks it safely into the floorboard of the truck. Toby dances from foot to foot in the moonlight, his bright red swimming trunks illuminated into an ugly brown. "Hurry up, Reed. We're gonna be late!"

Reed grabs my hand and pulls me toward the water. I hear, but don't actually see, Toby plunge in ahead of us. The disturbed water ripples around the point of entry, but it's obvious after a few moments that Toby doesn't have any intention of resurfacing.

"He's been here before?" It's a stupid question. The kid was antsy as soon as we turned down the dirt road to come here.

"He was practically raised in this creek," Reed says. "He knows his way around these caves better than I do, probably."

"Maybe I should be holding *his* hand," I say, pulling from his grasp. "You're sure this is the shortest way to get to the Huddle?" The incessant need to talk to the sheriff about Galen is almost overwhelming. I fuss with the decorative strings on the hip of my bathing suit.

"I'm sure," he says. "Don't worry. As soon as we get there, we'll get help, Emma. I promise."

When we're about knee-deep, Reed falls backward into the water, but not before he beckons me with a come-hither finger. I ease down, taking care not to forge ahead too quickly. I wasn't raised here, and I still can't see into the water from the surface like a full-blood Syrena can. The last thing I need is to rush, bust my nose on a rock or a log, and then greet Galen—because I will see him again—with two black eyes.

Because on my pale skin, black eyes shoot to a whole new level of hideous when they heal.

Apparently Toby has left us completely to ourselves. I stay close behind Reed, but my eyes don't adjust well in this crummy freshwater, and I have to give in and take his hand again. He leads me through a series of what I can't really call caves—they remind me of slides at a water park, only they're ridged, filled with water, and we're swimming through them instead of slid-ing. Sometimes the space gets cramped, and I'm forced to press my body against Reed's to fit, or else risk bumping my head on low-hanging stalactites.

I notice that during these close encounters, Reed seems to hold his breath. Then I freak out a little on the inside, because I hold mine, too. I try to push the thought aside, and not play the "What does this all mean?" game.

Because it means nothing except Reed is a member of the opposite sex and we're in a state of undress and I'm not totally unaware of it. We've got skin touching, for crying out loud. And, yes, I've noticed he's attractive, blah blah blah. But that's all it means.

So then why do I feel ashamed of simply being aware of him?

"Emma," Reed says, startling me from mortification. "It's wider now. You can, uh ... You can swim on your own. If you want."

I clear my throat of the nothing that's in there. "Oh. Yeah. Thanks. Sorry."

My eyes are adjusted well enough to see his small, satisfied grin. Or maybe I just imagine that I see it. Either way, he knows he's unnerved me, and I know he knows it. "It's not too far ahead now," he says. "And that's the last of the tight spots. If you really concentrate, you can sense others farther down. They're kind of the guardians of the cave."

But all I can really concentrate on is the fact that in a few minutes we will be out of the water, away from each other and physical contact and hopefully whatever source of light is in this cave won't be bright enough to expose the blush I know is smoldering on my freaking cheeks.

Then I remember something I can concentrate on. "Toby said you shaped a fin. Is that true?"

Reed glances at me but keeps moving. I've caught him off guard. "I'm going to beat the fool out of that kid when I see him next."

"So it is true."

He sighs and halts us. I really can see his face, though not all the details, but now I'm pretty sure I did catch a spy of a grin a few seconds ago. And I'm mortified all over again. "I didn't do it on purpose, though, is the thing," he says. "So I can't show you how to do it or whatever. It just sort of . . . happened."

"Tell me."

"I was about thirteen. Doc Schroeder says it had to do with premature hormone development. He's a real doctor, you know. He's mated to a Syrena, Jessa, and they have a son, Fin." He shakes his head. "Can you believe they named their son Fin?"

I take Reed by the shoulders and give him a good shake. "Hello? You in there? *Tell me how it happened.*" I can tell by the way he glances ahead of us that we're close to the Huddle. And I can tell he doesn't divulge this story to just anyone.

"Okay. Sorry." Reed actually backs away from me then, and I almost laugh, but I'm afraid that if I do, he'll get distracted again. "So one day I'm not feeling good, so I stay home from school. I'm not sick, not exactly, but I definitely don't feel like going to school. Which, since I never miss school—that's kind of a big deal—"

"Ohmysweetgoodness!"

"Okay, okay, sorry. So whenever I don't feel good, I like to go fishing. It's quiet and relaxing and . . . Anyway, I stand up for something in the boat, and I notice my legs hurt. I mean they *hurt*, like I had the flu or something. I tried stretching it out, because that's what it felt like I should do—stretch." He makes a show of bending slightly to stretch his legs. "Then I remember that's what Dad said it feels like when he's been out of the water too long. So I jump in the creek. As soon as I do, my legs start to twist and bend, and it feels hot, like my bones are melting together, but it doesn't hurt. Not much, anyways. It feels good, actually, in a painful sort of way." Reed looks at me incredulously, as if it's happening all over again. I can tell by his face that the experience would have unleashed Scared Senseless Emma. "So my skin gets real thin and stretchy, and it covers over my legs—which, by the way, twisted around themselves twice. But I don't shape a fin. Not a normal one, anyway. It's sickly looking. Like the whole length of it looks like the skin of a chicken after it's been plucked. Not smooth and badass, like Dad's. You can still see the knobs of my knees. I looked like a freak."

"Are you sure it was all that bad?"

He nods enthusiastically. "Absolutely. It was grotesque, Emma. I've never tried to do it again."

"Have you ever felt the need to stretch it out like that since?"

"One other time, a few months later. Never again though."

I wrap my arms around myself. "So . . . So our skin stretches like that?"

Reed grimaces. "According to Doc Schroeder, the skin cells of a full-blood Syrena are thick and stretchy. That's part of why things don't penetrate their skin as well. It kind of repels it, because of the flexibility. Half-Breeds inherit half the thickness, half the stretchiness, or whatever. That's why it pulled so thin over my legs and made me look like an anorexic chicken shark. I'm serious, Emma. You look like you're naked. And dying of something."

I can't help but laugh. He just looks so traumatized, rehashing how he came to sprout a bony, icky fin.

I'm pretty sure Dr. Milligan would be interested in this development. Maybe he and Doc Schroeder could get together over tea or crumpets or whatever doctors get together over. I'm sure they'd love to compare notes. But...I'm not sure Neptune would be willing to accept Dr. Milligan just yet. They do have their stranger filter on full effect.

I can tell Reed needs some comfort or a distraction or something to help bring him back. "You expected a kiss in exchange for a story about the diseased fin of a chicken?" This does the trick. Unfortunately. Stupid, stupid, stupid.

Without warning, he leans close to me, excessively close, so that barely any water can pass between our mouths. And my guilt about being "aware" of him knows no bounds.

He uses his thumb to trace the outline of my cheek. My instinct is to move back, but I get the feeling that he'll just ease closer. "Do I get one? Because if you've chosen me, Emma, tell me right now."

I close my mouth abruptly.

With that he withdraws, gently taking my wrist and pulling me back in the direction of the Huddle. Which is good, because Toby has come back for us.

"What is taking you two so long? Everyone is waiting." The twang in Toby's voice has devolved into a full country accent. "And anyways, I already told the sheriff about Galen, Emma. They're getting together a search thingy right now."

As if he spoke the sheriff into existence, a party of Syrena and Half-Breed—and one human with scuba gear—appear from around the next bend of tunnel. The Syrena at the head swims directly up to Reed. "Your father's waiting for you, son." Then he turns to Emma, and his face softens. "You must be Emma. I'm ashamed we haven't met yet." He extends his hand to me and I take it. "My name is Waden Grigsby. I'm the sheriff of Neptune and this lot behind me is my deputies. Except for the guy in the gear. He's lost."

My mouth pops open and Waden chuckles. "Just kidding. That's Darrel. He's with us." Then his face melts into all seriousness again. "Toby told us you're concerned that your friend— Grady is it?—is missing. Any idea where he would have gone?"

"His name is Galen," I say with more irritation than I should. He's leaving a party full of good company to help me, after all. "And he *is* missing. He wouldn't just leave me here alone like this." Right? *Right?*

"Were you two fighting?"

My lips pinch together as I try to stave off a full-blown scowl. "Why does everyone keep asking me that?"

Sheriff Grigsby gives an apologetic nod. "The thing is, if he left after a fight, then maybe he did intend to stay gone. Not that I know your friend or anything," he says quickly. "It's just that sometimes people need their space to cool off, so to speak.

Now if he ran to the store for some milk and never came back, that's quite a different scenario. You can see why I would need to ask then, right?"

Ugh. I do see, but Galen is too responsible—and thought-ful—to pull something like this. And helping a complete stranger understand that is like trying to seize a crab with your armpit. Not happening.

When I have no answer, the sheriff continues soothingly. "Now don't you worry, Emma. Go to the Huddle, enjoy your-self, and I bet by morning we'll have found your friend. In the meantime though, young lady, you should know that you're not as 'alone' as you think. You belong here." Then he asks me all sorts of questions about Galen's vehicle, which way we came from, if I thought he would take the same path home. And with that, Waden and his 'lot,' including Scuba Darrell, squeeze past us one by one. I watch until they disappear from sight, until I can't sense them anymore. I have no confidence in them at all.

Because maybe I'm wrong. Maybe Galen did leave me be-hind. Maybe I misjudged him like I have so many times before. It's not as if he doesn't have the whole freaking planet on his mind right now. What with our fight, his grieving over Rachel, his irritation at finding a certain illegal town called Neptune. Why *wouldn't* he need some time to step away and deal?

And what will he do if they find him? Be mad at me for sending them? Leave again? Maybe I should have left things alone.

"They'll find him," Reed says softly. And all of a sudden, that's what I'm afraid of.

22

THE ROOM is a whirpool of blur. Occasionally Galen will catch glimpses of Tyrden's back at the open door, of the men he's talking to. Is Reder there? He's not sure.

He only hears a few of the booted steps it takes for the group of strangers to approach the bed. The newcomers make no sense when they speak, are only capable of babbling. Sometimes they utter a coherent word. Those times the word is "search" or "Huddle" or "missing." Then there is "out of sight." The word "stubborn"—that's from Tyrden's mouth.

Emma's face flashes across Galen's mind, but he can't keep it there, can't make it stick. *Who are they talking about? Is Emma missing? Something isn't right, but it won't present itself. I have to find Emma. I have to protect her from these strangers.*

Then the strangers disappear. Suddenly, he's in the water.

He can escape. But every time he tries to swim deeper and deeper to safety, something grabs his fin and pulls him back to the surface, something stronger than he is. When he looks back, he stops fighting.

Rachel. He's pulled her too far in, she can't breathe, she can't breathe, why isn't she breathing? Her foot is no longer bound by the air cast. "Swim," he tells her frantically. "Swim!"

Now she's tied to a cement block, sinking sinking sinking. He reaches for the knife he knows is in her boot. He just needs to cut her ropes, and she'll be free. Like last time.

But there is no boot. Only feet. Bare, manicured feet. Bubbles escape her mouth in a desperate cry. The ropes have somehow weaved themselves into chains, handcuffs and chains. The cement block is there though. It's there and it keeps pulling her down down down into a box. No, a building. It pulls her into a building and there is nothing he can do. The roof swallows her up and she cries out and he's got her but he can't lift her. She's too heavy. The blocks are too heavy.

"Help me!" he screams around him. "Rayna! Toraf! Emma!"

Rachel is dying.

Rachel is dying.

Rachel is dying.

"Let me go, Galen," she whispers, but he can't let go.

"Galen, let me go," she says again. Her face is so peaceful. Decorated with her usual smile.

Rachel, please. Please don't die.

Rachel, no.

Rachel is dead.

Again.

23

WE FIND our way to a pool ladder attached to the rock. As I wait my turn, I take in our surroundings. On either side of us are huge red curtains, not the velvety kind you see at a theater, but a kind of thick tarp stretched across the walls, tethered top and bottom to the cave. I don't know if they're hiding something behind them, or if they're making a halfhearted attempt at decoration down here under the water.

Finally it's our turn to go up, and I watch as Reed's swimming trunks disappear to the surface. Beams of strong lights strike through the water, dancing around without much purpose, and it reminds me of the big lights at Hollywood. I wonder what kind of production I'm in store for as I follow Reed up the ladder, slipping a few times on algae congregated on some of the steps.

When I reach the top, and before I gather my bearings, a

cheer resounds through the cave. What exactly they're cheering about I'm not sure, since I've already met half of them or more. Maybe it's some sort of initiation to be taken here for a Huddle—wait for the stranger to come up the ladder, then scare the snot out of her when she surfaces. Yay for strangers. If it is some sort of Neptune tradition, Reed really should have told me. I would have at least braided my hair. Or something. Not to mention, being cheered while wearing a bathing suit reminds me of a nightmare I have sometimes about being naked in the middle of the school hallway. I do adore wearing clothes when I'm the center of attention.

And now I know where the word "cavernous" comes from. This inner chamber is as big as a ballroom. Smiling faces part for us as we make our way through the crowd. I don't like that Reed is holding my hand, don't like how it looks, but I decide not to struggle at this moment. Not when I've just been cheered.

Dozens and dozens of industrial-grade flashlights sit along the walls, sending columns of light to the uneven crevices of the ceiling. Lime formations cascade down the walls like huge curtains, only more beautiful than the plain red tarps below. A path has been roughly hewn that leads to the middle of the ginormous ballroom. In this new "room" are intricately carved wooden benches scattered around in a pattern that reminds me of the pews of a cathedral. The way they form a circle around the middle of the cave reminds me of the amphitheater at a summer camp Chloe and I once attended.

What draws my attention the most are the paintings on the walls between the intermittent deluges of limestone. Galen said that in the Cave of Memories back home, they keep paintings and murals and sculptures from the past. I wonder if this is Neptune's version of the Cave of Memories. The depictions seem to tell a story, possibly the one I'm about to hear.

To my left is a painting with a giant Syrena on it, wielding a humongloid trident in his hand. From the colossal waves in front of him and the mark of a trident on his stomach, my bet is that this is the General Triton sending destruction to Tartessos.

On my right is what looks like what all the history books depict as the first Thanksgiving. People—that is, a mix of humans, Syrena, and Half-Breeds—dressed in Pilgrim-like clothing are sharing a meal at a long picnic table outside. Children run around, chasing a happy-looking dog. The background of the painting shows wooden houses and buildings being constructed, and beyond that, the vast forest. I imagine this as the beginning of Neptune.

The middle wall illustrates a town of ancient times. Stone buildings, windows without glass, cobblestone pathways. The people—again, a mix of breeds—fill the small square in the center and children play in a fountain that has a Syrena statue on it. It's obvious that this is a marketplace of some sort; people can be seen trading things like necklaces and bracelets for things like loaves of bread and pigeons in small carrying cages. It's a peaceful scene—all the faces are painted with contented smiles.

I'm drawn back to the present when Reed puts a hand on my shoulder. I smile robotically, just in case I missed an introduction or something, but there is no one new nearby. It must be cool in here; everyone's breath ghosts in front of their face as they greet us. He leads me to the center of the circle of benches. I notice that everyone is quickly taking their seats.

I don't want to be in the center. It reminds me of the last time I was in the center of a crowd—the tribunal held to investigate all the Royals for fraud. Not a happy time.

Reder steps up to us. "Reed, what took you so long? We've been waiting. How did Toby get so far ahead of you two?" Reder smiles at me. I'd forgotten how friendly he is. "Toby told me about Galen," he says. "We'll do everything we can to help. If he wants to be found, we'll find him."

Why does everyone keep saying that?

"Thank you," I choke out, prying my hand from Reed's. Reder pretends not to notice the violence with which I do this. "Reed said we could form a private search party tomorrow. To aid the sheriff."

Reder's eyes dart to his son, then he purses his lips. "Absolutely. I'll make an announcement after the Retelling tonight."

"Retelling?" I ask.

Reder throws his head back and laughs as if I've told a joke. It catches the attention of several people already seated around us. Well, several more people who may or may not have already been paying attention to us. "I keep forgetting you're not from around here, Emma," he says. "That you're new to all of this. But, of course, you are. That's why we're holding a Huddle in the first place. And maybe after tonight, you won't feel so new." He nods to a front-row bench behind him. "I saved you the best seat in the house."

Reed says nothing, just drags me away by my wrist this time—which I guess is easier to keep hold of—hauling me toward the bench left open for us. "How did you guys build all of this?" I whisper as we sit. My attention is again drawn to the painted cave wall directly in front of us, where Triton sends the waves to shore. The small symbol on his stomach stands out to me. And of course, it reminds me of Galen. "Is that how you knew Galen was a Triton Royal?"

Reed shrugs. "Everyone knows about the mark. Our Archives keep their memories just as well as yours do. They wouldn't forget the mark of a Triton Royal. In fact, it was an Archive who painted that. Archives painted everything in here, since we don't have access to the Cave of Memories. Everything here has a special meaning."

Even this mini Cave of Memories is too much for me to take in all at once. I hope Reed and I can come back and explore this place. It would take a full day to get through the paintings alone.

He grins. "Impressed? You'll be more impressed to know we did this all the old-fashioned way."

I shake my head. He rolls his eyes. I contemplate pinching the "fool" out of him as they say in these parts. "These benches we're sitting on?" he says. "They're over a hundred years old. See that guy over there? He helped build this place. And that lady? The one talking to Dad? She's the one who found it when she was just a fingerling. Lucia is her name. She got lost in here, and when they found her, they found all this." He makes a sweeping motion toward the ceiling of the cave.

I allow myself to be impressed. Lucia must be pretty freaking ancient for a full-blooded Syrena to be sporting a head of white hair, wrinkles in abundance, and bony angles poking from her modest bathing suit. . . . She has to be older than the average geriatric Syrena—which puts her at more than three hundred years old.

Or maybe not. Mom and Galen both confirmed that Syrena age faster on land, but I'm not sure how much faster gravity speeds up the process. Doesn't look like gravity was all that kind to Lucia. . . .

Wait. *Syrena age faster on land.* Does that mean *I* would live longer if I stayed in the ocean? Is that what Galen was talking about?

He wants me to live in the ocean so he can have me longer? Probably I should have let him actually talk it out with me, instead of cutting him with all my sharp, negative words. Or am I connecting dots that aren't there? Am I reading between lines that haven't been written?

All I know is, my stomach is seriously considering vomiting, and for lack of a better place, Reed's lap seems to be the best target. If I aim in front of me, it might get on Reder. Besides, I've never seen Reed feel out of place. I'm betting a lap of upchuck will do the trick. It'll be fun.

Yep, my stomach just flopped over. I'm upchucking in three . . . two . . . one . . .

"Thank you all for coming tonight," Reder's voice booms.

Even my stomach is unwilling to trample on Reder's hospitality. It settles down all at once, as if chastising me for letting it act up in the first place. Still, a small corner of it aches, and I don't think that ache will go away until I see Galen again.

Until I confirm whether I'm a heartless butthole or seriously overthinking every little thing that Galen said. Either way, it's going to suck for me. Either way, I lose.

If I'm heartless, I've lost Galen for sure. If I'm overthinking things, and everything he said can be taken at face value . . . I've lost Galen.

So if I've lost him, why am I sending people out to find him?

Some questions can't be answered, some shouldn't, and some weren't questions to begin with. I can't decide which category this falls into.

But for now: life.

And I've entirely missed Reder's introduction to the Retelling and the fact that all the lights have been dimmed and adjusted to focus on him, and that the audience has grown maddeningly quiet while the voices in my head shout at each other.

"So Poseidon came ashore and made peace with mankind," Reder is saying. "Not just peace, though. He made friendships. Established a successful city where humans and Syrena could interact and live in harmony. Where they could form close bonds."

Reder chuckles. "And even Poseidon appreciated the curves of the land-dwelling women, did he not, friends?" This evokes a knowing laugh from the crowd. "So he took a human mate himself and had many children with her, Half-Breed sons and daughters who adored their father. Other Syrena were content to do the same, and so they, too, made sons and daughters with humans."

Then he focuses his attention directly on me, and I'm so grateful the lights don't follow his gaze. When you're sitting next to the speaker's son and the speaker's talking about taking a mate . . . *that's when you become hyperaware that maybe you've been giving the wrong impression—you stupid freaking idiot.*

Or you're just being pyscho again. Awesome.

"They continued on for almost a century, living prosperously. Poseidon used his Gift to feed his city; the words 'I'm hungry' could never be heard. What was left of the food they harvested from the oceans was traded to surrounding cities. In fact, the port of Tartessos became the epicenter for trading: It attracted merchants from around the world, eager to trade for its tin, bronze, and gold. Even human kings sent gifts to keep our great General Poseidon pleased."

"And that is when General Triton became jealous of his brother's prosperity. In a fit, he poisoned the minds of our Syrena brethren against humans, and he divided the kingdoms into two territories. Those who believed his lies about the humans moved to Triton territory; those who saw the good in humans, the potential of forming alliances with them, moved to Poseidon territory. After the Great Sunder, Triton still was not happy." At this Reder shakes his head. A disapproving moan moves through the audience. I glance at Reed beside me, but he doesn't notice. He sits expressionlessly, engrossed in the tale, though he's doubtless heard it many times. So far, the rendition of what Galen told me is fair, except of course in the Retelling, a more negative light is cast on Triton instead of Poseidon. And this is the first time I've heard mention of a Great Sunder. I look past that though, and try to be objective about what really did happen all those years ago.

"Afraid that his brother would gain too much power by forging such strong alliances with the humans," Reder continues, "the inconsolable general set out to ruin Tartessos. He sent forth messengers to the human rulers in the areas surrounding the cities, telling of horrifying things such as enslavement of humans and the unnatural breeding of them. He even sent word that Poseidon had taken another human ruler's wife as his own and that their own queens were not safe from him if he gained more power." A wave of agitation roars behind me. Some shout things like, "Triton is a liar!" and "He's no general of ours!"

After a few seconds, Reder holds up his hands. The Huddle sends a percussive *shhhh* resounding through the meeting cave. In Galen's version, Poseidon actually did take a human's wife as his own, though now I'm not sure how he could have accomplished that. I'm finding it difficult to glean the actual truth from the two stories.

When the crowd is sufficiently hushed, Reder begins again. "When Poseidon learned of the armies marching against him on land, he appealed to his good friend and well-respected Archive, Neptune, for assistance. Neptune called an emergency council with the other Archives. It was then that Triton made his final move to destroy all Poseidon had worked for. He told the Archive council that he would be willing to use his Gift to save his brother, as long as Poseidon admitted to making a mistake in forging bonds with the humans, and that they could not be trusted. He insisted that Poseidon abandon his city, everything he created there, to live as a Syrena from then on. In exchange for his help against the humans, Triton also demanded that all Syrena stay in the ocean henceforth. Having no other options presented—they couldn't outnumber the humans after all—the Archive council agreed. Neptune was devastated, of course, to deliver the news to Poseidon. Faced with the decision of the council, the king was outraged, to say the least, but was terrified for his mate and his Half-Breed children who could not return to the ocean with him. That is when Neptune, the Great Archive, became our founding father. He told General Poseidon that he would secretly remain behind on land, never to return to the Syrena realm, and care for Poseidon's family—and any who wished to abandon the way of life of the ocean dweller. Many did, as we well know. Those who chose to stay on land were believed to have died by the humans' swords. And hence began the secret."

"Neptune kept his self-sacrificing promise, friends, helping all who wished to stay ashore escape before the human armies arrived to meet their deaths by the great waves of Triton. He took the refugees farther inland, forbidding them to step foot in the oceans again, because they might be sensed by Trackers. After a time, they realized they could utilize the rivers and other freshwater sources without being detected, and so they did. Our brave descendants not only adapted to a new way of life on land, they embraced it, friends. They became as humans, so as not to be discovered by either species. At first, they were a lost, wandering people, but Neptune led them to a place of their own, a land of their own. They lived there in the fertile valley, unbothered for centuries until the Great Wars began—the humans call it the Spanish Reconquista. Caught in the crosshairs of human disagreement, our brethren were forced to find a more neutral place to etch out their lives. Though long dead, they knew Neptune would want them to seek safety elsewhere. When they heard of Columbus's expeditions to the New Land, a large part of them made preparations to sail to it. When they arrived, they did as the human pioneers and forged their way to lands of their own, farther and farther inland. And when they happened upon this small vale nestled between the protection of the mountains and surrounded by freshwater springs and caves, they knew they'd found home."

I become aware of sniffling behind me, and I can understand why. Reder really is a great storyteller, putting emotion and meaning into each syllable—and who doesn't like happy endings? A great exodus and a homecoming. If it weren't for the Galen-ache in my stomach, I'd be afloat with all the feel-good emotions like the rest of the gathering.

I wonder what Galen would think of this rendition. He probably would not approve, but who is he to say which story is the truth? From his perspective, Triton's motive was not envy: He sought to protect the Syrena realm by limiting communication with humans. He disagreed with Poseidon's lenient view of dealings with them and believed humans would one day turn on his brother. Also, in Galen's version, Poseidon appealed to Triton for help against the human armies; Reder's portrayal makes that sound very unlikely.

Still, both stories sound plausible. But there is more detail in this one. More explanation. And given the recent events in the underwater realms, I'm a tad inclined to believe there was dissention before. But what Reder says next is un-freaking-believable.

"Our society is a great secret, friends, kept from generation to generation of Poseidon kings. We have proof of this tonight, with our dear visitor Emma sent here from King Antonis himself. And with her help, we'll unite the territories once more. She is a sign, friends, a Half-Breed accepted among our ocean-dwelling brethren. A living symbol that we are on the horizon of great change."

Ohmysweetgoodness.

Reder takes the seat across from me at his kitchen table, easing into the chair like it might break. It reminds me of when, in the movies, psychiatrists approach a mental patient with slow, deliberate movements so as not to freak him or her out. They use a monotone voice and neutral words, like "okay" and "fine" and "comfortable."

This might be why Reder sent Reed and Toby out for ice cream—to remove everyone from this conversation except for him and me. The two variables that matter most. To make it seem like even though this is his kitchen, it's neutral territory and I should be comfortable here.

Or maybe I really enjoy overthinking things.

My hands encircle a mug of hot chocolate—also a typical scene in the movies when trying to reassure a traumatized person—and I watch as the liquid heat melts the marshmallows into tiny puddles of goo on the surface. I realize then that my attentiveness to my mug and the lack of eye contact I've offered Reder in general could be discerned as weakness.

And now is not the time for weakness. "I am not a symbol for Neptune." There. Conversation started.

Reder seems relieved that I've chosen to dive right into the subject. "You could be," he says, wasting no effort on tact. "If you choose to be."

"I'm here because my grandfather sent me. It's not some fulfilled prophecy or anything like that."

Reder smiles. "Prophecy? Of course not. But why do you think Antonis sent you here?"

The truth is, I still don't know. I'm sure he wanted me to see that there are other Half-Breeds out there, that I'm not the outcast that I think I am. But what I'm supposed to do with that information, I have no clue.

When I don't offer an immediate answer, Reder leans back in his chair. "I met your grandfather when he visited all those years ago. He was, of course, primarily concerned with finding your mother. He thought she may have heard of Neptune, may have sought it out."

"My grandfather said he stumbled across Neptune when he was looking for her." He never mentioned that he knew about it all along. But that is what the Retelling claims. That all Poseidon kings, generation after generation, have known all about the existence of Half-Breeds. I suddenly feel betrayed. He could have just told me that to begin with. Then again, he probably worried that I would share the info with Galen—and I probably would have.

"Your grandfather has always been a supporter of peace between the ocean dwellers and the citizens of Neptune. But like us, he didn't know how to go about pursuing it. Until now. Until you. I believe that's why he sent you here."

"Be more specific."

"You've already said the Archive council accepted your existence. That they even approved your mating with Galen, a Triton prince. Do you realize the significance in that?"

Maybe I look at the world with a smaller lens than Reder does. "I see why you would see it as significant. But I was the exception."

Reder nods. "Yes, you were. Think of all the lessons history has to teach us, Emma. Exceptions have always opened the door to bigger change. Your grandfather knows that."

"I think you're overestimating my influence in the kingdoms." By a long shot. When they made the exception for me, the lone Half-Breed, it was that I could *live*. It didn't mean I was granted voting powers or anything. "Besides, why would you—why would *Neptune*—want to unite with them anyway?"

Reder's eyes light up. "Think of what Neptune can offer the ocean dwellers. We can provide eyes and ears on land."

"Galen already does that. He's ambassador to the humans."

"Galen is one person. Don't get me wrong, I'm sure Galen has done an outstanding job in that respect. He seems very loyal to the kingdoms. But think of how much more effective an entire town of ambassadors could be. Plus, many of us have the Gift of Poseidon. We could ensure that all Syrena are fed for centuries to come."

I'm about to bring up the fact that I would never let the kingdoms starve—I have the Gift, too, after all—but I know he'll use the "how much more so" comparison again. And I can't bring myself to argue that point. It makes too much sense. "But what does *Neptune* have to gain?"

Reder considers, tilting his head. "When did your father die, Emma?"

This is unexpected, and I almost sputter into my hot chocolate. "Three years ago. What does that have to do with anything?"

"Was your father rich?"

I shrug. He was a doctor, so we weren't poor by any means. But we didn't have a maid and a butler, either. "No."

"Say he was. Say he was abundantly wealthy. And say, he left most of his wealth to you. How would you feel?"

Still not getting where this is going. "Grateful?" is what I hope he's looking for.

"Of course you would. But—what if your attorneys found a glitch in your father's will, a technicality that, by law, kept you from enjoying your inheritance? What if other people named in the will could enjoy what they inherited, but not you? Because of that one little legal stipulation, you were kept from what you were meant to have. Then how would you feel?"

Ahhhh. Reder views the ocean as the legacy of all Syrena. Except there is that one glitch, as Reder said, that one tiny law separating Half-Breeds from their birthright. And in his eyes, I've overcome that glitch. "I still don't understand how I can help." That one tiny law, after all, is centuries old and deeply entrenched in the minds of the kingdoms.

"I'm not asking you to shoulder the burden of the world, Emma. I'm just asking you to try to open up communications between Neptune and the underwater realm. Starting with your grandfather."

Deep down, I know what my answer is. Because deep down I want it, too.

24

"LET ME go, Galen," are the words he wakes up to. At first, they echo around him in Rachel's voice. Then gradually they manifest themselves into Emma's. *Why would Emma be telling me to let her go?*

His mind floods with images of their last words together, their heated exchange. *Surely she's not giving up on us?*

It takes several moments for his brain to register that it was all just a dream, then several more for his eyes to open, to focus on reality. When they do, he's startled to find Tyrden sitting in front of him. His expression is grim. In his hand he turns his knife over and over. *What now?* "It's time for you to make the phone call. You can thank Reder for that." He pulls out Galen's cell phone and starts scrolling through the numbers.

Think. His consciousness fights for orientation, for a grasp on what might have happened while he was out. *Why can I thank*

Reder? Inevitably, he wonders if Emma is okay. But his brain stops at the possibility that she might not be.

He wiggles his wrists and tests the ropes on his ankles. Somehow they feel even tighter than before. Then he remembers that Tyrden noticed his efforts to loosen the knots. *Was that before or after he drugged me?* Galen can't remember.

All he knows is that he has to get away. Life or death. If Tyrden dials Grom, Galen has to warn him of danger. He can't let his brother walk into the trap that is Neptune. He squirms in his seat, not caring if Tyrden notices or not. The ropes hold him in place, offering no comfort for what's coming.

It's not ideal circumstances for his escape, not by any means. The ropes are inflexible, no matter how hard he strains against them. Tyrden is armed and hostile, getting angrier by the second as Galen struggles to free himself. But it's his last chance. His only chance. He feels it in every cell of his body. There is a crisp look of irrationality in Tyrden's eyes, of instability.

This is going to hurt.

Tyrden holds up the phone. Grom's name and number light up in front of him. One touch to the screen is all that stands between Galen and Grom.

"Listen to me very carefully, Galen." Tyrden's voice is calm. Controlled. "Before we call Big Brother, I want to rehearse what you're going to say."

Galen licks his lips, then makes a show of eyeing the blade in Tyrden's hand. He needs the element of surprise. *Tyrden needs to believe I'm afraid, that I'm cooperating.*

And I have to get closer to him.

A brief look of relief flashes across Tyrden's face. "Good." He clutches the phone against his chest, tapping his index finger against the back of it. His eyes go blank for a few seconds. "You're going to warn your brother of an attack."

Galen blinks. "What?"

Tyrden nods hurriedly. "Yes, yes. That's what you'll say. That you and Emma are being held hostage in Neptune."

"Emma? Where is Emma?" His gut flips over in his belly. All this time, he'd assumed she was safe, what with the barrage of pictures of her and Reed that Tyrden insists on showing him. But something has definitely changed. Something that Reder has done.

"Shut up, boy!" Tyrden springs from the chair, sending it sprawling toward the wall behind him. "I'm talking." He scratches the back of his neck. "You'll tell Grom that you are hostages. That Reder is holding you. Yes, tell Grom that when he comes, he'll need to bring plenty of reinforcements. That the best strategy is an offensive attack on Neptune. To take out Reder first."

What? Now Galen is conflicted. This is exactly what he was going to tell his brother, provided he had time to fit it all in—and with the exception of eliminating Reder before hearing his side of the story. *Now Tyrden wants me to warn Grom of danger?* Something is off.

Galen works quickly to process this new information. In his grueling experience of Tyrden, he's learned that the old Syrena doesn't have a charitable bone in his body. What's more, he's displayed a vendetta against Reder the whole time. *Is Reder really holding me here? Or is Tyrden?*

Whatever Reder has supposedly done, it has foiled Tyrden's plans—which Galen hasn't quite figured out yet either. "Why do you want to help Grom?" Galen blurts.

Tyrden stops pacing and gives him a severe look. "We're friends now, remember, Highness? We're on the same side, you and I."

Galen nods slowly. Tyrden really has lost his mind—or what was left of it. Somehow he has to earn Tyrden's trust. Somehow he's got to close the physical distance between himself and his captor. *Not yet*, he tells himself. *Be patient.* "I couldn't help but notice that I'm still tied up. That's not very friendly, if you ask me."

Tyrden shakes his head slowly. "You think you're so clever," he growls.

"I'm clever for wanting to be untied?"

Tyrden considers this. The fact that he considers this alerts Galen to the possibility that Tyrden is not paying as much attention as he should. "I'll untie you as soon as you call your brother."

"What if he doesn't come?" Galen tries to sound concerned. This is what Rachel used to call buying time.

"It's your job to convince him."

Galen shakes his head. "But what if Emma and I are not important enough to him to risk coming to land? Or what if he wants peace?" He nearly rolls his eyes at that unlikely scenario. Grom will come, and he'll bring an army with him, just as Tyrden wants.

Tyrden's face darkens. There are shadowy circles under his eyes that Galen hadn't noticed before. His mouth tugs down in a scowl, the lines of which cut deep into his features. It would appear something has been bothering his captor. "If you and the girl are not important enough to Grom, then you're not important enough to me. I hope we understand each other."

He said "me" not "Reder." Reluctantly, Galen nods. "I'll need one of my hands untied. It will sound more natural to Grom if I'm holding the phone." He glances meaningfully at Tyrden's own hands, which are now shaking uncontrollably. "Do you need help dialing?" Galen offers.

"Why do you want to help me now, Triton prince? What game are you playing at?"

Galen keeps his expression solemn. "Emma is my life, Tyrden. I can't let you hurt her. If calling Grom is the only way to prevent that, so be it." The sincerity in Galen's voice is bittersweet and genuine. Emma is his life. But he's not going to call Grom.

Satisfied, Tyrden stalks toward him, and with one stout tug on the rope, Galen's left hand falls free. Tyrden offers the phone in his outstretched hand. *Now is the time.* Galen fights the hesitation, fights the self-preservation screaming at him not to do this. Everything is at stake, he tells himself. *This could break your fin,* his subconscious screams back.

But he does it anyway.

His transformation to Syrena form knocks Tyrden off his feet.

25

I WATCH as Reed impales the egg yolks on his plate, then whisks them into the grits with his fork. All the while, he holds his coffee cup level, ready to sip at all times. A true breakfast artist.

"We don't have time to eat." I move the scrambled eggs around on my plate.

The sheriff and his posse didn't turn up anything last night with their search. Which means today—and every day until I find him—will be devoted to searching for Galen. No more playtime in Neptune.

Especially now that Reder thinks I'm the Chosen One or whatever. But I don't mention that to Reed. It's not that I don't want to help, that I don't want Neptune and the underwater kingdoms to come to peaceful terms and coexist. It's just that I don't have any pull whatsoever in the territories. The confidence

I felt in myself and in Reder's cause has definitely faded since last night when we discussed everything over a comforting mug of hot chocolate. I mean, as far as usefulness goes, I'm as effective as cutting a rib eye with a plastic spork. What business do I have promising to help with this mess? I don't even know where to begin.

Maybe I just need more time to think about it. To contemplate what I'll possibly say to my mother when I call her and tell her what I've really been doing. And that I've misplaced Galen in the process.

Galen.

Galen will know what to do about this. He might still be angry with me, but this involves the kingdoms. He'll put off his grudge and handle this with Grom. Undo the damage I've done under pressure. Oh, the damage. With all eyes on me, I'd agreed to help Neptune negotiate peaceful terms with the underwater kingdoms by saying nothing at the Huddle. Then again in private, with Reder, I verbally agreed to help. I put it in actual words. I promised.

But Reder put me on the spot. What was I supposed to do? Laugh in his face in front of the entire Huddle? Uh, no. Besides, he's so irritatingly *reasonable.*

"We're wise to eat breakfast," Reed says, shoveling his concoction into his mouth, all but oblivious to my internal plight. "Number one, we're going to need our energy if we're trekking around the woods all day. And two, it's still too dark out. We've got another half hour before the woods will be light enough to see."

All good points. Still, I'm freaking out here. I need Galen back now more than ever. I'm about to tell Reed to hurry up, when Mr. Kennedy turns around in the booth behind Reed. "I couldn't help but overhear that you're heading out in the woods today, Reed," he says, dabbing at the corner of his mouth with a napkin.

Reed does a half turn in his seat. A few degrees less and the angle would have been rude. "That's right, Mr. Kennedy." What Reed doesn't say is, *What of it?* But it's all over his face. I fidget with my fork. I see that Reed's patience has an expiration date. I suppose he could be irritated with the fact that we might actually find Galen today and that these could be the last few moments he has me to himself.

"Well," Mr. Kennedy says, obviously put out by Reed's small but distinct attitude. "I feel obligated to share with you that I saw the most enormous bear—a black bear I think—but as you know, animals are not my expertise. I was washing up on the north bank of the river, and he was pawing the rocks on the south bank right before the beaver dam. And thank the stars for that! I may not look like much, but back in my day, I was on the varsity track team. I might have had a sporting chance then, but now . . ." He shudders. When Reed seems unimpressed, Mr. Kennedy continues. I lean in, trying to act intensely interested to make up for Reed's lack of enthusiasm. "Of course, you were born and raised here. I suppose you would know if black bears pose a danger, but I thought it would be best to share instead of let you both go blindly without knowing."

Reed grins. "Letting us go blindly without knowing that

there are black bears in the woods of Tennessee?" I kick Reed under the table. He ignores me.

Mr. Kennedy purses his lips. "Right. Well. Of course, there are black bears. It's just . . . Well, this one seemed rather large." The embarrassed scientist turns sharply in his seat and resumes whatever it is that he'd neglected on our behalf. Half a second later, he's standing, his check in his hand. I wait for the cashier at the front to check him out before I turn my ire on Reed.

"He was just trying to help," I hiss at Reed, who's smothering a biscuit with white-peppered gravy. "And if the bear's that big, it wouldn't hurt anything to avoid the area where he saw it."

He shrugs. "There are bears all over the place," he says, voice low. "And I have a feeling Mr. Kennedy doesn't know what constitutes 'big.' But if it'll make you feel better, we'll stay away from the south side. It will just cut down on our search area."

Which isn't what I want either.

"I'm just saying the search will be complicated enough without running into—"

"Emma, calm down. It's fine. We won't go south." He gulps the last of his coffee. "Are you so antsy because of what you and Dad talked about last night?"

"You think?"

Reed smiles. "Look, he wasn't asking you to stop the sun from rising. He was just hoping that since you were accepted among the ocean dwellers, maybe you could open the door to all of us being accepted. One day. Not like, tomorrow, or like next Tuesday or anything."

My mouth drops open. "You knew he was going to do that

last night. Make it about me helping everyone. How long have you known?"

Reed grimaces with appropriate guilt. "Since the night you and Galen had dinner with us. My parents were so excited after you left."

"That could be because they were happy to get Galen out of their house."

"That, too," Reed admits. "He's a horrible liar, by the way. They knew right away he was a Triton Royal. And if a Triton Royal is hanging out *on land* with a Half-Breed, something had to have changed. Emma, *you* changed them somehow."

I shake my head. "You're giving me too much credit. The Archives . . . They needed me, is all. It was all about the timing and circumstances, I guess." Really, they needed Galen and Rayna's Gift to help rescue some captured Syrena from humans— and my acceptance among them came as a package deal they couldn't refuse. Oh, the Archives didn't *need* me by any means.

But I'm not about to tell that to Reed. First of all, I feel a bit waylaid that he kept this big Emma's-Our-Savior thing from me. His eyes look like big balloons filled tight with hope right now. And don't I know what it feels like to cling to something as fickle as hope?

Reed crunches his napkin in his fist, then dumps it on the empty plate in front of him. "Then explain why your grandfather sent you here."

Why does this question keep surprising me? I should really find a default answer to it. "So that I could find a place to fit in," I blurt. "So I know I'm not alone."

Reed makes a show of looking around. "Maybe he sent you here to find me. Is that what you're saying?"

"Yes. No. Not exactly." I swirl the orange juice in my glass until it makes a miniature whirlpool. "Not you, as a person. But I think he wanted to give me another option."

"Option? Instead of Galen, you mean?"

Okay, this is sounding really bad. What's worse, Galen might have thought the same thing when we arrived in Neptune. That could be one reason he was instantly on guard. "I mean an optional way of life. Instead of being an outcast in the Syrena world and a weirdo in the human world."

Reed isn't convinced. "I don't think so. Oh, don't get me wrong. I'm sure that was definitely part of sending you here. But Antonis met my dad all those years ago when he came looking for your mother. Dad told you that, right? They were friends. They've kept in touch, in fact. Every couple of years or so. If I had to guess, I'd say this is some small part of their bigger plan to unite all of our kind, not just the ones who shape fins. Have you checked in with your mom since a few days ago, by the way?"

I shrug. I had called, but she hadn't answered, which probably means she's still back in Triton territory. Hopefully, she'll check in soon. Then again, I hope she doesn't. Because Reder will expect me to talk to her about all this. He made that clear. And I don't know how to pitch it to her yet.

Also, I'm going to kill Grandfather.

"You should invite her to come. And your grandfather. I know Dad would love to see him again."

Now I'm the one brimming with hope. "It's just that Mom's mate, Grom, he would never agree to come." Even Galen had said as much before he left.

"Who says he's invited? He's only the Triton king, right?" Reed grins. Then his face gets all serious and coddle-y. "One step at a time, okay? Don't get ahead of yourself."

One step at a time. Why not? That was our plan for me easing into Syrena society after I became Galen's mate. *If I become Galen's mate...* "We should go now. The sun is out."

"Just think about it, Emma. It's not like you have to demand a Tribunal in ten minutes. Just start thinking about ways we can connect with the ocean dwellers. How we can show them that we're not demons or something."

I turn my nose up. "Why should you have to show them anything? What's wrong with what you have here? You're all doing great without them." I sound angrier than I'd intended, which I immediately regret, but it's the truth. To me, Neptune gets the best of both worlds. Why fix something that isn't broken? To me, belittling the potential of Neptune sounds more like cudgeling something pristine and priceless.

Then again, I know what it's like to want something you can't have. And I have to look at it from Neptune's perspective: The oceans are something they view as their rightful inheritance. It's not about what the oceans have that Neptune doesn't. It's about Neptune having a share in what is justly theirs.

The waitress sets our bill in front of Reed. I go to grab it, but his hand is over mine in turbo-point-three seconds. "I've never been in the ocean, Emma," he says without removing his hand from mine. "I want to know what the saltwater feels like. I want to see all the colors of the fish outside an aquarium. I want to be BFFs with a whale named Goliath. Wherever you go, I want to be able to go, too."

"Reed—"

"Look, I'm not saying it's because of you. I've always wanted to see the ocean, see what it has to offer. But now that I know what it has to offer . . ." He squeezes my hand. "I want it so badly I can taste it. Look at what I'm missing out on." His eyes burn into mine, and I can't look away.

"But I'm not from the ocean," I say softly. Too softly.

"But you will be. If you mate with Galen. He'll find some way to steal you away."

The words reverberate through me. I can't let Reed know that Galen already suggested that very thing. He'd use it against me, in favor of himself, in favor of Neptune. *And is that so wrong? Shouldn't I have options?* Obviously Grandfather thought so. What if I'm selling myself short by making a decision so early?

Then I think of Galen, the way his lips feel against mine, the way his smile sends my stomach into a tumult more substantial than the innocent flutter of mere butterflies. The way his body fits around mine like a missing part and the way his laugh swarms through me like an intoxicating drink.

I am not selling myself short with Galen.

But when I said yes to Galen, I said no to all other options. Before I even knew what those options were. I would be a fool not to admit that right now I'm sitting in front of another option. Not just a good-looking guy who just happens to be consuming the space between us with those big violet eyes, that intense gaze.

This option comes with acceptance, others of my kind, a life on land *and* in the water. As far as I can tell, this option comes without baggage. Like, for instance, without wearing an invisible scarlet letter every time I visit the underwater kingdoms with Galen.

But I would be losing Galen.

Reed sighs. I'm obviously not making major life decisions fast enough for him. He pulls out a twenty and leaves it on the table for the bill. "Let's go, beautiful. We've got a lot of ground to cover."

And so we go.

26

THE FORCE of shaping his fin sends Galen flying backward. Beneath him, he hears metal scrape against the floor, the crash twisting his wrist until he cries out. A sharp snap coincides with pain in his fingers.

Tyrden is still sprawled on the floor. When he sees Galen, he gives off a howl of indignation. His eyes hold a certain disbelief as he takes in the sight before him.

Galen doesn't have time to be self-conscious about his big fin. With one eye, he watches Tyrden floundering on his stomach, grasping for his knife. With the other, he frantically tries to untie his right hand. Just as before, the knot doesn't give; he has no idea how Tyrden untied his left hand so quickly. He struggles to bend the rest of the chair, ignoring the pain in his fin where the ropes from his feet had constricted as his fin took shape. He may be limping out of here, at best. With that thought in mind, he punches the metal frame of the chair, willing it to break. With some luck, he might even be able to sever off a piece of chair sharp enough to cut the rope.

Tyrden pulls himself off the floor with a grunt. He approaches cautiously, knife in the ready position. Galen waits until he's within reach, then swipes his fin across the floor. The Syrena expects it this time and jumps, landing steadily on his feet. Beyond enraged, he breaks into a rabid run.

Galen abandons his efforts with the chair and flips over, slicing his fin through the air again, lifting it almost to the ceiling. Tyrden can't outjump this. The powerful stroke sends Tyrden against the wall with a loud crack. He falls to the floor in a thud, his knife several feet away. Taking advantage of Tyrden's disorientation, Galen pulls himself toward it on his elbows, dragging the warped metal chair with him.

Get the knife, get the knife, get the knife.

Tyrden doesn't recover as quickly this time, but the sight of Galen heading toward the blade seems to bring him to his senses. He shakes his head as if relieving it of dust.

Almost there. He grabs at the knife just as Tyrden kicks it across the room. Galen is forced to roll away as Tyrden brings his boot down hard on the floor, just missing Galen's head. Galen grabs the metal chair and uses it as a shield as Tyrden rears back for another kick. The clash reverberates off the walls; Tyrden is jolted backward, giving Galen a slight reprieve from another attack.

He turns his attention toward the knife again, shielding his back with the metal chair, dragging himself across the room as before. Galen debates whether or not to change back into human form, but with the rope injury to his fin he's not sure what his human legs will be capable of. Damage to the fin doesn't necessarily mean damage to his legs—or, at least, not both of them. Still, right now he needs the power and range of motion the Gift of Triton gives him.

Just as Galen reaches the knife again, Tyrden kicks the chair from his back, sending his right arm flying into an angry position. Even so, Galen's left hand closes around the grip of the knife, and he lifts the blade in front of him just as the crazed Syrena is ready to pounce.

Tyrden stops immediately. Galen uses his hesitation to jerk the chair back to him, making quick work of the rope with the knife. While Tyrden is distracted by the blade in his hand, Galen sweeps his fin across the floor. His tail connects painfully with Tyrden's hard boots, lifting the older Syrena off his feet and onto his back. His head slams against the floor in a sickening thump.

Galen lets out a grunt of agony. His tail is definitely twisted or bent or both. For several intense moments, he waits for his captor to get up. With a sense of dread, he watches the steady rise and fall of Tyrden's chest for longer than he should. He can't help but be cautious. This could be another mind game.

Galen makes the snap decision to change to human form. Keeping an eye on Tyrden, he tests his balance on each leg. His left ankle throbs with a deep ache but can still hold his weight. Everything else is in working order.

Picking up what's left of his jeans, Galen takes the longest piece and wraps it around his waist, trying to at least cover up. He uses the pads of his feet to tread quietly toward where Tyrden lies.

Galen squats down slowly, alert for any sudden movements. He places the tip of the blade on Tyrden's chest, where his heart beats the strongest. The Syrena does nothing. Galen rears back and slaps the unconscious Syrena across the face.

Tyrden doesn't wake up.

27

WE CRASH through the woods in a sort of irreverent way. It's as if Reed is taking care to disturb every plant and animal in our wake. Which I suppose is good if we're looking for someone who needs our help.

And bad if we're looking to avoid bears.

"We don't want to sneak up on anybody," he says, as if reading my mind. "Not a bear, not someone who doesn't want to be found." I didn't think of it like that.

By now I'm out of breath and a bit irritated at our speed, which I know is unreasonable because it helps us cover as much ground as possible. "He wants to be found," I blurt.

Without warning, Reed stops and faces me. "I don't buy that. Not if he's in these woods, Emma. If he's here, if he's been this close all along, then he doesn't want to be found." He takes a step closer to me. "And if he doesn't want to be found, then what?" He pulls me to him. "But here *I* am, Emma. Here *I* am not hiding from you, not running away, not pitching fits."

It's then I realize that Reed isn't stomping around for the heck of it, and not even because he doesn't want to surprise a sleeping cheetah or whatever. He's trampling his way through the forest like a human machete because he's mad. Not mad exactly, not with the torment in his eyes.

He's frustrated. And he's taking it out on nature.

But now it looks like he's about to direct it all back to its source. Me. "I would never have left you, Emma. He's a fool to have done it. And selfish. He thinks he's too good for the little ol' town of Neptune. And that means he thinks he's too good for you."

"That's not what he—"

"And how are we supposed to know what he really thinks? Because he isn't here, Emma. I am. I have been all along." He lowers his head. His lips are impossibly close to mine.

Reed smells good. The mix of his usual scent mingles with the smell of the earthy forest and the sweetness of some honey-suckle that he must have brushed through. "I was wrong, Emma. Kissing me doesn't make up your mind. It's not end all, say all. It's not choosing, at least it doesn't have to be. Give me permission, Emma. Let me have a chance."

My hands tighten on his arms and I swallow. Once. Twice. I can't blink. I can only stare into him.

"Give me permission," he whispers. "It's already too late for me anyway."

Did I just nod? Surely not, not enough for a definite yes. But I must have, because he's leaning in, brushing his lips against mine. They are soft lips, more gentle than I'd imagined.

And I consider the universe. I consider what this could be the start of, what this could be the end of. I consider who I am, where I've been, and how I got here. I remember Chloe, my dad, running into Galen on the beach, throwing Rayna through hurricane-proof glass, making Toraf jump out of a helicopter, bringing a wall of fish to an underwater Tribunal. I remember tingles and kisses and blushes and inside jokes and winks and knowing glances.

And none of it, not any of it, has anything to do with this kiss.

So I stop it.

Reed seems to know. That I'm not just stopping this kiss. I'm stopping any chance we might have together. That I've made my choice. That it's not about water or land, Neptune or New Jersey or the Atlantic Ocean. It's about choosing between Reed and Galen.

And I've chosen Galen.

He nods, backing away slowly. "All right then." He sucks in a breath of air. "Okay."

"I'm sorry," I tell him.

He rakes a hand through his hair and holds up his other, halting me. "No, it's fine. No need for apologies. That's what I wanted to know, right? That was the whole point. And now I know."

We embrace a perpetual silence then, as if letting the cosmos settle from our decisive kiss. After a while, the peaceful quiet turns into tangible awkward. I'm about to announce as much, but a bush rustles behind Reed.

Mr. Kennedy steps out. "Oh, goodness, you two gave me an awful fright."

Reed is almost successful at not rolling his eyes. Almost. "Hi, Mr. Kennedy."

The older man smiles. He must just be starting for the day, because his lab coat is still immaculate and pressed and smudge free. The smear of white sunscreen on his nose hasn't absorbed in yet. "Reed, Emma. Lovely to see you two again this morning." But by his tone, it isn't lovely to see us. In fact, I've never heard Mr. Kennedy sound . . . egotistical before. And I've never ever seen him sneer. "I'm so happy you decided not to gallivant south of the river, though there is a mother black bear and her two cubs close by in that direction." He points, letting his thumb linger in the air. Something is off. "Of course, with Davy Crocket here, you very well might have gone against my advice to stay north of the river. But, Emma, you talked him into listening, didn't you? You're a good girl, aren't you, Emma?"

And then Mr. Kennedy pulls a gun on us.

28

THINGS COULD *be worse.*

The sun is rising, giving Galen a general sense of direction as he makes his way through the forest. He has no idea where he is—or if he's headed the right way—but the logical thing to do would be to find a water source. In water, he'll be able to sense other pulses around him and trace them back to Neptune.

Back to Neptune, where he hopes he'll find Emma.

He slows his pace just long enough to bring up Grom's name on his cell phone. It's difficult to focus on multiple tasks when both of your hands are full, he decides. In one hand he holds Tyrden's large knife; in the other, his cell phone. Dialing with his thumb and only half his concentration, he speeds up again, trying to put as much distance between himself and Tyrden as possible. *No telling how long he'll be out.*

Galen had taken care to use the remnants of rope to tie

Tyrden's hands and feet together, but he's no expert in tying effective knots, and Tyrden is undeniably strong—not to mention too heavy to carry through the woods. Otherwise, he wouldn't have left him behind at all.

The phone rings and rings, but Grom doesn't answer. Galen hangs up and tries again. And again. Finally he leaves a message on voice mail. "Grom. Call me back. Don't go to Neptune. Just . . . Just call me back!"

After a few more minutes, he stops and rests against a tree, trying to put most of his weight on his right ankle. He works his left in a circular motion in an effort to stretch out the soreness. Triton's trident, but he's lucky there are no breaks, that he came through the scuffle without more alarming injuries. Groaning, he points his big toe at the ground to stretch out his aching calf muscle—another excellent reason to find a water source. It had felt good to shape a fin, even with the ropes constricting around his tail. He stands on the other foot then, repeating the stretches.

That's when he hears shouting behind him.

Shouting. And dogs.

Rachel told him once that humans use dogs to sniff out other humans when they're missing—or wanted. All these dogs need to find him is an item from his SUV or his hotel room, and they will be able to hone in on his scent. Galen pushes away from the tree and breaks into a jog, grimacing with each stride. *Has Tyrden already sent a search party after me?*

He flies past trees and bushes, scraping his forehead on low-hanging branches and reopening his busted lip on one of them.

It's difficult for his swollen eyes to adjust to his pace and after a time, one of them closes altogether. *Perfect.*

Still, he presses onward as fast as he can, the sun both helping him and hurting him as he becomes more visible in the woods. In the distance, a glint of white stops him in his tracks. It's the unmistakable hair of a Half-Breed.

Galen crouches down, crunching twigs and sticks and leaves beneath his heavy, clumsy feet. Fish were not meant to be stealthy on land, he decides. *But there could be more behind me than there are in front of me. If I can just sneak past this one . . .*

He resorts to crawling on the forest floor, ducking behind anything that will shield him and cursing himself for making so much noise in the process. When he's several fin lengths ahead of the Half-Breed, he hears a new sound.

The roar of rushing water. He takes off in a sprint—or as close to a sprint as he can manage—and heads toward the noise of his salvation. In his haste, he drops the knife he'd confiscated from Tyrden. *I can't go back for it. I won't need it if I can just reach the water.*

Behind him, the Half-Breed calls out to him. "Galen? Is that you? Stop!"

Not in a million years.

He doesn't stop until he reaches the rocky bank of the river. Hastily, he removes the remnants of his jeans and ties them farther up on his waist to use as a covering for later. His muscles scream at him to change, to shift to his fin. But he's afraid of what he'll find when he does. Back in the shed he was in fight mode. Now, his fin may not hold up as well.

Still, there are more voices behind him, and they're growing louder by the second, calling him by name. He wades in. If they haven't spotted him yet, they will soon. Just as he's about to dive in, his phone rings on the bank behind him, where he had to ditch it in favor of escape; the water would destroy it anyway.

But there is no time to go back.

As Galen dives in, he hears a gunshot in the distance.

29

REED ISN'T behind me.

Reed isn't behind me.

I'm too terrified to scream, which will only alert Mr. Kennedy to my location. So I keep running. I don't know where I'm going. I don't know what happened to Reed. I pray and beg and pray for him not to be shot. But I'm not brave enough to turn back.

Suddenly, voices tickle my ear. Voices and barking and shouting. Hunters, maybe? There is a chance they could be with Mr. Kennedy, but so far I haven't seen Mr. Kennedy warm up to anyone else. I have to assume he's working alone—on whatever he's working on. And couldn't it be another search party looking for Galen?

"Help me!" I screech, changing my direction slightly. "Help me—I'm over here!" Voices, shouting, barking. The roar of the river. If my heart beats any faster, my chest will explode. At this point that would be mercy. "Help me!"

My knees almost give out as I recognize the sheriff of Neptune standing barefoot on the water's edge. "Sheriff Grigsby!"

He turns toward me, startled. Bet he's even more surprised when I pitch myself into his arms and cling for what's left of life. "Sheriff Grigsby. Mr. Kennedy. Reeeeeed," I cry into his chest.

"Emma, what are you doing here? Do you know how dangerous it is to be in the woods by yourself?" The sheriff would sound really stern and uncaring if not for the fact that he's shaking beneath the security of his uniform.

I shake my head. "Not . . . Alone . . . Mr. Kennedy . . ." I've never been so breathless in my entire life, not even underwater. "Took . . . Reed . . . *Hehasagun.*"

Sheriff Grigsby stiffens in my arms. I'm beginning to think I have that effect on all males. "Did you say . . . You're saying Mr. Kennedy . . . What are you saying, Emma? Take a second to breathe. That's right. Calm down. In . . . Out . . . Good."

The mini Lamaze session does help. My heart beat slows to just outside the range of palpitations. "I was in the woods with Reed, and Mr. Kennedy found us. He grabbed Reed, held a gun to him. I ran and he started shooting at me."

Grigsby nods vigorously. "We heard gunfire. Tell me where you were. Where you saw Kennedy."

"I don't know if Reed . . . Reed might be . . ."

And if he is, it's all my fault. I'm the one who insisted on coming out here, who wouldn't take no for an answer. Mr. Kennedy was right: I played right into his hands. But what hands?

How was I supposed to know that there were even hands to be played into?

Grigsby grabs my wrist and starts hauling me away from the river. He stops briefly to put on his shoes, then there I am again, trampling through the woods. At least, this time I'm with someone who's armed.

"We saw Galen," he says abruptly. "He ran from us. Jumped in the river."

I dig my heels into the dirt. "You saw Galen? Was he okay? Where is he now?" What? Just when I think I'm catching my breath . . .

The sheriff shakes his head and pulls me forward with a jerk. "I told you, he jumped in the river. We can't sense him anymore. He . . . He's a very fast swimmer, isn't he?"

I nod. "Very."

"As soon as we get back to town, I'll send some Trackers to the river. If we can spare any."

I close my eyes against the frustration. *Spare any. Of course.* Now that Reed has been taken, all of Neptune's resources will be allocated toward finding him instead of Galen, who, from the looks of it, obviously doesn't want to be bothered. I know that's as it should be. Reed is in danger and Galen—well, Galen is obviously healthy enough to run and hide.

The thought of us being so close to each other in the woods has me reeling. Did he see me? Is he running from me? I practically bulldoze that thought out of my head. Still, why would he run from the search party?

What am I missing here?

30

JUST PERFECT.

It's been a long time since Galen has found himself caught in a net. But caught he is. Which is not a little embarrassing.

At least, he reasons, it's probably not a Neptune net. For starters, it's human made, probably by a machine. There are tiny flaws in the knots and weaves, flaws that were made because of industrial-grade bends and tangles in the line, not because of someone's handiwork gone awry. He's seen this kind of net before, and Galen can't imagine that any citizen of Neptune would choose a factory substitute over the fine art of weaving quality nets they've no doubt passed down from generation to generation.

Plus, the good people of Neptune do not need fishing nets. Not when the Gift of Poseidon swims so rampantly through their veins.

No, it's a human fisherman's net that caught Galen fairly and squarely. He was paying attention to all that happened behind him—and to the way he moves his tender fin so as not to hurt it more—instead of all that lay ahead of him. He's not sure what triggered the trap to spring, or really, what the fishermen intended to entangle. He hasn't seen anything in these waters that would warrant such a large net. But now he must wait for the fisherman to come back and retrieve his prize.

And Galen intends for that prize to look a whole lot like a dead body when the unsuspecting fisherman finally gets around to reeling him in from the north riverbank. That's the direction the line is coming from anyway. But how long he'll have to wait to shock the poor guy is the true question. If Galen is right, and he didn't spend too much time at Tyrden's mercy, then it should be close to the weekend, though he's not sure exactly which day it is. *Any good fisherman checks his net on the weekend, right?*

In the meantime, he should at least pass the time by trying to tear through the netting—with what, he's not sure. His teeth already proved no match for the commercial-grade rope and he's still berating himself for dropping Tyrden's knife in the woods. Stretching each square only makes the net tighter—as it should. The idea is to make the space tinier and tinier—and clearly, it does its job where that's concerned.

The good news is that he's well out of range of any of Tyrden's search parties. Even now, he senses no one. Of course, he'd made sure of that as soon as he hit the water. Though possibly injured and sore, his fin is still faster than that of most other Syrena.

From this spot in the river he tastes more salt in the water than he did upstream, which hopefully means he's getting that much closer to the ocean. Getting caught in a net is a setback—and humiliating—but it's exponentially better than getting caught by Tyrden or his men again.

Galen settles in for the wait, willing his body to let go of some of the tension of the past few hours. He has to concentrate on getting back to Neptune. There's a good chance that the Royals are already on their way. An ominous directive like, "Don't come to Neptune," is the perfect way to get Grom to do just that. He should have known better than to leave clipped phone messages like that without further explanation.

They must be so confused now. As is Galen.

Clearly Tyrden wants an attack on Neptune, but why? And if Tyrden wants an attack, what does Reder want? Galen doubts that Reder had anything to do with his abduction.

Galen shakes his head. *If Reder truly wanted hostages as Tyrden said, he could have taken me and Emma the night we came to his house for dinner.*

"Emma," he says aloud, changing the subject in his head. The sound of her name sends a refreshing jolt through his body. He thinks of how she must be feeling right now. Confused. Abandoned. Angry. Probably regretting coming on this road trip with him. *I'll make it up to you, I swear.*

Trying not to focus on the new, deep ache battering his chest, Galen massages the tip of his tail where the most damage was done by the ropes. The corners are slightly bent and will take some time to fully heal, to take their original shape. It reminds him of how a dolphin's fin might become misshapen if kept too long in captivity. The bridge where his fin turns into tail is tender; he's careful not to twist it. In fact, he'll have to be careful for a long time. He's hoping Nalia will know how to help it mend faster. If not, he'll make a trip to see Dr. Milligan after they've put all this behind them.

If *we put all this behind us.*

All at once, there's a tug on the net, and Galen feels himself being slowly pulled toward shore. Given the lengthy process, he assumes there is only one person on the other end of this line, which would be the best-case scenario. The net drags the bottom through several strong currents, and Galen is tempted to help it by swimming along and keeping it unstuck. But he saves his energy and his fin.

Besides, a smooth transition to shore just wouldn't coincide with the behavior of the dead body he's pretending to be at the moment. He shifts from fin to legs to make the haul more realistic. Minutes pass and the net slowly but surely moves closer and closer to shore. Galen nestles into the bottom, going limp as he's pulled to the surface.

Several maddening seconds pass by as Galen allows his unfortunate fisherman to behold the corpse he caught. He has to wait until his unsuspecting victim actually loosens the net before he can make his move—which means the poor guy will be close enough to touch.

But the net doesn't loosen. And then there is a sharp pain in Galen's thigh, so sharp he's forced to cry out. His eyes fly open and to his leg. A long metal rod protrudes from it, with a red feather at the end.

Galen jerks his head toward the fisherman standing over him with a dart gun. And there stands Mr. Kennedy. His face is blank, calculating, garnished only by the hint of a satisfied smile.

Galen's vision suddenly swirls into a tunnel, then disappears altogether.

31

FOR THE second time in my life, I find myself in the back of a police car. "Where are you taking me?"

Grigsby barely makes a show of glancing in the rearview at me. I wish I could sit up front; I feel like a criminal all slouched in the back. "We're going to Reder's. You need to tell him what happened to Reed."

What kind of backward country-bumpkin town is this? Shouldn't the sheriff be hauling me to the station and getting a witness report and calling Reed's parents and all that? Or am I a victim of watching too many reality shows? But then again, while Grigsby is the sheriff, Reder is the obvious leader.

The car pulls into the driveway of Reed's house. Grigsby opens the door for me, only to grab me by the upper arm again and all but escort me up the porch steps and to the front door.

"Um. Ow," I tell him.

He lets go immediately. "Sorry. Habit." *Just how many arrests does it take to make a habit out of grabbing someone's arm?* Neptune didn't seem like the kind of town that would have need of a seasoned sheriff.

Reed's mom answers the doorbell. "Emma, so good to see you! Oh. Sheriff Grigsby. Is . . . Is there a problem? Where's Reed? Now what has he done?" I can tell she's trying to discern if Reed is really the problem, or if I am.

Grigsby's face is grim. "Reder home? We need to speak with him."

She grabs the dish towel she'd tucked into her apron and wipes her already dry hands on it as she calls over her shoulder for Reder. "You've got visitors, honey." The tightness in her voice is noticeable even to an oblivious being like myself.

Reder's heavy footsteps fall on the stairs, and when he reaches us at the bottom, he takes one look at me and ushers us into the adjoining living room. The weird thing is, Grigsby's hold actually gets tighter once we're seated on the couch. *What does he think will happen here? I'll tell Reder that his son has been kidnapped or worse and then I'll lunge for his jugular?*

But I know it must be nerves. After all, Reed disappeared on his shift, *while he was in the woods close by.* It's kind of humiliating, being the sheriff and all.

Grigsby clears his throat when Reder's heavy glare falls on him. By Reder's expression, he's already heard through the radio grapevine what has happened. "We were in the woods looking for the boy," the sheriff starts. By that, I assume he means searching for Galen, just as we were. "The dogs caught his scent, and we were on him until we got to the river. He wouldn't stop running from us."

Reder turns to me, surprised. "Why would Galen run from our search parties?"

"I . . . I don't know."

"He could have been running from Kennedy," Grigsby says. "Maybe Kennedy got to him first."

Ohmysweetgoodness. The thought hadn't occurred to me but makes perfect sense now. If Kennedy has a habit of kidnapping people, and Galen disappeared almost as soon as we came to town . . .

"Go on," Reder says.

Grigsby swallows, nodding toward me. "Emma says she was in the woods with Reed, looking for the boy. Says Kennedy pulled a gun on them and took Reed."

"He took Reed and shot at me," I blurt. "We're wasting time here. We've got to find them."

Reder stands. Panic washes over his face. I wonder for an isolated second if my hysteria is contagious. It's the first time I've ever seen Reder unnerved. "Are you okay, Emma?" he says.

I nod, wrapping my arms around myself as if to the contrary. He puts a gentle hand on my shoulder. The alarm is gone from his expression, replaced by a look I know well. It's the face Mom makes when she's acting like a nurse—the face of an emergency responder. Calm, collected, courageous. "Did Kennedy say anything before he took Reed?"

I nod, then tell him word for word what went down. I'll never forget that conversation for the rest of my life. When I'm finished, Reder looks at Grigsby. "Escort Emma to the basement of city hall. Put two guards on her. It sounds like Kennedy was targeting Reed, but he could be after Emma as well. He could have been holding Galen, too. Obviously he's not hiding them in town anywhere or they would have been spotted."

Grigsby nods. "He supposedly goes to the woods every day looking for his plants. That'd be the first place I'd check."

"Take every warm body you can find and go back out there. Spread out, but no one goes alone. Make sure everyone who knows how to use a gun has one." Reder shifts his gaze to me. He is all business now. "Emma, go with Grigsby. You'll be safe with him. In the meantime, I think it's time you called your mother, don't you?"

32

GALEN COMES to, his pulse heavy and threatening to pummel through his temple. He can't open his eyes gently enough. First one, then the other. The light of day lances through his line of vision, and it feels like a thousand grains of sand are stuck to his eyeballs.

Each pound of his heartbeat seems to shake the room around him. As if that weren't enough, the new hole in his leg throbs with the pain of being recently moved. He groans.

"Hey, man," a voice says in front of him.

Galen squints into the sunlight streaming in through the window on the opposite side of the room. Reed sits under it.

"Hey, Galen," Reed says. "Are you okay?" Reed is in the same position as Galen. Sitting on the floor, chained with hands above his head, legs stretched out in front of him.

Galen nods. "You?" The word feels tangy in his mouth.

"I'm good. Well, as good as I can be, you know." Reed swallows. "So, um, where have you been? We've been looking for you everywhere. Everyone has. And what happened to your face?"

Everything, Galen wants to say. "I've been Tyrden's guest the past few days." Galen waits for a false reaction from Reed. Delayed remorse, counterfeit shock. Any sign that he or his father could be in on his imprisonment.

But Reed's eyes instantly go round as lily pads. "Tyrden did that to you? What did you do to piss him off?"

But Galen is distracted—the hands of grogginess haven't quite released him yet. Reed is supposed to be with Emma, not tied up and held prisoner in a dingy old house in the woods. *Where is Emma?* is all he wants to know, but right now, his mouth won't move to make the words. Because what if she's not okay?

Galen scans their surroundings. A wood building made with logs—which explains the damp musty odor he smelled before he could open his eyes. A lonely wooden stool sits in one corner, and a full table and chairs sit off to the left of Galen. A pair of muddy rain boots stands guard at the only door in the cabin. And none of it matters. Because he's ready to ask now. The only question that matters is the one Galen finally forces out: "Where is Emma?"

"I don't know. She ran away, but . . . I don't know if she . . . But the best I can figure is that she did escape, because if not, he would have brought her here, too. . . . But I swear he was a horrible shot, actually. I'm not worried." His voice speaks volumes to the opposite.

The idea of Kennedy shooting at Emma makes Galen's

stomach feel like a self-contained waterfall, roiling and raging. "Why is he doing this? Where is he now?" The thought *What else could possibly happen* crosses his mind, too.

"I don't know. He's not the only one, though. I mean, I haven't seen anyone else here, but he keeps talking to someone on the radio."

"Radio?"

"He has a satellite radio, so I figure we're well out of town if his phone doesn't have a signal. He must have been planning this forever." Reed's voice is tainted with a begrudging sort of admiration. "I thought he was just a crazy scientist," he grumbles. "We all did."

"Planning what? You said he was interested in plants."

"I said what he said. Which was obviously a lie, don't you think? He did say, 'mermaid,' to whoever he was talking to on the other end of that radio. We're screwed."

Nice. A botanist turned mermaid enthusiast? To Galen, that'd be the best-case scenario. But Mr. Kennedy has an air of knowledge about him. A familiarity. The way he set the trap in the river, for instance. Galen had wondered what river fish he'd been trying to catch with such an odd net arrangement. The net was large; obviously the prey was, too.

Galen has the sinking feeling that it caught exactly what it was supposed to.

"We've got to get out of here," Galen says, pulling and testing the chains above his head. "We've got to find Emma before he does."

Reed shakes his head. "The chains are bolted in, man. I sat here and watched him drill it myself. The wood's not rotten enough to give."

Galen beats his head against the wall. "We can't stay here. I can't stay here."

"What, but I can just put on some sunscreen and relax?" Reed spits. "That's grand of you."

"You don't understand," Galen starts. Then he tilts his head. "Or maybe you do understand. Maybe you know everything. You are Reder's son, after all."

"Oh, geez, let's just be as indirect as possible. Yes, I know, okay? I know he wanted Emma to help unite Neptune with the underwater kingdoms. And I don't expect a Royal like you to understand. And for the record, Emma knows that I know. Everyone knows. So you don't have to worry about bringing that up when you try to drag my name through the mud."

Galen scrutinizes Reed's face, looking for any morsel of a lie. He finds none. He decides to push further. If Reder wants to unite Neptune with the underwater kingdoms, then what does Tyrden want? "You're telling me you didn't know your father held me prisoner?"

"You said Tyrden did that to you."

"He was acting on orders from your father."

At this, Reed laughs. "My father would never trust Tyrden with any kind of orders. That guy's crazy as a raccoon in daylight."

Tell me about it. "What do you mean?"

"Did Tyrden happen to tell you that he used to be the leader of Neptune? That the citizens voted him out in favor of my dad?"

No, but he did tell me democracy wasn't working lately. And that Reder wasn't as good a leader as everyone thinks he is. The whole pictures paints itself in Galen's head. "Why did they vote him out?"

Reed shrugs. "It was before I was born. All Dad will say is that he was more like a dictator than an elected leader. I've heard some people call him cruel."

Sounds about right. "Why didn't your father force him to leave?"

"You can't force someone to leave just because they have a personality disorder. We have to abide by human laws on land, remember?"

A shame, to be sure. "Tyrden wanted me to call my brother. He wanted me to get Grom to attack Neptune. To tell him that Reder was holding me and Emma as hostages."

Reed licks his lips. "Did you do it?"

"Of course not." Galen rolls his eyes. "He wants your father dead."

"We've got to get out of here, Galen. We have to warn my dad."

"I left a message with my brother. I told him not to come to Neptune."

"Oh, well that's nice. We should just stay here then. Do you mind passing the cookies?"

Galen grins. Finally, they have something in common with each other—the urgent need to get back to Neptune.

A problem that leaves them both speechless. Both of them survey the room, as if in a contest to see who can come up with the best escape plan first. In all truthfulness, Galen has nothing. Mr. Kennedy had been very thorough in selecting strong chains and bolts for his prisoners. So thorough that none of this could have been chance.

His presence in Neptune.

The trap in the river.

The obviously predetermined location to house his victims.

Not a plant or flower in sight.

If Mr. Kennedy is a botanist, Galen is Triton himself.

Which wouldn't help him escape anyway.

"I have an idea," Reed says, his features brightened by what Galen recognizes as naive hope. "Is it true that you have the Gift of Triton?"

Galen blinks.

"Oh, don't be shy about it now." Reed rolls his eyes. "Emma swore me to secrecy. And anyway, we need to combine our skills to get out of here, don't you think?"

Jealousy seeps through Galen's veins, burning every part of him like the venom of a scorpion fish. Every second Galen has spent away from Emma, every inch apart they've been, Reed has filled in with his own presence. His questions. His flirty smiles.

Galen pushes the thought aside. "Oh? Why don't you use your gift to send a few fish to untie us then?"

Reed bangs his head against the wood behind him. "What is your deal, man? Don't you want to get out of here?"

Galen pulls his knees up to his chest, as if they can protect his heart in some way against what he's about to say. "Tyrden showed me pictures of you. With Emma," he chokes out. The words feel like tiny sharp fish bones in his throat. This isn't the time to confront Reed and he knows it. *But what if I never get another chance?*

Reed stiffens. "What? How?"

"It didn't look like you cared much about privacy." In all honesty, it would be hard to convince Galen that Reed didn't actually pose for the camera. "You're saying you didn't know?"

"Of course I didn't know!"

"How could he get that close without you noticing him?"

Reed shakes his head, looking every bit as confused as Galen feels. "I never noticed Tyrden. He must have someone else working with him. Someone who could get close to me and Emma without setting off any alarms."

Galen concedes with a half nod. *Or you're an idiot.* "Yes, there were others at first. He wasn't the one who actually took me. There were men with trucks. Full-blooded Syrena. When I woke up, I was with Tyrden."

"What did they look like?"

What did they look like? "I told you. They were full-blooded Syrena. One of them had a big nose, as far as I could tell."

Reed rolls his eyes. "Awesome. That's super-helpful. Thanks."

If Galen had use of his hands, he'd be massaging his temple right now. Or dotting Reed's eye. "It was dark and they knocked me out. I never really got to see their faces."

A silence falls between them then, one filled with aggravation and helplessness. Minutes come and go with nothing useful presenting itself as an escape. Just when Galen thinks they're done with the conversation for good, Reed pollutes the air with a question. "So if you saw pictures of us together . . . does that mean you know I kissed her?"

33

THE COUCH in the basement of city hall is everything a basement couch should be. Comfy. Pastel floral. Fuzzy in spots. A true relic from the 1990s. And it's the only piece of furniture in the entire room, aside from bookshelves and filing cabinets lining the walls.

So this couch is where I'll be sitting when I call Mom. When I tell her where I've been, what I've been doing, who I've been doing it with. I'll be perched atop this cushion like a vulture, shoulders scrunched, head hanging, waiting to be chastised.

I gently toss the phone back and forth between my hands. The universal symbol of stalling.

It's time.

As I dial, I'm hoping and praying that she won't answer. She didn't answer any of my check-in calls yesterday and hasn't returned them either. And if anyone had a mother to be suspicious of when she doesn't answer the phone, it would be me.

This time she does answer. Breathless. "Emma, I was just about to call you."

"I called you several times yesterday," I say, enjoying the upper hand while it lasts. I'm sure I can hear the quiet thrum of a vehicle in the background. I can't tell if I'm on speakerphone.

"Did you? My phone accidentally fell in the fish tank, so I had to get a new one."

"The fish tank?" Our fish tank is built into our living room wall. You literally have to reach underneath the wall to feed the fish or change the filter. Accidentally dropping a cell phone in it is a feat of clumsiness even I couldn't achieve.

"Yes, sweetie. Your grandfather told me where he sent you, and when I threw the phone at his head, I missed and hit the fish tank, shattering it everywhere."

Great. "I was just calling to tell you all about that, actually." I wonder how much Grandfather actually spilled.

"No need." Her voice is smooth and sweet as molasses. I'm in huge trouble. "I'm on my way to get you."

This makes my stomach feel like a nest of hornets. "I don't need to be rescued, Mom." This is not going how I planned.

"Apparently, Galen thinks you do."

"You talked to Galen?"

"He called Grom and left a message for him not to come to Neptune. Any idea why?"

"When was that? Where did he call from? Is he okay?" Why is everyone except me experiencing Galen sightings?

"He called from his own cell phone this morning. Grom called him back, but he never answered. It just goes straight to voice mail. I've called the phone company to have them track the location." She's quiet for a minute, then says, "He sounded panicked, Emma. We think he's in trouble."

I think he is, too. This morning he was spotted running through the woods, toward the river. Now I find out he called Grom and warned him away from Neptune. "It's got to be Kennedy," I blurt.

"Kennedy?"

So then I explain everything that happened in the woods with Reed. Mom is quiet for a long time. "Where are you now?"

"For my protection they put me in the basement of city hall. There are two guards at the door."

"Sounds a lot like keeping you prisoner."

"All I have to do is ask one of the guards, and they'll get me whatever I need. I'm not a prisoner."

"Emma, what exactly is going on here? What have you been doing in Neptune all this time? I'm getting mixed information here. Galen wants us to stay away, but you want us to come?"

Here is the moment of truth. "I mean, I want you to come to Neptune, but just to visit. Not to like, get me or whatever." Or like, grab my ear and use it to escort me to the car in front of the entire town. Nalia Poseidon Princess McIntosh still thinks doing things like that is okay. *Deep breath.* "I don't know why Galen doesn't want you to come. We had a fight, and he said he was going to tell Grom about Neptune—that's all he told me before he left. I want you to come because . . . because I've made friends here. And they want peace. With the ocean king-doms. With the Royals. They want to be able to swim in the oceans. They're like me." Yep, I'm screwing it up. I feel like a telegram machine firing off fragments and incomplete sentences with the eloquence of a woodpecker. I'm glad Reder's not here to see just how effective I am in the ambassador role.

Mom takes a minute to decipher my word vomit. "Your grandfather was wrong to send you there by yourself."

"Indeed I wasn't!" I hear in the background.

"You brought *Grandfather?*"

"I brought everyone," Mom says defensively. "Just in case."

I imagine Rayna and Toraf and Grom and Grandfather cramped in Mom's tiny car. I wonder whose lap Toraf is going to sit on for the ride home, because it's not going to be mine. "Where are you anyway?"

"We just left the airport. We're only about an hour out."

The airport? How did she get everyone on a plane on such short notice? They must have started making plans as soon as Grandfather spilled the beans yesterday.

Also, Mom is starting to remind me of Rachel.

"Listen, sweetie, are you alone?"

"Yes. Why?"

"It's important that you don't tell anyone we're coming."

"They know I'm calling you right now. They're expecting you."

Mom huffs into the phone. "It never occurred to you that you could be in danger, Emma? That these people could be lying to you?"

"What part of *'Grandfather sent me here'* don't you understand?"

"He's over two hundred years old, Emma. And so is his brain. Use your common sense!"

If the phone had guts, I would have squeezed them out by now. I loosen my grip and try to control my voice. "And if I am in danger? Then what are you going to do? This is an entire town, Mom. You're outnumbered."

Mom laughs softly into the phone. I recognize it immediately. It's the "Try me" laugh. "We'll simply have to do a hostage exchange."

"Hostage exchange?" I whisper-yell. "You've taken a hostage?"

"Not yet. But with an entire town, like you said, one shouldn't be too hard to come by."

"Ohmysweetgoodness this is not happening." What a great ambassador I am. My family now thinks I'm imprisoned and are planning a hostage exchange. Awesome.

"Don't be so dramatic. We're going to be on the outskirts of town. We'll get you out of there as soon as we can."

"I don't want to be out of here," I say through clenched teeth.

"We'll talk about this later. Keep in touch. Remember, don't tell anyone anything."

And then she hangs up.

34

HOW MANY kisses were there? Have I lost Emma entirely? Did I throw away everything I ever wanted with one disagreement?

The questions contend for the forefront of his mind.

How could she do this? But he knows that's not fair of him. After all, he left on bad terms and never came back. Who knows what she could be thinking? Who knows what she's been through without him? And if Reed was there to comfort her, then of course she would grow close to him.

And is that so horrible? Reed is just like her. He's a Half-Breed. He has the Gift of Poseidon. He has a normal "human" life. Everything Emma wants, all wrapped up in pale muscular packaging.

If I really loved her, wouldn't I want her to be happy?

He grits his teeth. *Yes, I do want her to be happy—I want her to be happy with* me. And no pasty pile of bones is going to get in the way of that.

"Galen, you have to talk to me. We're getting out of here, remember?" says the pasty pile of bones.

Galen slowly turns his attention away from the chains above him and assesses Reed with a cold look. "When we get out of here, I'm going to knock every one of your teeth out, then do a recount to make sure I've gotten them all."

"I understand that you're mad."

"Mad?" *Murderous* would be more accurate. The thought of Reed's lips on Emma's sends lava through Galen's veins. It reminds him of the time Toraf kissed Emma to make him jealous. Only this is much worse. That was before he and Emma were together, before he'd tasted her for the first time. Now she is going to be his mate.

Reed knew that, yet still disrespected that very important boundary.

And now I am going to disrespect his face.

"You know what I would be worried about if I were you?" Reed says pleasantly.

Galen decides Reed doesn't seem to value his tongue. "Stop talking."

"It's just that you're not asking the most important question here. It's something I would want to know. If I were you."

A growl erupts from deep within Galen. His curiosity is piqued and Reed knows it. Morbid as it sounds, he wants the details, to know exactly what happened. How did it happen? Where were they? How did Emma react?

And then again, he doesn't want to know any of it. The images in his head will never go away as it is. It's a soft sort of rot, the idea of them kissing. A rot that will always hide in the confines of his organized heart, like an underlying illness or a scar. "You said that already."

Reed kicks out in futile frustration. "Galen, stop being an idiot. Oh, yes, I'm talking to you. What I'm trying to tell you is, she didn't kiss me back."

"Of course, she didn't." He says it with all the air of a Triton Royal, but deep down, relief swirls through Galen. Emma rejected Reed. *Even after our fight and all the things I said.* The realization has a calming effect, cooling the lava running through his veins, slowing the pulse in his temple threatening to burst through his thick skin.

Even his teeth remember to ungrind.

"Well, you don't have to say it like that."

"I trust Emma."

"Yeah, I get that. But I mean if you think about it, I would be considered a good catch."

"Be serious."

Reed leans his head back against the wall. "Do you know she actually apologized to me for choosing you?"

"I would have rather she dislocated your nose." Still, Galen acknowledges the significance here. She didn't just reject Reed—she chose Galen. Out loud. Even when he disappeared for three days without calling.

Even when she has another option—and a good one at that. Reed is a good catch, he knows. He has the ease of a human life to offer her. She could have Neptune and everything it represents—companionship, belonging, safety. To Galen, such circumstances seem perfect.

But she chose me. I'm going to make this up to her. All of it.

Galen sits up straight. "A few minutes ago when you were babbling—did you say you had an idea to get us out of here?"

35

A KNOCK on the door startles me awake.

One of the guards—I think his name is Tyrden—pokes his head in. "Everything okay in here?" he says. Tyrden is the friendlier of the two. The other one was assigned to duty, and he seemed disappointed to be supervising a teenage girl when he could be out looking for Reed's kidnapper. But Tyrden volunteered to keep an eye out for me. So that was nice.

I sit up on the couch and motion for him to come in. "I guess I fell asleep."

"Oh, I didn't mean to wake you." He folds his hands in front of him, like he doesn't have any intention of leaving. Obviously, he takes this whole babysitting thing seriously.

I'm not really in the mood for company though. Not with the thought of Galen out there in the wild, alone and possibly in danger—plus, the very real probability that my mom is going to go all Rambo on Neptune. Still, I can't be rude to Tyrden—he might be the only person left in this town genuinely concerned for my welfare.

I give him a tight smile. In the light, I notice that he has a black eye. His lip looks swollen, too. He observes me observing him. "Don't mind my little cuts and scrapes," he chuckles. "I just fell down some stairs."

I nod knowingly. I get war wounds like that all the time. It's a clumsy-person thing. "Have they found Reed yet?"

"Not yet."

I stretch my arms up over my head. Then I reach for my phone in my back pocket and check the time. Mom should be strategizing World War III from just outside of town right about now.

"Expecting a call?" Tyrden says.

"No, just checking the time."

He nods absently, walking to each of the basement windows and locking them with a kind of careful deliberation. After he secures every one, he slides the shades down as well. "It'll be dark out soon. Don't need Kennedy snooping around and finding you."

I didn't think the windows posed any kind of threat, but I suppose if Kennedy were super-ambitious, he could finagle himself through one of them—with enough grease and wriggling. And of course, if the goal is to kill me, he did have a gun. Good for Tyrden for being meticulous. "Thank you," I tell him.

He nods graciously, then eases down on the couch next to me, coming close to invading my space. Aw-kward.

"I thought I could tell you a story," he says. "To keep your mind off things."

"Um. Okay." Because what else am I supposed to say?

"Let's see. Where to begin? Oh, yes." He leans toward me. "Did you know I used to run this town?"

"No," I say, trying to sound interested. The same polite interest you show when a person starts talking about how they knitted a sweater for their pet hamster.

He nods. "Well, I did. That was before Reder decided he would be better at it, you see. Though I don't really think he's proven himself, do you?"

Talk about being put on the spot. "Um. I haven't really been here long enough to judge one way or the other, you know?" I should get a trophy for my evasion skills.

Tyrden purses his lips. "That's a good point. And how rude of me. I'd forgotten to ask how you're enjoying your stay here in Neptune? Current circumstances aside, of course."

"I like Neptune. Everyone here is so friendly." I would expound on that with things like, "I fit right in," or "It's nice not to be an outcast here," but I'm sticking with short answers for Tyrden. I mean, he might be one of those people who doesn't shut up after they've started talking, and he's already promised to tell me a story. I'd rather get on with it.

"Word is your grandfather sent you here. Does he plan on visiting anytime soon?"

Yep. In about an hour. "He never mentioned visiting. I think he just wanted me to see this place for myself."

Tyrden nods knowingly. "He probably still has his hands full back home, huh? What with the uprising Jagen caused."

My stomach feels like I swallowed an anvil. "What? You know about that?"

The smile that Tyrden gives me sends chills just about everywhere. "Of course, I do, Emma. The whole thing was my idea."

Suddenly, there's a thump against the basement door. Still reeling from our conversation, I fold my knees up to my chest as Tyrden gets up to investigate. He pulls a gun I didn't know he had from the back of his jeans and aims it toward the door, walking with slow purpose. I feel fear and hope melting through me. Fear that Kennedy has found me. Hope that someone else has and is here to rescue me from Tyrden.

Several long seconds pass, and still nobody knocks on the door.

"Frank, is that you?" Tyrden calls, then presses his ear close to the door. I think Frank is the name of the other guard. When Tyrden gets no answer, he unlocks the door, careful not to make any noise. With one quick, smooth motion he pulls it open and repositions his gun for firing.

And the other guard slumps to Tyrden's feet in a pile. My throat closes up around a scream.

"Ah, Frank," Tyrden says, hauling him into the room by his limp arm, dragging him across the carpet behind him as if he were carry-on luggage. "So glad you could join us. I was just about to tell Emma a story." He dumps Frank along the basement wall, then pats him down, which produces a small handgun. Tyrden tucks it behind him and smiles at me. His eyes are wild.

"Is . . . Is he dead?" I ask. I'm holding myself tightly together with my arms, but I can't stop shaking.

Tyrden shrugs. "Not from what I gave him. But the fall down those steep stairs?" He shakes his head, making a *tsk-tsk*ing sound. "Lots of broken bones if you ask me." Then he kicks Frank in the stomach—hard. "But at least he's unconscious enough not to feel it, right?"

All at once, the room becomes smaller. The locked windows, the drawn shades, the unconscious guard strewn against the wall like a bag of trash. It all closes in on me, suffocating my hope.

The detached look in Tyrden's eyes as he raises his gun at me. I am not safe. "Let me tell you about how I came to know Jagen."

36

OBVIOUSLY MR. Kennedy isn't concerned that his prisoners will escape; it's been hours since Galen woke up, and there has been no sign of their captor. Still, Galen and Reed sit at the ready, waiting to spring their trap, growing stiff and sore with the tension of anticipation.

"If the Archives accepted Emma as a Half-Breed, why wouldn't they accept Neptune?" Reed drawls, rubbing his cheek with the back of his hand. He and Galen have been sitting long enough to scratch the surface of a few topics. And for Reed, it keeps going back to the subject of Half-Breeds. "I mean, what's the big deal now?"

"Why are you so interested in what the ocean dwellers think? You're here, aren't you? You exist, don't you? It seems to me that what they think about Neptune never really mattered in the first place. What's the point in worrying about it?"

Reed's jaw hardens. "Maybe it does matter. Maybe some of us would like the freedom to explore the oceans, too. Without, you know, getting speared in the shorts and whatnot."

Galen grins despite himself. "I didn't say they wouldn't accept Neptune." *I didn't say they would, either.*

"But you don't think the Archives will go for it."

"It's a big decision."

"The Archives have too much power if you ask me."

"Saying things like that won't help your cause, idiot."

"What, are you going to tell on me?"

Galen rolls his eyes. "Of course not. I'm helping you out, remember? You won't be able to run your mouth with a broken jaw."

"You're never going to get over it, are you? It was just a test kiss. I'll never do it again. I'm not a stalker, you know. But there was this one second where I thought she might—"

"I swear by Triton's trident if you don't stop talking about it—"

"Did Triton really have a trident?"

"I'm done talking."

Reed grimaces. "Sorry." But after a few more minutes, Reed opens his mouth again. "Can I ask you a question? Why are you wearing a diaper?"

"I had to tie my jeans around my . . . Just shut up."

But Reed has no filter. "You know, my dad's a great negotiator. All he needs is a chance to talk to the Archives. Do you think Grom would—did you hear that? Someone's coming."

Both Galen and Reed make a show of relaxing, though

every muscle in Galen's body threatens to riot. They have to be smarter than Mr. Kennedy this time around. And so far, they haven't shown any promise in that regard.

Heavy boots resound on the wooden steps outside, and there's the squeaky rustling sound of metal on metal. A latch, maybe? Mr. Kennedy strides in, all confidence, standing taller than before, his hair in perfect order, his glasses gone. "Hello, boys," he says in a deeper voice than Galen remembered.

There's something familiar about Kennedy when he's not wearing glasses.

With a loud clunk, Mr. Kennedy sets a large metal lock on the table. They'd been locked in from the outside. Good to know—if this plan doesn't work.

Which it probably won't, Galen thinks to himself.

But his job is to be all confident and stubborn. It's Reed's job to be scared and nervous and pliable. Mr. Kennedy smiles at Galen, then at Reed across the room. "You two been plotting on how to escape, I hope? Oh," Kennedy says, slapping his knee as he sits on the table. "I do hope it's interesting. It'll be at least a day before my backup arrives. Ooops? Did I give you a tidbit of information for you to steal away and compute and think about when you should be resting or planning an escape?" Then he throws his head back and laughs. "I've never considered myself the bad guy before. Bad guys are always much cooler than me, after all. I'm just a lonely, awkward botanist, right?"

Galen thinks Mr. Kennedy might have lost his mind. And he's weary of dealing with lunatics.

"But at least, I'll be a rich botanist," Mr. Kennedy continues. "Oh, Galen, look at your fists. You'll just have to relax. Or

I can give you something to relax, hmmm?" He pulls a dart out of his lab coat pocket. "Remember your little friend here? Probably the best sleep you've ever experienced, eh?"

The sound of rustling chains draws Kennedy's attention from Galen. "And Reed, are you actually shaking? I tried to warn you of the dangers of being in the woods, didn't I though? But you had none of it. So gallant you are, willing to brave the dangers of predators just to impress little Emma. That backfired, huh? At first, I didn't want it to be you, Reed. Because you were so helpful to me all those other times. But at the café, something about you changed. You got cocky. Rude. And you idiotically divulged where you two would be alone that afternoon. I can't afford to miss such gift-wrapped opportunities. Of course, you understand, right?"

Reed's lip quivers. He's doing a good job of portraying petrified. "Wh-wh-what are you going to do to us? My dad will come looking for us."

Kennedy's lips press together. "Yes, Emma will see to it that he does. Oh, in case you were wondering, your little love interest got away. I'm a terrible shot, I have to say."

Galen springs from the wall and is jolted back by the heavy chains. He couldn't act this angry if he wanted to. Real, unfiltered fury wells in his chest. "If you hurt her—"

"Oh, now," Mr. Kennedy says, "aren't you the wild card, Galen? You leave, you come back, you leave again.... Where have you been, anyway? But don't worry. Good ol' Reed has been keeping an eye on Emma for you. He's been most attentive if I do say so myself."

"But not as attentive as you, apparently," Galen growls. "You're not a botanist, are you?" He pulls at his chains with all the aggression of a caged shark.

Mr. Kennedy readjusts to get a better look at Galen. "You're smarter than you look, now aren't you?" He chuckles. "Not all balls and brawn after all, eh?" Mr. Kennedy sighs dramatically. "Well, you've caught me, Galen. I am indeed *not* a botanist. And can I just say how boring it is to pretend to be a botanist? But Neptune would have run me off if they'd known I was a marine biologist."

Galen's gut twists like one of the pretzel's Rachel was so fond of. A marine biologist. Just like Dr. Milligan—the only other human, besides Rachel, whom Galen has ever trusted. He's devoted to helping preserve the Syrena way of life, and he's in a good position to do just that—a marine biologist himself, he keeps Galen updated on the human world as it relates to ocean exploration. In exchange, Galen allows him to run tests on him in order to study his species.

Dr. Milligan certainly doesn't go around kidnapping his specimens.

"Oh, Galen, just wait until your memory kicks in, then you'll be really impressed," Kennedy is saying.

My memory? Did the dart do something to my memory?

But Reed is unconcerned, quickly turning the conversation back to plan. "What are you going to do to us?" he whimpers, a little more convincing than Galen would like. *Is he breaking? Is he losing it?*

Galen tries to make eye contact with Reed but he won't look

at him. He keeps his frightened gaze on Mr. Kennedy. Galen is officially impressed with the acting skills of the Half-Breed across from him. If they're real.

"Oh, now, shush, little Reed. I'm just going to run a few tests. And by a few, I'm afraid I mean a lot," Kennedy says. "Unfortunately, some of them will hurt. But of course, I'll keep you as comfortable as possible and show you the same hospitality you've shown me, Reed." He shoves his hands in his pockets and rocks back on his heels, smirking down at Reed. Galen has seen that look before. Rayna wears it right before she does something bad to Toraf.

At this, Reed's face darkens so briefly Galen wonders if he imagined it, but then he recovers beautifully, showing himself the terrified companion he needs him to be. "I didn't mean to be rude to you, Mr. Kennedy, I swear," Reed says. He shifts his weight against the wall. "I was just frustrated, that's all."

Mr. Kennedy waves at him in dismissal, then pivots on his heel to examine Galen. "You're in luck, Galen. Since you've been such a scandalous absentee and Reed has been so very . . . congenial, I'm pleased to inform you that Reed will be the first in my tests. Once we get you out of here."

Out of here? He's moving them? Galen tries to decide if this changes things, and he hopes Reed's thinking the same thing. Galen knows that Kennedy isn't stupid enough to move them without tranquilizing them first. Or without help. Maybe that's who he was talking to on the satellite radio.

No, they have to stick with the plan. Which is why Galen is pleased that Reed seems to agree.

"No!" Reed shouts. "No! You don't want me to go first."

Mr. Kennedy turns on him. "And why is that Reed? Because right now, if I had the equipment, I'd be taking all kinds of painful samples from you."

Reed shakes his head. "I'm not that interesting, I swear. I'm pretty ordinary, in fact. I can only Blend, but——"

"Blend? What do you mean blend?"

Reed's mouth snaps shut. "Nothing."

Kennedy nods and walks calmly to the table, retrieving the lock there and gingerly testing the weight of it in his hand. Then without word or warning, he closes his fist around it and strides toward Reed, his expression blank. The Half-Breed makes himself small against the wall, and Galen knows this is real, healthy fear, but no matter how compressed he can make his body, it will be of no help. Kennedy's fist connects with Reed's jaw, sending him sprawling to the side. The chains catch him violently and force him to sit back up, or possibly dislocate his arm. "In case you're not aware," Kennedy sneers. "That was not a test." Reed's lip is swollen and red in the corner where a small tear has begun. "Now that we've set the bar," Kennedy continues, "I'll ask again. What do you mean you can *blend*?"

"Please don't hurt me," Reed says. "But I'm not supposed to show our Gifts——"

And Galen is again impressed.

Kennedy is not. He clutches the lock with one finger, striking Reed with the body of it across his nose. This time blood spurts across the room with the force of the blow, and when Reed opens his eyes, there are real tears in them. Galen knows the nose and face area are sensitive places for humans. He wonders how much of the pain registers with a Half-Breed. Not much, he hopes. If it were Emma in Reed's place, Galen might have broken through his chains by now.

Kennedy hovers over Reed as he gains his composure. Reed slides up with great effort, using the wall to straighten his back. Galen doubts the trembling of his hands is fake.

The biologist lightly tosses the lock back and forth in front of him, keeping it in Reed's line of vision. "I shouldn't like this as much as I do. I suppose that makes me a bad person. Maybe it's all the years I've spent as a laughingstock in my profession, eh? All the disapproving looks from my colleagues. The invitations to parties and award ceremonies that stopped coming. All the grant requests for research denied. No one wants to throw their lot in with a crazy mermaid hunter, right?" He nudges Reed's ankle with the tip of his boot. "But *you* won't deny me, will you, Reed."

Reed groans. "Please stop. I'll show you. I will. Just please stop."

Still, Kennedy raises the lock, taking aim again.

"Enough!" Galen barks. "He's had enough."

Kennedy spins on him, scrutinizing his face with malice. "You'd spare him, Galen? This pathetic girlfriend stealer? I'd think you'd be the first to see him suffer. Perhaps, you don't know the extent of their relationship, hmm? How accommodating Emma has been?"

Galen swallows the unvarnished fury spreading through his veins like hot liquid steel, fortifying any cracks of brokenness he had left in him about the kiss. Reed kissed Emma. She didn't kiss him. And if Galen gets out of here, Kennedy will pay for what he said.

Kennedy can tell he's hit a nerve, an entire army of nerves really, and his mouth smiles in a way that says he has more where that came from. Galen's body is near shaking with contempt, but he strains against it. Allowing himself to become provoked is not a good strategy for this game they're playing. Or maybe it is. *Rage tends to be useful. . . .*

Through clenched teeth, he says, "Reed is just a Half-Breed. He can't take hits like that. I can. Take your anger out on me."

Reed flashes him a questioning look. Galen offers the slightest of shrugs. Telling Kennedy about the existence of Half-Breeds is not a great idea, Galen knows. But telling him fragments of information to lead him on is.

"A Half-Breed," Kennedy says, interest sparkling in his eyes. "Very well, Galen. Tell me about Half-Breeds."

Galen leans his head back against the wall and grunts as if he's disappointed in himself. Kennedy falls for it. "Oh, now," he chuckles, "you've spilled the beans, Galen. You might as well tell me."

Galen doesn't hesitate to answer. "You're supposed to be studying the town of Neptune, and you haven't figured that out yet? Some marine biologist."

Reed nearly brains himself on the wall in frustration. This was not the plan and Galen knows it. Somehow, he needs to put everything back on track. Which means keeping his mouth shut. *I'm the quiet one. I'm the quiet one. I'm the quiet one.*

Kennedy presses his fist against his chin, cracking his neck from side to side. Galen has seen this done before on television. The actor did this to intimidate someone. To Galen, cracking joints just shows how fragile humans are.

"I'll tell you if you don't hurt him," Galen blurts as Kennedy takes two slow steps toward him.

Kennedy's nostrils flare. "Truth be told, Galen, I was thinking about testing your pain tolerance. You have a few wounds I could easily reopen, don't you think?"

Galen relaxes against the wall, exuding as much cockiness as he can—a trick he learned from Toraf. "By all means. Whenever you're ready." He can take countless hits from a human and recover without much effort. After all, he's just been through worse—Tyrden's hard Syrena fists do much more damage than a mere human's—and even Reed seems sturdy enough against the wrath of a lock-wielding scientist.

The two dilated orbs that used to be Kennedy's eyes narrow down at Galen. "If it weren't a waste of time, I'd be tempted to call you on your bluff. As it is, you have five seconds to explain."

Galen nods. "Half-Breeds are half human, half Syrena. The result of the two mating together. As such, their bones and skin are weakened by their human genes. Not like a full-blooded Syrena. I could take blow after blow from you." Galen laughs for effect. "I'm afraid you'd tire out before me."

Not entirely true, especially given his all but fresh bruises already, but at least the somewhat altered facts appear to slow Kennedy's rage. "A cross species? Really?" Now the man looks like an eager, attentive child. He turns to Reed. "So that explains the stark contrast in coloring. You're not two separate species, but a mix of two. Fascinating."

Reed allows his lips to quiver. "He wasn't supposed to tell you those things." He casts Galen a defensive look.

Galen rolls his eyes. "Show him how you Blend before he beats you senseless. My patience only goes so far, Half-Breed."

Kennedy gives off what can only be described as a cackle. "You two are delightfully at odds, eh? But now now, Reed. Let's see about all this Blending business."

Reed's shoulders slump. "I'll need a glass of water."

37

NO ONE can really get comfortable when they have a gun pointed at them.

Yet Tyrden sits and talks as if we're in his living room and I am his guest. As if we have cookies and milk before us, instead of an unconscious injured man who is now bleeding from the nose.

And he's such an illustrious storyteller, I'm afraid he'll get too excited and pull the trigger by accident.

"So when Antonis sent another messenger to Reder, I decided to take advantage of it. Can you guess who the messenger was?" By his expectant expression, he's waiting for an answer.

"Jagen?"

Tyrden slaps his knee. "Correct!" He shakes his head. "Jagen and I hit it off as soon as we met. He understood that Neptune—and the kingdoms, of course—were capable of so much more. It's adorable how some people are just contented to exist, isn't it?"

As for me, I'd love to keep existing. And so far, asking questions is doing the job. "So you and Jagen wanted to . . . improve the kingdoms?"

"And Neptune," he says.

"How?"

"By improving the leadership, obviously."

In other words, by taking over and running things how they saw fit.

"You see, Jagen saw how poorly your grandfather ruled. The only reason he sent messengers to land was because he was constantly looking for news of your mother. Otherwise, I believe he would have severed his relationship with Neptune as well. Old fool."

My grandfather did become a recluse after my mom disappeared. I'm not saying it was right or wrong; I'm just saying it was understandable. Grief does strange things to people.

"We couldn't get close to Antonis in order to overtake him, but we could get close to Grom. As luck would have it, he was in need of a mate, and Jagen just happened to have a daughter of age."

"Paca."

"Paca," Tyrden says gleefully.

"So you're the one who taught her how to train dolphins? When she disappeared on land, she came to Neptune?"

"Oh, no, of course not. Do I look like I know how to train dolphins?" He huffs. "I taught her how to act human, dress human, do human things. Then I sent her to Florida to learn how to train the dolphins."

Toraf said he tracked Paca to the coast of Florida after she had gone "missing." So that's where she learned the hand signals she used to convince the entire Archive council—even Grom—that she had the Gift of Poseidon. She was purposely found after she had learned her skill. And so started the conspiracy to take over the Triton kingdom. Of course, the reappearance of my mother, the long lost Poseidon princess threw a huge wrench in those plans. What would have happened if Mom didn't show up? If Grom had remained mated to Paca?

"But Grom still would have been king," I say. "I don't think he would have agreed to—"

"How dare you interrupt me," Tyrden says in a low, calm voice. The look in his eyes has changed from carefree and pleasant to cold and calculating. "Do you think I'm a fool?"

"Sorry," I say quickly. "I think you're brilliant." And I think you have a gun pointed at me. "But I was just wondering how Grom played into all this."

Tyrden sneers. "He doesn't. We were going to kill him."

38

REED TAKES the cup of water and dumps it onto his forearm, then starts rubbing the damp skin furiously. Galen admits that he's just as enraptured as Kennedy—the idea of a Half-Breed with the ability to Blend is beyond Galen's wildest imaginings. Even Dr. Milligan had dismissed the possibility.

Will he be surprised, Galen thinks to himself. *If I ever get the chance to tell him.*

After what seems like enough time for the friction to cause a small fire, Reed's skin begins to camouflage itself. Kennedy gasps, and Galen wonders if Reed used the same trick to impress Emma.

What he concludes is *probably.* And he wonders if Emma can do it, too.

Reed starts to breathe heavily with his exertions. "If I stop rubbing, it will turn back to normal," he explains to Kennedy.

"Why?" Kennedy wonders aloud.

"I don't have a clue," Reed admits.

Kennedy nods, thoughtful. "Does your whole body have this ability?"

Reed shrugs, stretching out his arm. "My arms, legs, and stomach do. I assume the rest of it is fair game."

"We'll see about that." Kennedy turns on his heel to face Galen. "Can you Blend, Galen?"

"I can Blend, but I have to be completely submerged," Galen lies. He does need water, but not a whole lot of it. And he doesn't need to rub five layers of his skin off, like Reed does.

"Hmm," Kennedy says. "I'm guessing it's some sort of defense mechanism. Like the way an octopus cloaks itself by changing color?"

Galen shrugs, uninterested. "Sorry. I haven't had the opportunity to ask an octopus how it Blends."

Kennedy raises a brow. "You're not very likable, are you, Galen? Tell me, Reed, is this all you can do?"

Reed nods, rubbing his arm now for comfort instead of necessity. "That's all I can do. But him?" He nods toward Galen. "He can do something even more special than Blend. Galen has the Gift of Triton."

And the plan is officially in action.

"The gift of . . . of Triton? What on earth is that?"

"Tell him, Galen," Reed says.

"No," Galen says with finality.

Kennedy doesn't like this answer. "Galen, I feel there's a

lack of communication between us. It would be in your best interest if we resolved it quickly."

"I already told you. I'm not afraid of you and your scary metal lock."

Kennedy's mouth becomes a straight line. Galen can tell he's on the verge of throwing a Rayna-level fit. "Yes, you've made that very clear, haven't you? But how do you think your Half-Breed frenemy here feels about me and my scary lock?"

At this, Reed stiffens. "What? I've told you everything! He's the one not opening up!"

"I told you he's had enough," Galen protests calmly. "He can't take anymore. He wouldn't make a very good test subject if he were dead." At least, that's what Dr. Milligan always says when Galen gets himself into trouble.

Kennedy chuckles. "No, not dead, of course not. But I can work with 'damaged.' So what do you say, Galen?"

"I say go to hale." Or was it hell that Rachel was always talking about? He can't remember.

At any rate, Kennedy seems to grasp his meaning. He fists the lock in his hands and strides once again toward Reed. Galen allows him to strike him a first time, right in the jaw. It's something Galen had intended to do anyway, possibly worse, ever since he learned Reed put his lips on Emma. One more blow is not going to make or break Reed, just hurt his feelings a tad.

When Kennedy raises his arm again, Galen intervenes.

"Stop. I'll show you." Galen says it with a sigh, and not only for Mr. Kennedy's benefit.

Reed spits blood on the floor beside him and glowers at Galen from across the room.

Kennedy raises his fist further. "Are you sure? You seem wishy-washy, Galen." He goes in for another blow, and Galen is tempted to let him do it. But he knows it's not right anymore. Well, not that it was right to begin with but . . .

"I said I'll show you. Are all humans hard of hearing?"

Why Kennedy continues to put up with his smart remarks is beyond Galen. He must, in a way, like to be bullied. Or maybe after all these years as a laughingstock he could just be used to it. "I'm beginning to wonder what Emma sees in you, Galen. You're not very charming at all."

Galen shakes his chains for emphasis. Kennedy says, "I have good news. I'm going to remove those chains very shortly, Galen. But first I want to show you something." From the back of his shirt he retrieves a small handgun. Galen knows what they can do. Rachel had a few of those little things in crevices all over the house.

"This is a gun, you ignorant fish. Maybe my fists and my puny little lock won't penetrate your skin, but I can assure you that at close range, these bullets will tear through your flesh in a most unpleasant way. Shall I give you a demonstration?" He turns to face the far end of the cabin and takes aim at nothing. The shot is loud and splinters the wood on the far wall. A long, straight rod of sunlight streams in through the hole it produced.

"Up close, I'm a fair shot, Galen. Don't make me waste

bullets on you. Not when we've just really started to develop a relationship."

"You were an unhappy child, weren't you," Reed drolls. "Sounds like Daddy issues."

Whatever that means. *If Reed keeps distracting him, how will I lure him outside?* Besides, Reed is supposed to be afraid for his life right now, or something close to it. His sudden burst of confidence is ill-planned, to say the least.

"Surely you of all people don't want to talk about Daddy issues, Reed." Kennedy laughs. "Not the shadow of the almighty Reder."

Reed grimaces. He knows he's said too much, and yet he's been provoked badly enough to keep talking. Galen can see war on his face. Talk back, no don't, yes let's. Reed's pride has taken a harder hit than his face ever did.

"Why don't you just let him go?" Galen says, bringing the attention back to him. "He's just a Half-Breed. I'm full-blooded."

Kennedy rolls his eyes. "Oh, yes, let Reed go so he can run away to his pa and tell him everything so the entire town of Neptune can go on a witch hunt looking for us. No, thank you." Kennedy does something to make the gun in his hand click, then pops two more bullets into it from his jeans' pocket. "Fully loaded. Now, Galen, what is this gift of yours?"

Galen says, "It's a surprise," at the same time Reed says, "He can talk to fish!"

If it wouldn't make a fantastic noise with the chains and all,

Galen would run a frustrated hand through his hair. Galen decides Reed is officially an idiot.

Kennedy laughs. "This smells like a trap, boys. I mean, don't tell anyone, but even I can talk to fish."

Reed rolls his eyes. "Except when Galen does it, the fish listen and obey him."

This ignites a fire in Kennedy's eyes. "You're bluffing."

"Really? I'm going to have to take another beating because you won't just go get proof for yourself?"

And Galen decides that Reed is actually a genius. The plan was to tell Kennedy about his gift of speed, but that would put the lunatic biologist on high alert as soon as they got to the water. Telling him Galen has the Gift of Poseidon is much better. Kennedy will be so intent on watching the fish's reaction to Galen's voice, Galen will be able to catch him off guard long enough to get into the water and swim away as fast as his Gift of Triton will take him.

Reed adjusted according to Kennedy's intelligence.

Brilliant.

"Is this true, Galen?"

Galen turns away, doing his best to act betrayed. Kennedy takes it as a yes.

He strolls over to Reed and grabs his face, sticking the gun in his left eye socket. "I hope you're not lying to me, Reed. Because if you are," Kennedy moves the gun lower, to Reed's hand.

Then he pulls the trigger. Reed shrieks and squirms as Kennedy backs away slowly. Blood oozes down his forearm, dripping off at his elbow.

"If you are lying—hush now, pay attention, Reed—I'll cut out your tongue."

With that, Kennedy pulls a small key from his jeans' pocket. "Shall we, Galen?"

Guilt tightens around Galen's chest like a giant crab claw as they leave Reed behind to suffer alone.

The afterglow of the sun filters through the trees behind them, staving off the full effect of dusk at the shore. "If you keep yelling like that, you'll scare away all the fish," Galen whispers to Kennedy. Which Galen couldn't care less about. "Stop splashing around."

But Kennedy is in danger of popping several blood vessels, pacing barefoot back and forth along a small patch of the beach. Already, he's allowed Galen to get calf deep, distracted by his own fit throwing. Which might do more than scare away the fish; all this noise could attract attention. And Tyrden's men could be anywhere.

"Did Reed really lie to me?" Kennedy shrieks. "Did he really send me down here to the lake knowing I'll carve out his tongue?"

Galen sighs. "You've gone and spooked the fish again. I think we should move deeper into the water."

"Oh, I'm sure you do!" Kennedy yells. "What, so you can swim away?"

This catches Galen off guard. Obviously Kennedy isn't as distracted as Galen had fervently hoped he was. A breeze wrestles through the trees, and Kennedy points the gun in the woods. "Who's there? Show yourself."

Galen rolls his eyes. "It's the wind. Look, you're making too much noise. People are going to be looking for you since you took Reed. If you want to stay hidden, then shut up."

"I've made tracks all over the place. They'll be going in circles for days looking for us." Kennedy eyes Galen curiously. "You don't want to get caught in the grasp of Neptune either, I take it."

"It's not my favorite town."

"But Emma is there."

Galen considers. "Apparently Emma is safe there. I'm not."

"Ahhh, so they accepted your girlfriend but not you. Interesting." Kennedy taps his finger on his cheek, thoughtful. "You really don't remember me, do you? Oh, but I would recognize you anywhere. You're the reason I'm here, after all."

Galen stiffens. "What?"

Kennedy laughs. "Maybe if I donned a mask and snorkel it would jog your memory. You know, I've always wondered, did you know Jerry before our little run-in at the reef?"

Jerry? *Dr. Milligan.* It all comes back to Galen in a tidal wave. He was just a fingerling then, playing around the reef with Toraf and Rayna when he spotted a human—Dr. Milligan—lying on the ocean floor, clutching his leg. The doctor had strayed from his snorkeling group and developed a cramp and was on the verge of passing out. Galen pulled him to the surface immediately and to his boat. Dr. Milligan had been with two friends—one whom Galen realizes now was Kennedy—and when they saw Galen's fin, they tried pulling him into the boat as well. But Dr. Milligan put the boat in gear, full-speed. The other two snorkelers lost their balance and dropped Galen.

That was the first time he'd met Dr. Milligan. And the first time he'd come in contact with Kennedy. Later, Kennedy and the other man claimed they'd seen a merman. Dr. Milligan contradicted them, and the sighting was dismissed as a hoax.

Kennedy smiles as the astonishment washes over Galen. "Ah, so you do remember. It was starting to hurt my feelings." His face turns hard. "How fitting that I've recaptured you after all these years. You're my unicorn, you know that?"

Galen remembers what Kennedy said in the cabin. That he considers himself a mermaid hunter, which has made him a laughingstock among his peers. *And I'm the reason for it.*

What are the odds that he would ever find me again? Galen shakes his head at the unlikelihood of it all.

Kennedy nods. "Yes, let it all sink in, Galen. I bet you're wondering why I haven't just shot you yet, aren't you? Because you and I are going to have a long life together. One exhibition after another. Can you just imagine the millions of dollars we'll make together showing the world that mermaids really do exist?"

He wants to put me on display? "If money is what you want, I have plenty of that. I'll pay you to let me go. And Reed."

Kennedy purses his lips. "I think we both know it's not about money, Galen. You ruined me, you little snot. You ruined my future, my credibility. I couldn't even get a teaching job."

Galen can tell that the bitterness is beginning to really fester inside Kennedy. *He might think better of all this talk about living and decide to shoot me. Now would be a really good time to think about escaping again.*

Galen nods. "I'm sorry."

This strikes Kennedy by surprise. "Are you? For what, exactly? Getting caught?"

"For doing it to you again."

And Galen dives in, shocking even himself.

His fin rips through what's left of his twisted jeans, which is a worthy sacrifice for the chance at escape. He's stretched to his full length when a bullet whizzes by his head, then a staccato of shots all around, making thin water tunnels ahead and beside him. Galen's tail is still sore, and it takes careful maneuvering to keep a straight course, but he shoots forward as fast as he can, remembering that Kennedy is a terrible shot but that he's desperate. Plus, luck hasn't exactly been on Galen's side lately— and he's not sure how many bullets the gun has left.

He's mindful to keep low, toward the bottom, in case Kennedy set any traps this far down the river. He hears more gunshots in the distance but sees no bullets hurtling by.

Truth be told, he's torn between going back and helping Reed or pressing on. *But what can I do against a gun? And how would I get Reed free of the chains? I could hardly help myself when I was tied to a chair.*

No, if he's going to go back, he needs help.

And he needs to find Emma.

39

TYRDEN PEEKS out the window shade. "Looks like the streets have died down a bit. Everyone who's not looking for Reed is at home enjoying their dinner. Probably waiting by the phone for news." He turns back to me, rubbing the back of his neck. "This little town runs like clockwork. Day in and day out. Everything shuts down by five thirty."

Beside his foot, Frank stirs, moving one leg and groaning. The other leg is bent at an odd angle probably broken from his plunge down the stairs. Tyrden nudges that one with his boot and Frank whimpers.

"Stop hurting him," I say, closing my eyes. I sound braver than I am. I still don't know what Tyrden wants from me. Why is he keeping me here? I keep hoping and praying someone will come check on us, that they'll come through the door and see what he's done.

Then again, he'd probably shoot them on the spot.

"It's almost time to go." He walks back toward the couch.

"Go where?"

"I have a special place for you, princess. I dug it this morning."

He's going to kill me. I swallow the vomit and terror as it rises from deep within me. "Why?" My voice is shaky now. In fact, my whole body seems to quiver from the inside out. "Why are you doing this?"

He gives me a pouty face. "Oh, Emma, how naive can you be? Don't you remember the story I just told you?"

Is he worried that he'll be punished for his role in the conspiracy? I wish he hadn't told me about it. Now I'm a liability to him. Now he feels he has to eliminate me. "No one else knows about that. If you let me go, I won't tell anyone, I swear." But that isn't true. Jagen and Paca know about the conspiracy and about Neptune, and they haven't told anyone, despite their sentence to the Ice Caverns.

Why is that?

"Jagen and Paca kept the secret. I will, too."

Tyrden sneers. "You think I actually trust Jagen and Paca?"

"Don't you?"

He clinks the barrel of the gun to his head. "Think, Emma. Why would they hide anything now that they've been caught? Why would they continue to keep the secret?"

He's getting frustrated with me, I can tell. There's a turbulence in his eyes that hints at unpredictability. His behavior is all over the place, too. Calm then agitated. Mild then excitable.

I have to at least guess at the answer, if it'll make him happy—for the moment. "Because you're their friend and they wouldn't betray you?"

He laughs pityingly, crossing his arms. "I don't believe I've ever met someone so obtuse."

Insult me, fine. But keep pointing that gun everywhere but at me.

Tyrden shakes his head. "Jagen still has an interest on land, Emma. A Half-Breed son. His name is Asten. Lives two towns over with his mother. I check in on them every once in a while. He's getting big. Almost two years old now."

The realization of what he's saying slaps me in the face. "You threatened to kill his son if he told."

He tilts his head, giving me an off-balance smile. "You see, I have to make sure my secrets are safe."

"If you let me go, I promise I won't tell. I'll keep your secret, too." But we both know it's a lie. As soon as I was in the clear, I'd go straight to Reder and tell him about Asten, that his life is in danger. I'd make sure the baby was safe, that Tyrden couldn't do him any harm.

"Of course, our situation is different, Emma. You and I have already reached an impasse."

"I still don't understand."

"You remember the part of my story where Jagen and Paca had the Royals right where they wanted them?" He takes several slow steps toward me. I nod, eyeing the end of the barrel now pointed at me again. "Then of course you recall who showed up with a wall of fish and ruined everything."

40

GALEN PRESSES himself against the wall, listening for any movements or noise coming from Reder's house. There are no lights on, and like the entire town of Neptune, it seems deserted—which Galen couldn't be more thankful for, considering he's naked.

He creeps up the steps to the front porch and jiggles the doorknob as quietly as he can. Peering in the window, he finds no one in the living room or dining room. He decides to make an entrance in the back of the house; if he has to break a window to get in, he doesn't want to be seen by any passersby from the road.

He tiptoes around the side of the house, using the moonlight as his guide, and nearly trips on the coiled-up water hose lying close to the back porch. Opening the screen door, he cringes when it gives off a boisterous creak, which reminds him a little of the way Toraf belches after he's had too much to eat.

To Galen's surprise—and relief—the back door is unlocked. *Thank Triton for small neighborly towns.* He inches through the house, checking each corner and room for signs of life and finding none. Deciding clothes would make this whole break-in less stressful, he makes his way up the stairs to find Reder's closet. Reder's build is more like Galen's than Reed's is.

He pulls on the first pair of jeans he can find and slides into a worn T-shirt. He tests out some of Reder's shoes and finds them a bit big, but if the laces are tight enough, they won't fall off.

Galen had hoped to find Emma here. It's the one place he thought she would be. Now that she isn't, he's not sure where else to look. *I'll try calling her.*

He eases his way back down the stairs and into the kitchen where he remembers seeing a telephone hanging on the wall. Dialing her number, he holds his breath, knowing already that it would be too easy if she answered, that tonight is not going to work out that way.

When it goes to voice mail, he hangs up and dials Dr. Milligan. Though he's quite certain no one else is in the house with him, he still whispers when his friend picks up.

"Dr. Milligan, it's Galen. I need you to come to Neptune. Kennedy is here, and he's taken Reed. He's going to expose the Syrena."

"Galen? Neptune? What?"

"Kennedy—one of the men you were snorkeling with when we first met—he's here in Neptune. Neptune is a town in Tennessee full of Half-Breeds and Syrena. He's got Reed. And I can't find Emma."

After a long pause, Dr. Milligan says, "Okay, okay, just calm down." But to Galen, it's Dr. Milligan who seems alarmed. "Kennedy you say? Greg Kennedy? I haven't seen him in years."

"He's been busy hunting Syrena. And now he's found some." Galen describes all that has happened in short, choppy sentences that may or may not serve as a decent explanation. He's hoping Dr. Milligan can follow—and that he picks up on the urgency of the situation. Apparently, he does.

"Oh, dear. This isn't good."

Galen nods into the phone. "I know. Can you come?"

"I'll catch the next flight out."

When they hang up, Galen dials Grom. He's surprised when his brother answers. "Galen, where are you?"

"I'm in Reder's house. I can't find Emma and she's in danger."

Galen hears a slight shuffle on the other end of the phone, and suddenly he's talking to Nalia. "Emma's in the basement of city hall."

"How . . . How do you know that?"

"We've spoken on the phone. Go get her. And tell Toraf we don't need a hostage."

"Toraf? Where's Toraf? A hostage?" Didn't he tell them not to come to Neptune? Still, he's glad they didn't listen. He could use their help right about now. Especially since they've been in touch with Emma.

"He's on his way to town to kidnap someone for us. We were going to do a hostage exchange."

Galen shakes his head. "Nevermind. I don't even want to know. I'm going to find Emma. Where should we meet you?"

"We're in a picnic area right outside of town. It's a little off the road."

Galen nods. "I remember seeing a sign for it on the way in."

"Good. Hurry. Oh, and Galen?"

"Yes?"

"I'm going to beat you senseless for leaving Emma all alone there." And then Nalia hangs up.

Galen beats his head against the wall. How could this possibly get worse?

Before he leaves, he takes the magnetic dry erase board from the refrigerator and scribbles a message on it. Hopefully someone will come home and see it before anything else bad happens.

Tyrden and Kennedy are your enemies.

He places the board on the kitchen table and leaves.

When Galen gets back into town, he's forced to dodge into alleyways between buildings. The streets of Neptune are flooded with people wearing orange vests and carrying flashlights. Probably search parties for Reed. By their downtrodden expressions, they haven't found him yet.

Galen ducks behind a dumpster just as a couple passes by

on the sidewalk in front of him. He has to get to city hall without being detected, but he's not sure exactly where it is.

"I knew I smelled something," a voice says behind him.

He turns to face Toraf. "How long have you been there?" Galen hisses. Still, he's never been so glad to see his friend.

"I was here first. You almost stepped on my foot. Not very observant, minnow."

"Have you found Emma yet?"

Toraf shakes his head. "She's not at city hall. I already checked."

"How did you know where city hall was?"

Toraf shrugs. "I asked someone. They're pretty friendly here."

Galen massages his temples with his fingers. "And have you already gotten yourself a hostage?"

"Nope. That's what I was in the process of doing before you almost head-butted me, trying not to get noticed."

"You can't just take someone out in the open in the middle of town."

"I was going to call a cab and get them to take me to the picnic area where everyone else is. Boom. Hostage taken. What's with your face? I hope the other guy looks worse."

"This town is too small to need cabs." He wonders where Toraf learned about calling for cabs but decides to put the question off for later. Now is not the time to go off on a tangent especially where Toraf is involved. Still, his friend's plan was rather impressive.

"Um, minnow? Not to interrupt your expert strategizing,

but . . ." Toraf points to the street behind them. "Isn't that Emma?"

Galen whips around. Sure enough, Emma is in the passenger seat of a car stopped at the only stoplight in town. And Tyrden is driving.

41

I WANT to scream at the people around me. To beat on the window and yell for help. But Tyrden is pointing the gun at my stomach, and I know he'll shoot before anyone can come to my aid. Before anyone will realize what happened.

So my choice is getting shot now or later. It's just that I think I have a better chance for escape later. Now, if I even move, I'm dead. Later, when we stop wherever we're going, he'll have to get out of the car at some point. There will be that brief second when the gun isn't pointed at me. At least, that's what I'm hoping. That's when I'll make my move.

Rachel taught me that when someone has a gun, the best chance you've got is to run away in a zigzag pattern, that it's harder to hit a moving target. She says that way, even if they do shoot and hit, it lowers the odds of them striking a vital organ—and increases your chances of getting away.

I'm startled from my thoughts when one of the pedestrians knocks on my window. I'm too terrified to look up at whoever it is. "What should I do?" I ask Tyrden quietly.

"See what he wants," he says. "And remember what I've got in my hand." Tyrden lowers the gun to rest it on the seat between us, hiding it in a shadow cast by a streetlamp.

I roll down the window. And come face to face with Toraf. My eyes feel like they've doubled in size. *Toraf is here. Toraf is here. Toraf is here.*

"Hi," he says, poking his head in. I want to push him out, to tell him to run, to tell him to help me, to tell him there's a gun. My mouth is hung on the hinges, unwilling to make the words. "Can I get a ride to city hall?" he says.

There's no way Toraf doesn't see the gun. *What is he doing?*

"Sorry, we're not going that way," Tyrden says, his voice all friendly and cheerful. He presses the gun into my hip. "And we're late getting to where we're going."

"Oh, sorry. Could you just give me some quick directions then?"

"Sure." A bit of his impatience shines through. "Turn right at this light and—"

The sound of shattering glass hits me from the driver's side before the actual shards do. Toraf flings the passenger door open, and I spill out of the car on top of him as I hear the gun go off behind me. It makes contact with the door panel inches from my head.

"Get up, get up," Toraf says, pulling me to my feet. He wraps his arm around my waist and hauls me to the curb.

There are screams all around us. The car bounces up and down, squeaking the suspension, which is made more horrifying by a succession of male grunts resounding from the front seat. After a few seconds, another shot rings out and with a clink, the gun falls onto the pavement beside the car.

"I'll be right back," Toraf says, kicking it away. Then he all but dives into the passenger seat.

In a matter of milliseconds, Galen appears from the driver's side, and my stomach does cartwheels. He drags an unconscious Tyrden out of the car by his armpits and unceremoniously throws him in the backseat. He seems oblivious to the crowd that has gathered around him. He spots me on the sidewalk, doing nothing at all to save myself or him. Galen appears relieved that I'm not being useful.

"Emma!" he yells. "Get in the car."

Robotically, I scramble back to the passenger side just as Toraf's feet fly over the bench seat and he takes his place next to Tyrden's limp body in the back. "Go go go," Toraf says, and Galen stomps on the gas, parting the crowd.

The advantage of being in a small town is that you can get out of it quickly. Two minutes, and we're speeding down the highway. I'm clutching the door panel, trying not to think about the bullet hole in it. Also, trying to absorb what just freaking happened.

"Angelfish," Galen says beside me. He puts a gentle hand on my leg, and I instinctively cover it with mine. "Are you okay?"

I nod, eyes wide. "You?" It's a valid question. He's got bruises all over his face, a puffy eye, and both his top and bottom lips are split. Some of the bruises are yellowing already, which means they're older than the recent scuffle with Tyrden in this car. I've never seen him look so rough.

"I'm going to be," he says with confidence. "Once I get you safe."

"What should I do if he wakes up?" Toraf says behind us. I glance back at Tyrden, who is folded up into an almost ball in the seat. He looks like he's been packed in a suitcase in a hurry.

Galen looks in the rearview. "Keep your boot in his face and get ready to use it."

"Will do."

"Galen?" I say softly. I don't know whether to laugh or cry, but whichever I choose is going to be done in a state of hysteria.

"Hmm?"

"Where have you been?"

He takes a deep breath and squeezes my knee. "You're not going to believe everything that has happened."

I take in Galen's face, the bullet holes in the car, the man we've kidnapped in the backseat, and the fact that he was holding me hostage not ten minutes before. "Try me."

42

GALEN DUMPS Tyrden in the back of the SUV Nalia rented from the airport. With concentrated movements, he starts wrapping him in layer after layer of rope she'd gotten from a hardware store a few towns down. *She really was prepared to take a hostage.* With his teeth, he tears off a piece of duct tape and places it carefully over Tyrden's mouth.

"You should put it around his whole head," Rayna says from behind him. "It'll hurt more if he has to pull it out of his hair." Then she smacks the sleeping man on the cheek. Hard. "He's really out of it."

Triton's trident, but Galen has missed his twin sister. "Hopefully he won't get the chance to pull it off at all."

"He won't." She leans against the back of the SUV and slowly raises a hand to touch his face. "This guy did that to you?"

"It doesn't feel as bad as it looks." Which isn't a lie. His lips will tear themselves back open if he's not careful, but other than that, everything seems to be healing well. At least, that's what Nalia had said.

He shuts the hatch to the SUV and turns toward the picnic tables where everyone is gathered. "You coming?" he asks Rayna.

Slowly, she shakes her head. She walks around to the side of vehicle and opens the rear passenger door. "I'm going to keep an eye on him."

Galen is about to tell her that their hostage is not to be toyed with, but he sees the hard look in her eyes and thinks better of it. She knows exactly what she's doing. "If he moves I'm going to beat the smell out of him," she says. Then she hops in and shuts the door behind her.

Maybe it's best that it is Rayna standing guard over Tyrden. Out of all of them, Rayna might be the only one who wouldn't hesitate if the situation called for it. His sister has always been fond of asking for forgiveness rather than permission. And her temper is unmatched in all the kingdoms.

Which is exactly the kind of vigilance Tyrden deserves.

Galen walks to the picnic tables and takes the seat next to Emma and across from Grom and Nalia. Toraf stands against a tree behind them, watching Rayna watch Tyrden. Antonis sits at the picnic table beside them, waiting expectantly.

Galen and Emma have much to tell about their individual experiences in Neptune. Emma starts by telling them about the town itself, how it came to be, how Reder wants peace and unity between the ocean dwellers and the land dwellers, and how

Tyrden was involved in Jagen and Paca's conspiracy to overtake the Triton territory. And a fact which shocks everyone: Jagen has a Half-Breed son. "We have to make sure he's going to be okay," she says.

"We'll do the best we can," Grom says. "I would say that right now he's safe, since Tyrden is tied up in the back of a vehicle."

Galen tells them of his captivity with Tyrden, then with Kennedy. He nods toward the SUV. "We've got other problems besides him," he tells Grom. "Dr. Milligan is on his way here to help us deal with the Kennedy situation."

"What exactly is the situation?" Nalia folds her hands in front of her. "You escaped."

Galen tells them about Kennedy shooting Reed and his intention to run experiments on him. "I have to go back for him," he says with finality. "He helped me escape and I owe him that. We can't leave him there."

"And we can't let Kennedy run experiments on him," Nalia interjects. "All of us are at stake. Though I'm not sure I understand how Dr. Milligan can help us."

"Maybe he can talk some sense into Kennedy," Galen says. "Maybe we can buy him off." But Galen knows the unlikelihood of that. Still, he believes Dr. Milligan can help. He's just not sure how.

"But the whole town has been looking for him," Emma says. "If they can't find him, how can we?"

"He told me he purposely threw them off his trail," Galen says. "I need to get to the river. Then I'll be able to find my way back to the embankment where I escaped. From there, we'll find the cabin." *And hopefully Reed.*

"Then what?" Grom says. "Then we have two captives from Neptune, and a human scientist and no plan. I think that's a little more than we can handle."

"Tyrden isn't just a captive," Nalia corrects. "He's coming back with us to the ocean for his own tribunal. His crimes against the kingdoms are too great to ignore."

"Neptune won't like that," Grom says. "He's their citizen, after all."

"Ask me if I care," Nalia says. "And why do *you* care? Neptune shouldn't exist. We don't have to recognize their authority over anything. He screwed with my family. He's not getting away with it."

"But Neptune does exist," Antonis says gently. "And Grom is right—a little diplomacy goes a long way. I'll go back to the kingdoms and recruit some backup for us." He hops up from his seat and places a hand on Grom's shoulder. "The town of Neptune can no longer be ignored by the kingdoms. We must begin talks with them."

Grom shakes his head. "You put us in this position. You and your secrets."

"It's a secret that has been kept for thousands of years. It would be unfair to call it *my* secret." Antonis crosses his arms. "And they want peace. They always have. I think now might be the time to pursue it. The Archives accepted Emma, after all."

"Emma is one exception. One," Grom says. "This is asking too much too soon."

"Then maybe we shouldn't ask the council just yet," Antonis says. "Maybe we should limit the discussion to those present. Allow the Archives to ease into the idea over time."

"You've been thinking much about this," Grom says irritably. "You have this all worked out in your mind, haven't you?"

"Of course not," Antonis says. "Well, maybe a little. That being said, maybe recruiting backup isn't a good idea. We don't want to involve more than is necessary for—"

Nalia buries her face in her hands. "Unbelievable. All this time—"

"Look," Galen says. "I know this is an important discussion to have, but we're wasting time where Reed is concerned. I don't want to give Kennedy the chance to move him somewhere else." Everyone nods in silent agreement. "I think Grom and Toraf and I should go."

"I'm not leaving Rayna here with that lunatic," Toraf says.

"You would trade one lunatic for another?" Galen says, though he knows Toraf's mind is made up. Toraf is overprotective of his sister, which can be good and bad.

"Nalia, Emma, and Antonis can handle Tyrden. He's bound and gagged. There's no reason Rayna can't go with us."

Galen doesn't like the idea of leaving Emma behind with Tyrden either—especially since he just got her back. But the fact is, Tyrden is tied up, and Nalia is practically an expert at shooting a gun—three of which she happens to be in possession of right now. And since Emma can't shape a fin, she'll be slowing the group down in the river.

He and Emma exchange looks of understanding. She nods slightly, giving him her acceptance of what can't be helped.

"Okay," Galen says. "We'll take Rayna. Let's go. We can't wait for daylight. And watch for traps."

They wade from the river onto shore in the moonlight. The trees and bushes around them are black and blue shapes, barely discernible in places where the canopy of the forest blocks the night sky. Barefoot, Toraf, Rayna, Galen, and Grom make their way to the tree line.

"How far is it from here?" Rayna whispers.

"Not far," Galen says, taking the lead into the woods.

"How are we going to overtake him if he has a gun?" Grom says.

"We outnumber him," Galen says. "And there are trees to hide behind. Plus, he's not a great shot."

"Perfect," Toraf grumbles.

"You're the one who wanted to bring Rayna," Galen says.

"Can I change my mind?"

"No," the twins say in unison.

"All of you, quiet," Grom says. "Galen, stay focused."

Galen squints into the distance. The outline of a cabin shapes itself against the trees behind it. "We're here," he whispers, pointing ahead of them. He motions for them to come closer to him. "We're going to surround him and go from there."

"What if he won't come out?" Rayna says.

"He will once he knows we're armed."

"We're not armed," Toraf says.

Galen picks up a stick from the ground and breaks off a few twigs. He points the end of it at Toraf. "In the dark, we are armed."

Toraf nods and finds his own stick, then for effect, he makes a shooting sound. Galen rolls his eyes.

As a group, they creep toward the cabin, sticks at the ready. Every time they break a sprig or crunch leaves under their feet, Galen cringes. *There is no way Kennedy doesn't know we're coming.* He takes off into a light jog, motioning for the others to circle the rest of the cabin. Galen claims a tree directly in front of the door.

When everyone is in place, Galen yells. "Kennedy, we've got you surrounded. Come out and we won't hurt you."

But Kennedy doesn't answer. In fact, there don't seem to be any sounds or movements coming from inside. Galen finds a rock and throws it at the lone window in the front, smashing out the bottom corner of it.

Still nothing.

There are no lights on within. Slowly Galen eases toward the steps, feeling a bit childish as he raises his stick like a gun. In the patch of moonlight, he can make out the padlock hanging from the door, locking it shut. *Kennedy is not here.*

"Reed?" Galen calls. "Reed, are you in there?" He peers in through the busted window. Reed's shackles lay sprawled out on the floor under the window on the other side. Kennedy has already moved him.

Toraf and Grom meet him around front, and Rayna is not far behind. "They could still be close," Galen tells them. "If he's smart, he'll be moving farther south. We should start—"

"Shhhh!" Rayna hisses. "Do you hear that sound?"

They all hold still. For a moment, the only noise that can be heard is the rustle of the windblown canopy above. Then a very distinct buzzing hits them from the direction of the river.

"A boat," Galen says. "It has to be them."

They sprint back to the embankment, not caring about the low-hanging limbs and branches whipping at their faces. In the distance, they see a small yellow light skitting across the river—heading south.

"They're moving fast," Grom says.

"Maybe I can catch them," Galen says, wading in. Rayna grabs his arm. "We all saw your fin, Galen. You need to rest it. Let me handle this."

"You'll never catch them," Galen says as Toraf huffs. "Absolutely not."

Without so much as a word of warning, Rayna opens her mouth. And the Gift of Triton moves down the river in a giant wave.

43

GRANDFATHER TAKES the seat next to me at the picnic table. He clears his throat and makes a show of smoothing out the wrinkles in his T-shirt. Finally he says, "Well?"

"Um. Well, what?" It sounds a tad disrespectful, so I make up for it with, "I mean, I'm not sure what you're asking me, Grandfather."

"Are you upset with me that I sent you to Neptune?"

"You could have told me what I'd find there."

"But you know why I didn't."

"Galen."

Grandfather sighs. "I find that Galen and Grom are of similar disposition, though neither would care to admit it. They both seek safety first, pleasure later. Sometimes this can be a good thing. Most times, in fact. But other times, this can be an inhibition to experiencing a full life."

I wonder if he's thinking about Grom forbidding Mom to go on land all those years ago, and thus starting the fight that separated them for decades. I'd like to think I've cured Galen of forbidding me to do things, but there are still times when I can see hesitation lurking in his eyes, a fight he doesn't quite let bubble to the surface. He doesn't like when I do certain things, but at least he doesn't tell me not to.

But with Neptune, I think Grandfather was right. I think Galen might have put his foot down, had he known what we'd find in city limits. "I'm not upset with you," I decide as I say it. "I know why you couldn't warn me beyond what you did." Our experience in Neptune wasn't the stuff of my wildest dreams, especially after what happened to Galen while we were there. But learning about the existence of other Half-Breeds, of a town that accepts both species and lives in unity? It gave me hope. A blossoming kind of hope that might be dead-headed after the events of tonight.

"And how do you feel about the peace Neptune wants with the kingdoms?" He lowers his voice then, probably to avoid the reach of Mom's hearing.

"I want it to happen." Period.

"Then let's work on it together, shall we?"

I'm about to ask him how he proposes to do that, but suddenly Galen and Toraf appear at the edge of the woods, hauling Reed between them, helping him walk. Grom and Rayna materialize behind them, Kennedy thrown over Grom's shoulder like a sleeping child. His arms sway back and forth like dangling banana peels.

Galen helps Reed sit at one of the tables and ushers for Mom. "His hand is injured." There's a cloth tied tightly around Reed's palm, and from the looks of Galen's tattered shirt, he was the donor of it.

Rayna cheerfully trades places with Mom, who's been standing guard at the SUV. Tyrden only woke up once, briefly—until Mom knocked him unconscious again with the butt of her handgun like some sort of gangster.

Mom brings a bottle of water to the table where Galen, Grom, and Reed sit. Toraf joins Rayna at the SUV, helping to bind up Kennedy the same way Tyrden is. I suddenly have an out-of-body experience, taking in the scene out of context.

If someone were to decide to have a picnic here right now, we'd be screwed.

I keep my seat next to Grandfather, adjusting on the bench to hide my nervousness. Right now, anything we do seems like a duty. This picnic table feels like my post for now, and I stand aside until I feel useful. This family-friendly picnic area has turned into a basecamp for mermaid gypsies.

Carefully removing the wrapping, Mom examines Reed's wound. He's a good sport, only grimacing here and there, but never verbally relaying the pain he's in. "You have several broken bones," she says after a few minutes. "I'll have to make a run to a drugstore and get some bandages and antibiotic ointment. You'll need a cast, so the bones can set correctly. You . . . Does the town of Neptune have a hospital?"

He shakes his head. "We have a doctor. We try to avoid the hospital. For obvious reasons."

Mom nods. I notice that she doesn't tell him we'll get him to the doctor right away; apparently we won't. "This is going to hurt," she says, holding up the water bottle. Reed looks away as she pours it onto his palm. I look away, too. I don't have the stomach for open flesh. After she's done cleaning it, Mom walks back to the SUV and retrieves a clean shirt, tearing it into usable strips, all but ignoring the two men tied up in the back. She rewraps Reed's wound and gives him some Tylenol. "It's all I have," she says.

Reed accepts it and takes a swig of the bottled water offered to him. He looks at Galen, then at Grom. "Are you going to take me home? Or did I go from one captor to the other?"

Galen folds his hands behind his head and lets out a breath. "I guess it's time to talk about our next move. My vote is to let the kings handle it."

"Of course they'll handle it," Mom says.

But I know that Galen made the statement for my benefit. He's letting me know that the world doesn't rest on my shoulders and that whatever they decide to do about the town of Neptune, it's not a decision I have to make. It's meant to bring me relief.

Or is he telling me I don't have a say? We'll see.

Grom begins to collect sticks and pieces of wood, piling them in one of the charcoal grills for a fire. Toraf helps him, and within minutes, we've got something to cook dinner with. Except, we don't have any dinner unless someone caught more than Kennedy when they went down to the river.

I notice that Galen doesn't help with the fire. He stares at it for a long time, as if hypnotized. For the several minutes he stares at it, I stare at him. That's how I know the exact moment he looks up. And I'm startled by the look in his eyes.

Abruptly, he strides across the camp and stands before me, his gaze piercing into me. There's an underlying torment there—and a hint of reserve. Something is bothering him. And it has to do with me. "I would like to speak to you, Emma. Alone."

44

GALEN LEADS her away from the picnic tables and into the woods. They can still see the campfire from here, but it's far enough away that his words will be for Emma's ears only. He stops them after a few more feet, glancing back at the camp then to her.

Her eyes are huge and filled with questions. He doesn't know where to begin.

"Galen, you're making me nervous," she whispers. Her voice is uneven, like she might be on the verge of tears. Which is exactly what he doesn't want.

He runs a hand through his hair. "I didn't bring you out here to upset you. I just . . . A lot has happened between us—*to* us—since our disagreement at the hotel. And I think we need to talk about it, before anything else happens."

She clears her throat. "When you didn't come back, I thought you'd left me. I thought it was over."

Of course she did. What else was she to think? "Did you want it to be over?" It's not the question he was going to ask, but it's the one he wants to know the most.

"Galen—"

"If you did, just tell me. I won't be mad." He feels himself losing control of his emotions and remembers how that fared last time. *Calm down. Talk it out.* "I said some things that didn't make any sense. I wasn't in a good frame of mind. I was in shock, I guess, from finding Reed and dealing with Reder—no. No excuses." He shifts his weight from one foot to the other. But it's not his physical weight making him feel heavy. "I've had plenty of time to think about things. To think about us."

"I didn't want it to be over."

He lifts his hand, caressing her cheek with the back of it. She closes her eyes against it. He doesn't know if that's good or bad. "The reason I wanted you to live in the ocean with me, the reason I wanted to get away from land is because . . ."

"You think I'll live longer. That ocean life will be easier on my body, like it is for Syrena."

"Humans are fragile."

"You're talking about Rachel."

"I guess I am. Yes, I'm talking about Rachel."

"What happened to her was an accident. It was no one's fault."

He shakes his head. They could argue that for several cycles of the moon. "It's not even that. It's . . . That can't happen to you. Dying, I mean."

"It's going to one day. It's going to happen to us all. Dying is a part of living."

"I try to tell myself that, I swear. I try to appreciate the quality-not-quantity thing. But I keep thinking about how you're going to die first. Unless . . . But I want you to be happy. I don't ever want you to feel like my prisoner."

She grimaces. "Oh. That. I was mad when I said that, Galen. I don't really feel that way. It's more like the other way around. I feel like *I'm* keeping *you* from the ocean. I feel that's really where you want to be."

"I want to be wherever you are." And he means it.

A tear slips down her cheek. "Galen, there's something you need to know. About Reed."

He uses his thumb to wipe away the new stream slipping down her face. He knows what she's going to tell him, and he decides to let her. To put what happened into her own words. To tell him from her point of view. No matter how badly it hurts him. It's obviously something that she has to get out.

He would have let her keep it, he never would have forced her to tell him. Because at the end of the day, she chose him and that's all that matters. "Tell me," he says softly. "If you want to."

"Reed and I were . . . We were in the woods looking for you. And then suddenly he's in my face, asking if he could kiss me."

Galen's gut twists. "And you said yes?"

"I must have, because he kissed me right after that."

Wow. He didn't realize how painful this was going to be,

reliving the details he'd worked so hard to banish from his mind. "Why . . . Why would you give him permission?"

Her lip quivers. "I don't know. I mean, you and I were fighting. You were gone. You wouldn't answer my calls, my texts. And there Reed was, being nice to be me, showing me how great it was to be a Half-Breed in Neptune. And . . . And . . ."

"You thought it might be something that you wanted."

"Yes. No! I mean, I knew I didn't want *him*, I knew all along that it was you I wanted. I just felt that he was giving me another option. An option that . . ."

"That I couldn't give you."

"Couldn't? Maybe. At the time, it felt more like you weren't willing to. I'm so sorry, Galen. I never should have let him. I should have pushed him away, stopped it before it happened."

"You didn't know where we stood. You thought I left you all alone in a strange place. I can't . . . I can't imagine what you must have thought of me."

"But I still shouldn't have let someone else kiss me. You and I were going to be mated."

Were? His next question burns in his throat, encapsulated by the heat of anxiety rising from his stomach. "Emma. Does that mean . . . Have I lost you?" He takes her face in his hands. The situation has become beyond urgent. *What does she mean we were going to be mated?* "Because I swear I'll make it up to you. All of it. Give me another chance. I'll give you all of the options. If you want Neptune to unite with the underwater kingdoms, I'll support that. I'll try to convince Grom that it's for the best. What do you want, Emma? Just tell me and it's yours."

She leans against him, sobbing into his chest. He pulls her to him, relishing the feel of her in his arms again. "You're asking me to give you another chance when it should be the other way around," she says. "This is so backward. You always do this. Put the blame on yourself."

He strokes the length of her hair. "You didn't kiss him though. He told me that you didn't, that you pulled away."

"Reed told you?"

"While we were at Kennedy's."

"And what else did Reed tell you?"

"He said that you chose me. You didn't have to. Not after how I acted. I was ready to leave Neptune that night, Emma. Ready to take you away from a place that could make you happy. I was being selfish and jealous. You had a right to explore other options."

"If you knew I told him that, then why did you ask me if you lost me?"

"I wanted to hear it from you. I *needed* to hear it from you. You could have changed your mind, you know."

But then she pulls his mouth down to hers. Her lips are an unrelenting frenzy, as if she's making up for lost time. Her body presses into his, as if she's seeking to eliminate the space between them altogether. Suddenly, he's lifting her in his arms, giving himself leverage to kiss her more deeply. She wraps her legs around his waist, holding herself in place so as not to break the kiss for a single moment.

He leans her against the closest tree, his hands frantic to touch every part of her. Just as he reaches for unexplored territory, Toraf clears his throat behind them. "Ahem," he says for emphasis.

I'm going to kill him.

Galen pulls away immediately, but stands in front of Emma to allow her to gain some composure. She smooths down her sundress and runs quick fingers through her hair. She nods when she's ready to face Toraf. Her mouth is swollen—and in danger of more kissing from him.

Galen looks away from her to his friend. "We've really got to work on your timing," he says, nearly breathless. His pulse is thrumming at a faster pace than even he can swim.

"Hmm," Toraf says. "From the looks of it, I was almost too *late*."

Before Emma can say all the irate things on the tip of her tongue, Galen covers her mouth with his hand. "What do you want, Toraf?"

His friend folds his hands in front of him. It's such a formal, controlled act. . . . *Could Toraf be embarrassed?* "It would seem that the two kings have concocted a plan," Toraf says, clearing his throat again. "They need Emma to call Reder."

Here we go.

45

"REDER, IT'S Emma." The words feel tight in my mouth. For some reason, I feel I've betrayed Reder, but in reality, I'm doing exactly what we talked about. At least, I hope it will be.

"Emma, sweet Neptune, are you okay? Where are you? Are you with Tyrden? Frank, he's—"

"Is Frank all right?"

There's a slight pause on the other end. Reder's voice changes from worry to suspicion, which hurts a little bit. *Wait till he hears all that I have to say.* "He's in rough shape. Emma, what happened? Where is Tyrden? People are telling me that there was an accident at the stoplight in town. That—"

"We have Tyrden," I say. "And it wasn't an accident." I sound sterner than I'd wanted, but the memory of Tyrden pointing his gun at me doesn't exactly delight me.

Another pause. "We?"

"My family is here. All of them."

"And . . . And you've taken Tyrden? Why?"

"We have Reed, too. And Kennedy." Anxiety bubbles in my stomach like seltzer. Mom told me to stack up our advantages in the very beginning, but it doesn't feel right. I don't have to alarm Reder into being reasonable. He's already as rational as they come. "I've told Grom and Grandfather about your wish for peace between the ocean dwellers and the land dwellers. They've agreed to meet with you."

Reder sighs. "Unfortunately, I can't trust your family anymore. They've already taken two of my people, including my own son. And look what they did to Frank. How do I know this isn't a trap, Emma?" In a lower voice, he says, "How do *you* know this isn't a trap?"

"How do I know? I don't. But I trust my family. And I trust you. I think this is legit. And it was Tyrden who did that to Frank, not us."

"What do you mean?"

And that's when I explain to Reder that Tyrden is a power-hungry sociopath with a side of torture fetish dipped in crazy sauce. And that Kennedy is his twin brother from another mother and all that. It takes the mayor a while to process all that has happened right under his nose.

Finally, he says, "I've failed you, Emma. I've failed my people. My son. I should have been more alert to the danger. I should have known these things were going on."

What am I supposed to say to that? Something generic and comforting, I decide. "Blaming yourself doesn't change anything," I tell him.

"And what will change anything? What are your family's terms for returning my son?"

"I mean, we're not holding him hostage or anything."

The phone is snatched from my hand. "Reder? This is Nalia, Poseidon princess, daughter of King Antonis. We *are* holding your son hostage, until such time as you agree to meet with us in a public place. I think we can agree trust is not something either of us can afford right now. As for Kennedy, your cover has been blown. He has contacted outsiders that may be on their way to Neptune. That said, it's in our best interest to help you clean this mess up. We're having someone fly in from Florida to assist with this. We're going to leave Kennedy at a picnic area outside of town, just inside the woods. You'll need to secure him until our friend, Dr. Milligan, arrives." She pauses. Apparently Reder would like to speak.

"I'm sorry, but until our terms are met," she says, "we're keeping your son. I assure you, he's being well-cared for. We are not like the wild animals you have lurking in your own town." *Oooh, low blow, Mom.* But in a way, she's right. We don't sound like animals.

We sound like freaking terrorists.

46

THE RIDE to the mutually decided-upon restaurant is interrupted only by a brief stop at a drugstore to get Reed some proper bandages and Tyrden some proper sedatives. He keeps waking up, and Rayna keeps punching him unconscious—not that Galen minds all that much.

What is bothering him though, is the fact that Reed and Toraf seem to get along right away. From the backseat they can be heard playing Slap, which is a game of reflex Rachel taught Rayna.

"That's cheating," Reed says. "Cheaters get slapped harder."

"Then I'll start slapping with a closed hand," Toraf says, unconcerned.

Sitting on Galen's lap, Emma turns around to look at them. Galen had thought she'd fallen asleep—though how she could have, he's not sure, with two renowned loudmouths cackling in her ear. "Can you guys play a different game? Something that doesn't involve making noise or being obnoxious?"

Toraf puts his hands down. "Well, how long until we're there anyway?"

"Yeah," Reed says. "We've been driving over an hour." Reed of all people should know how long it takes to get to Chattanooga from Neptune.

"Patience is a virtue," Nalia sings from the driver's seat. Everyone groans. She raises a brow in the rearview. "We're almost there, children." As if on cue, they pass a sign that says, WELCOME TO CHATTANOOGA.

Galen feels Emma tense up against him. "It will all be okay, angelfish," he whispers in her ear.

She eases back. "How do you know?"

The truth is, he doesn't. There is no telling what will happen at this meeting with Neptune officials, what the result will be. But the fact that there will be a meeting at all—on neutral ground—should be taken as a positive sign.

The cabin of the SUV grows quiet then. Rayna and Toraf point to the tall buildings lancing up into the sky all around them, farther than they can crane their necks to see. Reed appears occupied by watching traffic pass outside his window. Emma relaxes against Galen's chest, lost in her own thoughts.

He hopes today will not be a disappointment. Antonis is right—no matter the reason, they can no longer ignore the existence of Neptune. They have to work something out. And they'll have to tell the Archives.

When they arrive at a restaurant called Hennen's, Nalia lets everyone off at the door, except Rayna and Toraf, who've been commissioned to keep watch over Tyrden. At least, Galen thinks to himself, Rayna can give her fists a rest now that he's properly sedated.

They wait on the curb in front while Nalia parks the car. Apparently, it takes an additional few minutes to find an ideal location for hostage storage. When she joins them, she winks at Grom, then laces her arm through his, ushering him inside. Galen, Emma, Reed, and Antonis follow her lead. Why wouldn't they? She seems so at ease, like she's done this hundreds of times.

The hostess leads them into a large private room, to a single long wooden table that could easily seat thirty. After placing down menus for everyone, she eases the door closed behind her. The room is glass-walled; none of the sounds from other parts of the restaurants can be heard.

Reder is already seated, along with two other men Galen doesn't recognize. Reed takes the initiative to seat himself beside his father. It was decided on the way here that he would be permitted to do so in a show of generosity from the Royals.

Antonis's voice rattles through Galen's skull. *A little diplomacy goes a long way.*

Between father and son, they have a brief whispered conversation, wherein Reed holds up his injured hand for Reder's inspection. Galen can't tell what is running through the mayor's mind right now, but it looks a lot like anger and frustration. Then he wears an emotion Galen is very familiar with—self-loathing.

By the time a short brunette server comes, no one has yet spoken. Everyone obediently gives her their drink order. When she returns with nine glasses of water, Nalia motions to her. "We won't be ordering our dinner just yet," she says. "We'd like some privacy if you don't mind."

"Of course," the waitress says, bowing away from Nalia, her drink tray in tow. This time when she closes the door, Grom begins immediately.

"We are appreciative that you chose to meet with us today," he says.

Grom the diplomat. Just how appreciative he is remains to be seen, thinks Galen.

"That said, we are convening here without the knowledge or approval of the Archive council," continues Grom.

"Are you saying this meeting is worthless, then?" Reder says.

Grom is unaffected. "I'm saying that any solutions or conclusions reached during this meeting will be treated as theoretical, until such time as it has been discussed with the council."

Reder takes a sip of his water. "I suppose I'll take what I can get." His cell phone rings, then during the split second it takes for him to answer, the tune of a country song resounds through the glass-walled room. "Good," he says after a couple of minutes. "Keep me posted." When he hangs up, he looks at Galen. "Your friend Dr. Milligan has arrived in Neptune. He's talking to Kennedy now."

"Where are you keeping him?" Nalia says. "Somewhere secure, I hope."

"We only have one holding cell in our jail," Reder says. "That's where he is."

That they have a jail at all impresses Galen. What with a town whose inhabitants appear so in harmony with one another. "Has the NOAA arrived yet?" According to Dr. Milligan, the National Oceanic and Atmospheric Association had been notified—not good.

Reder shakes his head. "Turns out the NOAA sent one man out to investigate Kennedy's claims, and that gentleman was, unfortunately, given wrong directions to Neptune when he called Sylvia's inn from the interstate. Your Dr. Milligan will get a good half hour alone with Kennedy."

Grom leans on the table, folding his hands in front of him. "Emma has told us the story of how your town came to exist. Are there others like it?"

Reder nods. "How many, I'm not sure. Some of Poseidon's descendants remained behind in Europe rather than sail with Columbus. I assume they procreated. I hear that others traveled to Asia. Smaller groups started breaking off. I have no reason to doubt that they're all over the world. But again, if you want to talk numbers, I have no idea."

"Why haven't we heard from them before now? Why is this the first extension of peace from Poseidon's descendants?"

Reder shrugs. "It could be that they don't have the same inclinations we do in Neptune."

"Inclinations?"

"The same desire to explore the oceans," Reed explains. "As

far as we can figure, they're content with sticking to freshwater or assimilating as humans."

"Do you communicate with these other communities?" Nalia says.

Reder shakes his head. "Not really. Every now and then we get a visitor—whom we welcome, of course—but they are few and far between. The most recent was about thirty years back. From Italy. Had a nephew competing as an Olympic swimmer." Reder can't hide his small smile.

Grom wastes no time getting back to business, unimpressed. "Tyrden was recently involved in a conspiracy to overthrow the Triton kingdom. We would like to take him back to the ocean with us."

Reder crosses his arms. "What proof do you have of that?"

"He told Emma what he did while he held her hostage. That was after he injured your guard—what was his name, Frank? He also kept Galen in captivity and used methods of torture on him in order to secure more information about the kingdoms."

"Frank says he remembers waking up long enough for Tyrden to kick him. He thought maybe he was dreaming." Reder scowls. "Even so, Tyrden is a citizen of Neptune. We have procedures in place for wrongdoing. He won't go unpunished."

"This isn't just wrongdoing we're talking about," Nalia interjects. "His crimes are against the kingdoms. He abducted two Royals, conspired to overthrow Triton territory, and used fraud to simulate one of the sacred Gifts of the generals. We cannot leave him behind. He simply must return with us."

"You may have noticed that we don't abide by the laws of the kingdoms."

"If your true pursuit is peace with them, you'd do well to at least respect the laws they hold dear," Nalia says.

Reder considers. "You want me to turn over Tyrden. What am I getting in return? You've made me no promises."

"And as we've said," Grom says, "we are in no position to do so. But as king of the Triton territory, I can agree to an exchange."

"An exchange for what?"

"Your son," Grom says.

This evokes disturbed grunts from the other two Neptune officials sitting on either side of Reed and Reder. To Galen, these Syrena appear to be there for show. He wonders why the mayor bothered to bring them at all. It occurs to Galen that they could be bodyguards. Reder is, after all, outnumbered, no matter how public a restaurant this is.

"My son is sitting next to me," Reder says, raising his voice. "He's no longer in your custody. And you have the gall to offer him as an exchange? You'll take him back over my dead body." This makes the two "officials" tense up. *Definitely bodyguards.*

"You misunderstand me," Grom says calmly. "I mean for Reed to accompany us back to the kingdoms as our guest."

"For what purpose?" Reder says, alarm rattling in his voice.

Grom nods in understanding. "You must look at it from our perspective. You'll agree that Antonis and I have a fantastic story to tell the Archives when we return. A town on the big land called Neptune that harbors long-lost descendants of

Poseidon as well as Half-Breeds who have chosen to dispatch the laws of the generals. And then you want us to petition for peace and unity with them?" Grom shakes his head. "These things take time. We've just experienced upheaval in the kingdoms as it is. The Royals are being watched for even a small misstep."

"What I'm hearing is that you can't protect Reed if he goes with you," Reder says.

"I'll protect him," Galen says through gritted teeth. *For Emma's sake. She wants this so badly.*

"I appreciate the valiance, Galen, but you are one person. And you," Reder says, focusing his attention on Grom again, "you haven't explained how putting my son's life in danger will unite us. I'm not connecting the dots here."

"We can't promise that it will unite us," Antonis says. "But it will give us a better chance. I will go back and report that I, as well as all the generations of Poseidon kings before me, have known of your existence. That you have not pursued anything but peace with us, albeit from a distance. That you are not our enemies."

"You will already be sending Tyrden with us as a token of goodwill, for him to be punished according to our laws," Grom says. "That will not be viewed as a small thing. And by sending Reed with us, they will have a chance to see that he, too, has the Gift of Poseidon. I think they can be persuaded in time that an alliance with an entire town who possesses this Gift could prove beneficial to them."

Reder takes in a deep breath, massaging his temples with shaky fingertips. "And if they decide that he's an abomination under the law? If they decide my son should be put to death?"

"They accepted Emma," Antonis says. "They would have to explain why one Half-Breed is acceptable and not the other. The Archives are not unreasonable, Reder."

Reder nods, lifting his head higher. "You forget the other advantages we can offer the ocean dwellers."

"Such as?" Nalia says, surprised.

"We have eyes and ears on land," Reder says. "We can watch the human world for you. Galen has done a good job as ambassador to humans, I'm sure. But we have more connections. Better capability. It's a full-time job, one that Galen shouldn't have to shoulder alone."

"This is true," Grom says.

The whole room is silent then, heavy with contemplation. There are life-changing—world-changing—decisions being discussed over this glossy wood table. Any compromise reached here will carry with it a ripple effect for years to come. It will span generations on land and in the sea.

"If Reed is agreeable to it," Reder says finally, "I'll let him go. But it's his choice."

"I'm ready to go right now," Reed says. "Let's do this."

Galen's stomach tightens. Reed will be coming with them. Which means he'll have more access to Emma. He glances at her sideways. Oblivious to his jealousy, she gives him an enthusiastic smile. Which he can't help but return.

"Baby steps," she whispers to him.

Galen nods. *Baby food,* he thinks to himself. *Which is what Reed will be eating if he comes near you again.*

Reder holds up his hand. "It's inevitable that others of our kind will hear of this truce. What if they step forward?"

"We will put that worry off for another day, my friend," Grom says. "I believe it sensible to meet again, within one cycle of the moon. This is not a decision the Archives will make in haste. Of course, if you need to send word to us before then, you may have our phone numbers. And if Reed is truly ready, we will take him now and be on our way."

"There is one more thing," Galen says to Reder. "Tyrden wasn't working alone. There were other men who helped him take me. I would appreciate if you found out who."

Reder nods. "I still haven't formerly apologized for what happened to you both. I truly am sorry that these things took place on my shift, while I was in charge." He looks to Grom. "You're leaving already? What of Kennedy?" Reder says. "What if Dr. Milligan can't help us?"

"I'm sure this isn't the first time you've experienced human discovery," Antonis says, standing. "Even if it is, you can always resort to what you do best."

"What's that?" Reder asks.

"Adapt."

47

I DIAL Dr. Milligan's number. When he answers, I put him on speaker and set the phone in the cup holder of the console between us in Galen's rental car. It has been a long drive home in this cramped little compact, but it was all the airport had left. The rest of the Royal party is somewhere behind us on the interstate. They had to make a pit stop in Neptune in order to collect a few personal things for Reed, which Galen generously offered to keep at his house.

"Hello?" Dr. Milligan says. It sounds windy in the background. Or it could just be the suckiness of speakerphone.

"Dr. Milligan, it's Galen. Can you talk?"

"Indeed I can, my boy. I've just left Neptune. Interesting place, that."

"And Kennedy?"

Dr. Milligan sighs into the phone. "To be quite honest,

I hardly helped at all. Sadly, Greg's mental health has deteriorated since last I saw him. The NOAA agent was hard-pressed to get anything out of him at all. What he did get were fragments of what sounded like a fairy tale. The NOAA doesn't put much stock in magic."

"Magic?"

"Like people disappearing before your very eyes."

"Oh. Blending."

"That's what I figured."

"So where is he now?"

"From what I hear, Reed is pressing charges for a gunshot wound. I think Greg might be headed to jail."

"Do you think he'll be back?"

There's a long pause. "If not him, then someone else. Times are changing, Galen."

Galen glances at me and nods. "Then we'll just have to change with them."

Epilogue

ONE YEAR LATER

IT FEELS weird to latch on to Grandfather's shoulders and press my stomach into his back. It seems too intimate, too familiar. We never do things like hug, or even pat each other on the back, so to hitch a piggyback ride is just a tad awkward.

But how could I refuse? He was just too excited. He practically wouldn't take no for an answer. Not that I would deny him this one thing.

Especially this one thing.

Grandfather has become special to me in a short amount of time. A couple of nights each week, he sits with me on the beach after dinner, telling me stories of his childhood, of being groomed for kingship, of the times he spent with my grandmother before she died. Of how much my mother is just like me—even if we can't see it. He's teaching me how to make Syrena nets and how to make a squid ink itself without much effort.

Galen has had to begrudgingly allow room for Grandfather, to accept that he'll be taking up some of my time now, too. And Grandfather has come to terms with the fact that I'm not a child—or a fingerling, as he calls it—and that Galen and I need time alone. Oh, at first he was inconsolable. In fact, he threw such a tantrum when he found out we were going to share the same off-campus apartment—separate bedrooms for crying out loud—that we were barely able to get our deposit in on time and almost missed out on our dorm rooms.

Separate dorm rooms. On opposite sides of the campus.

But today everything changes, and Grandfather seems to recognize that. To be honest, he seems almost contented.

So we glide through the water in silence, Grandfather and his self-assurance and me and my jitters and my waterproof pack. The ocean is calm today, in stark contrast to the churning vortex that is my stomach. I try to appreciate the fish around us, the pod of dolphins playing below us, the beauty of the canyon-like drop-off ahead of us. There is more seaweed floating around than usual, which means that a few extra minutes will be devoted to washing it out of my hair tonight. Seaweed is like the Silly String of the ocean—it never comes out.

But those are short, fleeting thoughts. All I can really think of is Galen—and how all of him will be mine in a matter of hours. The delicious contours of his lips when he smiles. The silhouette of his body walking toward me in the moonlight.

The way his embrace seems to be the one thing I've been missing all my life. Everything that is Galen will belong to me.

And ohmysweetgoodness, I'm nervous.

I feel Grandfather slow down and I peer around him. We're almost there. The light from the sun becomes brighter, glistening off the surface like a sprinkling of diamonds. Just ahead of us, the ocean floor slants upward toward shallower water. In front of that, a mound of sand piles its way up to the surface, forming an island.

The island Galen picked for us.

Grandfather eases us to the surface, and I think my heart might stop. When we reach the top, I let out a breath I'd been holding for longer than I should. But I can't help it.

This is the day.

The island is a masterpiece of tropical beauty. Palm trees form a protective wall around the lush forest farther inland. Coconuts freckle the beach sand where low tide leaves a dark wet stripe across the shore. Seagulls overhead squawk in a chorus, lazily gliding in the breeze instead of flapping their wings.

The island is perfect.

Grandfather takes us to the beach where Mom waits for us, waving like a crazed person. As if we could miss the giant pink flower in her hair. Or the immense boat she rented rocking gently a few yards away—it's way bigger than we talked about. What she could possibly need a boat that humongous for is beyond me. It's like a three-story house cradled in an overgrown canoe.

When I think I can touch bottom, I let go of Grandfather's shoulders and fall slightly behind him.

He turns to me and smiles. "It was an honor to bring you to your island, Granddaughter."

I nod, suddenly feeling excessively shy. "Thank you." I don't know if there's something else I should say. This is a Syrena tradition. Traditionally, my father would be swimming with me to my mating ceremony, supposedly to impart last-minute words of wisdom or something like that. Kind of like how the father escorts the bride down the isle. But since Dad is gone, Grandfather volunteered. And he either forgot the words of wisdom, or he didn't have any.

He swims away then, probably to the other side of the island, where there is hopefully a change of clothes waiting for him. When he was informed he would be among those standing on the beach, he got all agitated, muttering to himself for a solid hour.

Old people.

I adjust my pack on my shoulders right before Mom slams into me. I'm still knee deep in the waves so the impact makes a healthy splash. Since Mom's not really a hugger, this affects me down to the most basic of levels. I had counted on her to be my rock today, the stable one. That might not work out.

"Galen is already here," she says, which I already know, but I feel a flutter in my stomach anyway at the sound of his name.

"What's with the yacht?"

She leads me by the wrist down the beach and to the plank connected to the boat. "Grom and I are going to have a second honeymoon after the ceremony."

"Ew."

Rayna materializes on the deck of the boat wearing honest-to-God coconut boobs and a grass skirt. She gives us the classic princess wave, all wrist wrist, elbow elbow. I toss Mom a questioning look. She shrugs. "She wanted to help with something, and Galen already ran her off the other side of the island. Something about catching the decorations on fire."

"Fan-flipping-tastic."

"Hush. She's just going to do your nails and hair." Just? She caught fire to decorations, and now she's going be to wielding a flat iron near my head mere hours before my mating ceremony? If there was a time when I didn't need singed hair, it would be rightfreakingnow.

Everyone is going to be at this ceremony. The Triton kingdom. The Poseidon kingdom. Half the town of Neptune, at least. All eyes on me. That's how I know something is going to happen. Rayna will crisp my hair, or burn a welt into the side of my face. A seagull will relieve itself on my dress. Or what could be more fitting than me tripping into Galen on our wedding day? Just like old times' sake.

"Emma, if you don't want to do this, you have to tell me right now."

That's when I notice I've stopped making progress in the sand toward the boat. I must look like a startled cat. "I'm just nervous," I tell her, licking lips gone dust dry. "What if something goes wrong?"

She smiles. "Years from now, you'll be able to look back on this day and laugh. No matter what happens." So she thinks today has disaster potential, too.

"Laugh at how I sobbed myself to sleep on my wedding day?"

She grasps a tendril of my hair being thrown around in the breeze and tucks it behind my ear. "In a few hours, all this will be behind you. Just hang on for a few more hours. And it's not likely you'll be sleeping anyway—"

"Mom!"

We take a few more steps and start up the plank, the heat of my blush creeping down my neck and up to my ears. Rayna has already disappeared inside the cabin. We hear the sound of something heavy being mishandled, possibly dropped.

"How has school been?" Mom says quickly. "Are your professors nice? Is Galen adjusting to college life?" This isn't the first time we've had this conversation, but the questions must come easily to her, just as the answers come easily to me. It's effortless chit-chat, which is what we both need right now.

"It's fine. I have a few cool professors, and then there are some who act like morticians. Galen...Galen is being a good sport." He's great at his classes and politely evading the female population of Monmouth University. His weaknesses are not quite being able to choke down the cafeteria food and keeping his fists to himself when an intoxicated undergrad propositions me.

But he's getting better. With the cafeteria food.

Once inside the boat, I follow Mom down the narrow hallway that leads to a rickety set of winding stairs, which takes us down to the next floor. At the bottom is one big room, probably meant for entertaining but that is now repurposed for the singular objective of prepping me for my wedding ceremony.

And it's beautiful.

The carpet is sprinkled with flower petals, and there are black and white and violet balloons floating everywhere in different states of levitation. Matching streamers hang from the ceiling, along with crystalline balls, which cast a kaleidoscope of light spinning around the room. It's all basic party gear, and taken separately it might be considered cheesy, but taken as a whole—including the fact that Mom and Rayna got along long enough for this to be done for me—brings it to a new level of special.

"Wow," is all I can get out. Mom is pleased.

Rayna grins. "It's going to be a girl party. You'll see. Your mom brought all my nail polish, and I found these super-shiny shells by the reef that I think would go great in your hair." Without asking, she comes right up to me, grabs a painful handful of hair, then pulls it back toward the crown of my head. "I'm thinking an updo like this. And forget the tiara. That's too fancy for Galen."

"I agree," Mom says, but she won't make eye contact with me. Oh schnap.

The mirror must be mistaken. The girl in the reflection cannot possibly be me. Because the girl staring back at me looks so . . . so . . . glamorous. But in ways that are so subtle I wouldn't have thought the sum of the parts could ever equal this whole image. The tiny shells in my hair—which is swept back into submission and curled into soft ringlets—look like shimmering gems in the light of the cabin. Though Mom took the simple approach with my makeup, it has a certain elegance to it. A touch of blush, a few swipes of mascara, and tinted lip gloss to complete the natural effect. (She was either going for natural, or this application represents the scope of her makeup knowledge. Either way, I'm happy with it.) I'm also the grateful recipient of Rayna's best French mani-pedi to date.

My white strapless dress falls just above the knee, hugging my curves, but the outer sheer material flows long in back, just past my ankles. I feel I've been transformed into a real princess, instead of just being one on a technicality.

I wonder if all brides feel this way.

"You're gorgeous," Mom says, and since she almost chokes on the words, I almost cry and ruin my mascara. "I can't believe this is happening."

"You and me both."

"Tell me about it," Rayna says. "I never thought Galen would be able to trick anyone into mating with him."

We all laugh then, because the idea is so ridiculous and because it's better than crying anyway, right? Mom lets out a big breath. "Are you ready? The sun is about to set. We still have to get you through the trees to the other side."

We walk the plank, so to speak, and plant our feet in the soft sand. I decide that whoever cleared the path from one side of the island to the other is an expert. I know the Syrena are skilled at prepping islands for mating ceremonies, but I don't think they've ever prepared one quite like this—making accommodations for barefoot Half-Breeds was probably never on their to-do list before. Still, my feet encounter nothing but velvety white sand, warmed by the setting sun.

The walk is single file and quiet, Mom taking the lead, Rayna in the middle, and me last. I'm supposed to be lagging behind a little more, but it's getting darker, and I'm just clumsy enough to trip over nothing at all, let alone some tropical obstacle blown in my way by the breeze or fate or whatever.

Through the trees ahead, I see a pathway of torches leading to the beach, to where I hear the waves lapping against the shore. Probably most beach weddings don't lure the bride and groom to the water—but this is not most beach weddings. After all, the majority of our guest list will be attending in the shallow water, sporting fins instead of tuxedos and dresses.

When we reach the edge of the tree line, I stay behind, giving Rayna and Mom time to take their places at the front of the procession. And by procession, I mean me. I don't know how long to wait—was it fifteen seconds or fifteen minutes? My lungs forget to breathe with my new dilemma. My heartbeat threatens the boundary of my veins. I'm going to make a fool of myself.

I'm going to make a fool of myself.

And all at once, I hear humming. It's soft but distinct, coming from the water. The gentle rise and fall of harmony. A song. They're giving me my cue.

And so I walk, using the pathway of torches as my guide, trying to fit my stride to match the rhythm of the gentle tune. I wonder if this is a traditional Syrena mating-ceremony song and conclude that it must be. They all know it so well. They all contribute to it so beautifully.

There is a slight hump in the sand before the beach can be seen, and as I make my way over it, my eyes are inevitably drawn to the figure on the right. Galen.

My destination.

My destiny.

He stands in low tide wearing a tuxedo tailor-made to hug his physical perfection. His expression is the only thing not sharp about him. I thought—worried—that today he might adapt Grom's impassive expression or maybe don an unruffled smile. That today would not be as nerve-racking for him as it is for me, and for some silly reason equating to something less special. I hoped that he would show some emotion. That he would reassure me with his eyes or a quick squeeze of my hand. That he wouldn't be the statue he's capable of being.

What I never expected to see is this kind of tenderness radiating from him, the profoundness of vulnerability on his face. His eyes are intense glowing orbs in the torchlight, and they show me everything. How he feels about me, what he thinks about my dress, and a slight impatience for me to reach him. I feel the worry leave me like beads from a broken necklace.

This is right. Galen knows it. I know it.

Behind Galen is the setting sun, which illuminates hundreds of heads bobbing just above the water. Dark Syrena hair intermittent with the shocking white of Half-Breed hair. Hundreds of guests, but I'm undaunted because with each step I get closer and closer to the thing I must have. To the thing I don't think I can live without.

Beside Galen, Toraf gives me a playful, brotherly wink. And I notice that Toraf cleans up nice. In a tux, he resembles a big, handsome child. I can tell he's uncomfortable wearing long pants, because he keeps scratching at his knees. His sleeves are a tad short, and he tugs them down obsessively. Rayna grabs his hand then to stop his fidgeting: A crooked smile spreads across her face when she sees me.

I think Rayna might like me now.

Mom is on my left and Grom stands directly in the middle—he'll be officiating the ceremony. Close to the shore, I spot Grandfather in the water. Grandfather, who is supposed to be standing on shore with the rest of us. Grandfather, who apparently had no intention of changing into a tux. And beside him is Reed—accompanied by not one, but two female Syrena. I think I recognize one of them from the Triton kingdom. Reed notices me noticing him, and he gives a little encouraging wave.

Galen raises a brow at him. Reed's smile falters, his hand lowering below the surface.

One day they'll get along. Maybe.

When I reach Galen, he takes both my hands in his. If I remember correctly, he's not supposed to do that until we're repeating the vows—or whatever the Syrena call them. When Grom sees that Galen is one step ahead, he calls the ceremony to order.

"Let it be known that we are all witnesses to the union of Galen, Triton prince, and Emma, bearer of the Gift of Poseidon.

As we all know, friends, this union is to be everlasting, a bond broken only by death." A solemn murmur breaks out through the water. Grom is undeterred. If anything, he sounds more official when he says, "Let it also be known, for the memory of the Archives, that this is the first legal union recognized by the kingdoms between a Syrena and a Half-Breed since the destruction of Tartessos. That this day will forever be remembered as a symbol of peace and unity between the ocean dwellers and the land dwellers."

This is unexpected.

Our mating ceremony is a symbol for all the kingdoms? It feels like it has taken on a life of its own now, a moment flash frozen in time. It's not just about Galen and me, and our dedication to each other anymore. It's an occasion that will be memorialized forevermore as something bigger than the union itself. But I distance myself from that thought.

Because to me, nothing could be bigger than becoming Galen's mate. I don't care if this is the last legal union between Syrena and Half-Breeds, so long as this one happens.

Grom keeps talking and I try to listen, I really do. He explains the separate and mutual duties of the male and female, how the law cherishes loyalty, and how it outlines punishment for infidelity. That as prince, Galen's first duty is to the kingdoms, his second to me. That my duties are the same, given my Gift of Poseidon. Then he drolls on, something about raising fingerlings to respect the law and the council of the Archives, especially during these times of change.

Not exactly the replica of a human wedding, but I've been

to half a dozen of those—who doesn't agree that they tend to drag on and on? Besides, these are things that Grom has already reviewed with me and Galen a few days ago when he sat us down and asked if we're really ready to do this.

I allow myself to let go then, to focus all my attention on Galen and his lips and his eyes and his hands in my hands. A warmth steals through me, a tiny wave of excitement that almost makes me squeal.

Here are the vows. And as Syrena tradition would have it, I go first. But I've got this. I've repeated it to myself a million times in front of the mirror. Behind me, I hear sniffling, and I tear up, knowing it can only be Mom.

Mom who doesn't cry.

I clear my throat and start spouting the words. "Galen, Triton prince, I vow to cherish you as my mate for time everlasting. I vow to serve you within the boundaries of the law and the council of the Archives. I vow to be faithful to you always, and to honor you in word and deed. Galen, Triton prince, I take you for my mate."

Galen doesn't have to be told when it's his turn. As soon as the last word leaves my lips, the first of his vows falls from his. "Emma, bearer of the Gift of Poseidon, I vow to cherish you as my mate for time everlasting. I vow to serve you within the boundaries of the law and the council of the Archives. I vow to be faithful to you always, and to honor you in word and deed. Emma, bearer of the Gift of Poseidon, I take you for my mate."

Grom gives his brother a solemn nod. This is where we're supposed to kiss each other's cheek. "Friends, I present—"

"I'm not done," Galen says. Then that Syrena prince gets on his knees in the wet sand. His eyes are wells leading to his soul, his very being. I think I'm going to swallow my own heart. "Emma, I will love you with every breath in my body, and beyond my own death. I swear to be your shield, your protector, your worshipper. There is nothing I will deny you. I am yours."

I drop to my knees then, too, brought down by everything that is Galen. My dress splashes into an oncoming wave, and the saltwater licks up my hips and thighs, but I couldn't care less. "I love you," I tell him, but I'm not sure he can make out the words through my tears.

His mouth is on mine, covering over my sobs. All that he said in words, he puts into this kiss. I'm vaguely aware of a distant cheer surging up over the sound of the waves and of the seagulls and my heartbeat. I'm vaguely aware of Grom clearing his throat, of Mom's hand on my shoulder, of Rayna giggling. But this kiss cannot be stopped.

And it shouldn't be.

I straighten the corners of the sheet over the sand and settle in the middle. Galen takes the spot behind me, wrapping his arms and a light blanket around me. He pulls me to him, leaning me back against his chest. Our nakedness feels natural, like we've always been this way with each other. It's odd to think that hours ago, this island was overrun with guests, congratulating us and cheering us, and bringing us fish for our first night together. To think that Mom was here, proudly clutching Grom's arm while Rayna fretted over my soaked dress. Even now, the noise of the crowd seems to swirl around us in the wind as a ghost that reminds us of all that took place. Of all the privacy we didn't have.

But the moment they were all gone, we took our solitude back with a vengeance.

Tonight Galen and I have loved each other fully, in a way we've never been able to before. I still feel breathless when I think of his touch, his tenderness, the warmth of his body. I will never be satisfied, and yet I am content, right now at this moment.

"I have a surprise for you," Galen whispers in my ear. Tingles shimmy through me, commandeering my spine and taking my senses hostage. He runs a hand down my arm and extends it out toward the ocean, pointing to the horizon. And then I see it.

The water is glowing. Thousands and thousands of blue lights swarm just below the surface, forming a wide ring around the island. The illumination from the jellyfish is magnificent, a radiant constellation in the water, which taken together looks like a spill of florescent paint into the ocean.

"How?" I breathe.

"You're not the only one with the Gift of Poseidon."

"It's like underwater fireworks." He nuzzles his nose into my neck, planting a kiss just below my ear, which evokes an involuntary sigh from my lips.

I don't want this night to end, but at the same time, I want tomorrow to begin.

And all the rest of the days with my Triton prince.

ACKNOWLEDGMENTS

Where to begin? They say it takes a town to raise a child. And it just so happens that writing a book is like rearing a child from birth (the idea), all the way into its dramatic late teens (edits). At first it's a delight, and you love playing with the child and just spending time with it in general. Then things get progressively more difficult to deal with. Terrible twos. Next thing you know it will be in middle school and back talking you like nobody's business, refusing to shape itself into the working plot you imagined. But you still love it because it's your baby. You created it. But you reach a threshold where you must cut it off (by copy edits, you're ready) and launch it out in to the world whether you're ready or not (seriously, by copy edits, you're ready).

It takes a town to write a book.

And I'd like to thank my town, in no specific order:

My agent, Lucy Carson, for being so supportive. More than

that, you've been absolutely vital to me. These have been a difficult few years and you've been nothing less than amazing. I'm so lucky to have you (and the rest of TFA team!). Liz Szabla, how could I have written this trilogy without you? There's no way I could have. Not without your insight, not without your understanding, not without your support. Jean Feiwel, you have a way of making me feel at home. I can't explain it.

Macmillan publicity. Holy crap, you guys are all rock stars. Do you sleep? Rich Deas, for designing the covers for the entire series. Fans might choose their favorite of the three, but they are all gorgeous, every one.

Thank you, Jessica Brody, for always being there with your positivity and support. Emmy Laybourne and Leigh Bardugo, we've grown up together. And I've loved every minute of it. Kaylie Austen, what would I do without your snarky-yet-encouraging texts? Heather Rebel, what would I do without you, in general?

All my sisters, Lisa, Teri, Tami, and Debbie. I'm a writer, but there are no words I can say that will adequately express my gratitude for all you've done for me. For all your support, even though it seemed like tragedy hunted us down at times. Maia, thank you so much for sharing me with the world and putting up with my absences. I love you. Jason, thanks for letting me talk it out with you, for being the constant recipient of my worries and fears and for putting up with me anyway.

Opa, you might be my biggest cheerleader. Thank you.

Thank you, Laura, for naming Reed.

To all my fans: Thank you. Infinity times infinity times

infinity squared. You made this series what it is. You. Not me. Thank you. So much.

To the book blogger community: You guys are fan-flipping-tastic. Seriously. But you already knew that, didn't you? Admit it. You know you own it. ☺

If I've missed your name I'm so deeply sorry. I'm writing these acknowledgments at 3:00 am—because my gratitude actually woke me from a dead sleep—so please forgive my brainlessness in not mentioning your vital contribution to this book, this series. Even if it's not listed here, I'm grateful for it, believe me. And I am indebted to you always.

Dear Fantabulous Reader,

Thank you so much for signing up for this crazy adventure with me, starting with *Of Poseidon* and ending with *Of Neptune*. Thank you for coming out to see me on tour, for e-mailing me your gushing reports of Galen, for rooting for Emma, for laughing at Toraf's antics, for washing your hands of Rayna, and for crying over Rachel. Thank you, from the bottom of my butt (my butt is bigger than my heart, so you're getting a good deal) for making *Of Triton* a *New York Times* Bestseller.

What I hope you're taking away from the Syrena Legacy Series is this: Be proud of *all* your gifts and embrace them, no matter how "different" they make you feel or how much they make you stand out from the crowd.

So, how's it going? Are you sad that the series is ending? Are you going to be lost without Galen and Emma, Toraf and Rayna? Me, too.

But here's the thing: Endings don't always mean good-bye. Sure, we're saying farewell to this cast of characters, but we're also saying hello to a whole new set in my upcoming novel, *Joyride*. You're going to meet Carly, a feisty young heroine who's trying to stay under everybody's radar because of her breathtaking secrets, and you'll also meet Arden, a swoon-worthy hero who's trying to convince Carly that she would make the perfect accomplice—but for what, you'll have to read to find out!

Now, who's with me???

Lots of love,

Anna Banks

Thank you for reading this FEIWEL AND FRIENDS book.
The Friends who made

OF NEPTUNE

possible are:

Jean Feiwel	publisher
Liz Szabla	editor in chief
Rich Deas	senior creative director
Holly West	associate editor
Dave Barrett	executive managing editor
Nicole Liebowitz Moulaison	production manager
LAUREN BURNIAC	editor
Anna Roberto	assistant editor

FOLLOW US ON FACEBOOK
OR VISIT US ONLINE
AT MACKIDS.COM

OUR BOOKS ARE
FRIENDS FOR LIFE